Also by Phyllis Moore

People of Akiane Trilogy
Pegasus Colony
Storm's Coming
Jessica's Mission

The Destiny Series
My Haunted Bed & Breakfast

People of Akiane
Book Two

Storm's Coming

Phyllis Moore

Myth Rider
Publishers

Novels are a ride into another world.

Moore, Phyllis
Storm's Coming / by Phyllis Moore — U.S. ed.
1st Edition

Summary: WSC Space Force ordered Lt. Jessica M. Hewett as negotiator to a rogue Earth colony in the Pegasus Constellation. Now for the sake of public relations, she's on Woden, an expedition to across the frozen planet. The conditions of the planet are so sever the likely of her surviving are slim.

ISBN 978-0-9907091-3-8 paper book
1. Science Fiction — Fiction. 2. Soft Science Fiction — Fiction.
4. Storm's Coming — Fiction.

First published in U.S.A. 2016
Typeset by Cheryl Barr
Printed by CreateSpace

Myth Rider Publishers
Mooresmyths@comcast.net

Cover image from IStock
Cover design Phyllis Moore
Front design by Ethereal Eakain
Book jacket design Cheryl Barr

III

Acknowledgments

It is said that writing is a lonely profession. That is somewhat true. There are many lonely hours of writing and rewriting, but without the help of friends, family, fellow authors, and professional help, books would never come into existence.

There are too many to give every name that has had an influence on the writing of Storm's Coming, but I will name those close to the end who encourage me not to give up.

Coworkers: Andy Dreissig, Bill Codere, and Justin Campbell

Fellow authors: Cassandra Amesley, Ronald Peterson and John Palmer

Thanks to all,
Phyllis Moore

Prologue

In the late 21st Century, the nations of Earth united to explore and colonize space. They pooled their financial and scientific resources into one civilian organization, World Space Coalition.

WSC built its base on the moon in an effort to keep it neutral. The coalition colonized the moon, Mars, and Europa, one of Jupiter's moons.

In 2132, 2,035 colonists left Moon Base in three space transports to be the first settlers of an alien world. Akiane was to be Earth's and WSC's greatest accomplishment, the colonization of a planet in the Pegasus Constellation.

WSC lost contact with the settlers and were never heard from again. It was believed the project had failed. Earth's dream of a galactic colony was soon forgotten.

Three hundred years later, a communication test revealed the colony had survived. *WSC Britannia* was immediately launched to make contact.

Pegasus Colonists insisted they'd been purposely abandoned from the very beginning, and refused all attempts of friendship. Lieutenant Jessica M. Hewitt was not acceptable as an official diplomat from WSC unless she made Woden.

Chapter 1

Rona Montgomery
Day One of the Expedition

"I DON'T believe Jess is doing this! I don't understand *why* she has to do it." Rona Montgomery knew why, she was having trouble *accepting* why. She was a scientist. Her thoughts were ruled by logic, but the colonists on this alien planet were ruled by tradition, religion, and emotion. "It's too dangerous. What if we never see her again? Jess could die!" Emotions confused Rona and at this moment, they overruled her logic making her vulnerable to the illogical.

Olivia Zeller flanked Rona on one side and Jorge Krause on the other. They were the last of Jess' friends to watch her expedition leave.

Olivia stood silently crying, both were a rare reaction for her.

Jorge dropped his head, shuffled his feet, and sniffed.

Rona held a gloved hand over her mouth. It didn't help. She pulled her turtleneck up and wiped her tears to keep them from freezing.

Winter lasted for five years on Akiane, plunging temperatures turned oceans into blocks of ice and land became a frozen tundra.

Despite the fact that the winter years were ending, and the planet was warming up, there was little evidence of the warmth this morning. It was bone-chilling cold.

They'd come outside at dawn, on the western side of the habitat just as the star Kahair was waking the day. Now, at mid-morning, the star had risen above the edge of the caldera and would soon bring some semblance of warmth to this crisp winter morning.

Jess no longer wore her usual dark blue WSC Space Force uniform but was bundled in her new red fur winter suit provided by the colonists. The sleds were packed, dogs hitched to the sleds, and good-byes had been said.

The journey had begun with Cameron calling, "Huk, huk." His companion Nu Venia walked directly behind him, heading northward. The two teams of dogs jumped to their feet and obediently followed, one after the other.

Reluctant to leave, Jess was the last to follow.

According to their religious tradition, the colonists demanded that Jess undertake an expedition called Woden to prove her worth. Woden was a dangerous, life-threatening journey into Akiane's frozen world.

"I can't bear to watch her go." Rona turned to face the habitat. "I shouldn't let Jess see me like this. I don't want her last memory of me to be crying."

"No, you're right to be worried," Jorge said. He draped an arm over her shoulders and pulled her close. "You're an excellent friend."

It felt good and comforting to be this close to him. They walked toward the habitat with her head on his shoulder.

"When she first moved into my room, Jess was so angry. I didn't think we'd ever become friends. Oh." Rona's memories of their first encounter came rushing back.

Jess was originally *WSC Britannia's* Communications Officer. When she was reassigned as negotiator to the colony, she was transferred to the civilian living quarters and became Rona's roommate.

It was clear from the moment Jess walked into the room, she was incensed. Rona had fully expected their living arrangements to be miserable. It only took a few months for them to become fast friends.

Now Rona couldn't imagine Jess not being in her life every single day.

The first time they had entered the Eatery together, Jorge was sitting with friends. He stopped talking and stared. For him, it was love at first sight. He left his table, and taking his meal with him, joined them. For the rest of the trip, he ate most meals with them.

Both women liked Jorge, but Jess refused to believe he preferred her.

Even though with all her heart she'd rather Jess not leave, Rona couldn't help but feel that there might be the faintest chance she and Jorge could rekindle what they'd had before Jess.

As they neared the habitat, Jorge released Rona so she could take the steps into the seven-meter long tunnel first. They exited into a much warmer habitat than the frigid morning outside.

Rona pulled her hood off, unzipped her orange military issue winter jacket, took her gloves off, and stuffed them in her pocket. She passed her hands along the back of her neck and pulled her thick, dark-mahogany tresses out, which spilled over her hood and down her shoulders perfectly complimenting her dark skin and eyes.

"If it weren't for you, Jorge, I don't think Jess would've ever gotten past her anger," Rona said.

He gave a little chuckle. His lightly freckled nose crinkled. "Yeah, Jessie was my biggest challenge." He unzipped his jacket a few centimeters as he pushed his hood back to reveal a mass of tousled blond hair.

Rona slightly tilted her head back to look up at him. "Jess will be ok, right? She will come back to us, won't she?"

"Sure she will. Jessie is a lot tougher than she thinks she is. Cameron is native to this planet. He knows what to do. He'll take good care of her. He won't let anything happen to her." His words of encouragement didn't ease Rona's fears.

She wasn't sure if he was trying to convince her or himself of Jess' safety.

The warmth of his arm wrapped around her again, but this time it didn't stay. After a quick hug, his arm fell back to his side just as she was leaning into him. Disappointed, she stepped away.

"Don't fret. We'll get Jessie back safe and sound." A quick smile exposed his dimples, both quickly faded.

They stepped onto a path made of pulverized colored rocks in the rocks and headed toward their living quarters on the opposite side of the habitat.

The colonists had allowed the planet's native plant life to flourish within the habitat. Just inside the habitat, against the western wall, was well manicured and picture perfect Chinese-like garden. Every alien blade of grass, leaf, flower, tree branch, and rock was placed and shaped for its aesthetic beauty. But the gardens beside the Earth visitors' living quarters were a different matter.

There the foliage was thick, cutting off the overhead view of the glass ceiling. Branches grew over paths and caught on sleeves, pant legs and long hair. They easily tripped those walking along the pathways. One might have thought they were in a real forest instead of a terrarium.

Rona and her fellow scientists were banned from the rest of the habitat. They were told to stay in their area and use the exits nearest them when they went outside.

No one listened. Walking inside where it was warm and where one could sit by the lake was too inviting.

Rona's brilliant teammate and very good friend, Chow Lu hurried down the path toward her and Jorge.

Lu was a petite Chinese woman. In the traditional Chinese manner, Chow was her family name and Lu her given name. She was the youngest of the scientists who'd come to study the planet Akiane. Her short, thick black hair was cut to her chin and bobbed and swayed with every step. Her orange one-piece winter suit was pulled up to her waist and zipped in place. The upper half of the suit flapped wildly behind her as she ran. She was always running somewhere.

"Has Jessica left already?" Lu asked breathlessly.

"Yes," Rona said.

"That was fast," Lu said. "I thought I'd have more time to get out there. I wanted to talk to her before she left. I have something important to tell her. Something, she should know."

"Then you should have been outside with us instead of playing with your dogs," Jorge said irritably.

Lu stuttered when she was nervous or flustered. Jorge's rebuke stirred her stuttering. With a guilty look, she said, "I-I-I w-wasn't with the dogs. I w-was with the t-t-tech guy. We were trying t-t-to get into . . ."

Jorge interrupted her before she could finish. "It couldn't have waited?" he demanded.

Rona had never seen Jorge snap at anyone before. He was the nicest guy in the world. He literally liked everyone, even the most disagreeable. And everyone liked him.

"Jorge, " she admonished, "don't take your frustrations out on Lu. It's not her fault Jess left."

"Right." He passed his hand through his hair. Then more gently, said, "Sorry, Lu."

"Tech Terzo says the colony's data is old. He was having trouble connecting . . ." Lu tried to explain, but Jorge wasn't listening.

He kicked at a black rock on the path. It tumbled past Lu's winter boot toward the edge of the path and stopped.

Lu stepped to the other side as if he'd kicked the rock at her.

Rona wanted to comfort Jorge. Or maybe she wanted him to comfort her. Either way, she wanted to be with him right then, not Lu. If only she could give Lu a hint to leave.

Lu didn't take hints. She didn't understand them.

Jorge sighed heavily like a little lost puppy. His head turned from side to side, then he said, "I'm going outside to the algae patch to collect samples."

That was his field of study, snow and algae, and their ecology. He often visited a large patch of algae just north of the habitat. He'd probably spend the rest of the day there.

It would be a nice quiet place for the two of them to be alone and talk. A pang of guilt at moving in on Jorge while Jess was away hit Rona.

No, she thought, *Jess had her chance and turned it down. I stepped aside so they could be together, but Jess never encouraged him. Now that she's gone, it's my turn.*

She and Jorge had been close before Jess, not in a romantic sense, but maybe this time they could be.

"Would you like company? I could come with you," she suggested hopefully.

"I'd kind of like to be alone for awhile. I'll catch up with you later," he said, and hurried toward their work area. He was going for his equipment bag and winter suite.

Rona sighed. *Perhaps it would be better to give him time. Don't rush him.*

"Jessica will be all right. It's not like she's alone. She's with Cameron and his daughter. They'll take good care of her," Lu said.

That was Rona's only consolation. Jess was traveling with two colonists, Cameron and Nu Venia. Still, she wouldn't be out there in the first place if it weren't for them. This expedition was their idea, and they were dragging her along.

"I hope you're right, Lu. Still, I'm in no mood to chase dogs right now," Rona said.

"Terzo and I learned something interesting," Lu said as soon as Jorge was out of hearing range.

"Lu, I'd like to be alone, too." Rona needed time to think, process, and get her emotions under control. She'd lost her best friend and the one person she wanted to comfort her was in love with that friend. She sat on a rock, conflicted.

"I had this feeling," Lu began, "I know it sounds strange, but I just..."

Once again, Lu wasn't taking the hint and kept talking. She remained standing, staring at the tunnel exit worry etched her young face.

Rona cut in. "I don't care, Lu. I don't want to hear about it. I don't want to talk about anything. Just leave me alone."

Now pain imprinted Lu's face.

Rona knew she'd hurt her feelings but resisted the urge to apologize.

Even at 20, she can still be such a child, sometimes.

After a moment's thought, she reconsidered. *Perhaps I should apologize.* But she knew if she did, Lu would start up again. Rona was in no mood to hear about it.

Lu sat on the rock next to Rona.

"I want to be alone," she said, for the third time.

Lu nodded as though she understood but didn't leave.

"I should have thought to read the Captain's logs sooner. Then we would have known," Lu rambled. "I'm not even sure it would have made a difference. I mean to the colonists." Lu shifted her feet, twisted her fingers. She fretted for a few more seconds before she started up again; this time she spoke quietly to herself, "Over time, facts can turn into legends and myths." She paused. "That was why I wanted to research Woden. I wanted to know what was fact and what was fiction."

Rona had no idea what she was talking about. She was in no mood to ask for an explanation. "Please, Lu."

Lu continued as though she hadn't heard. "It's just that over time, facts can become exaggerated. I thought it would be a good idea to check to the colony's ship logs. We, Terzo and I, were hoping to find some insight into this Woden—something the colonists were not telling us.

"Rona, the original Woden was nothing like what the colonists say it is today. Originally, it was a fishing trip. Woden was the name of a rain storm that . . ."

Rona wasn't listening. She was lost in the privacy of her thoughts. And those thoughts were mostly about Jorge.

Chapter 2

Jess Hewitt
Day One of the Expedition

"TEA?" I was flabbergasted.

I couldn't believe it. Cameron had dragged me out here. He was the one who wanted this expedition, insisted that we leave as soon as possible. Now one hour into our journey, he wanted to stop for a cup of tea!

Cameron was a huge over 200 centimeters all muscle no fat. Why did he need to stop for tea?

"Tea will warm us, Lieutenant," he said.

Lieutenant! He didn't even call me Jessica, Jess, or Jessie. Perhaps he thought to keep me in line by using my rank. Well, it wasn't going to work.

"I'm already warm. We'll be warmer if we keep moving," I said. "You wanted this trip. Let's get on with it. I don't want tea!"

"We have traveled for one hour. Chovis have need to rest for one hour," he said.

They were dogs but these people called them chovis as if that made them something special. I was prepared to walk until I dropped, then set up camp, and start all over the next day. That was the military way. But if Cameron pampered his dogs by stopping every stinking hour, this was going to be a very long journey.

"One hour?" This wasn't helping my frustrations. "One hour! I can still see the habitat!" Realizing, that I was yelling, I yelled louder. "Maybe I should go back and wait until you've had your tea! Then I'll come back and join you."

"We have a long journey ahead of us," he said ever so patiently, "that will become more rugged. Chovis have need to build stamina. As do we."

He knelt and unhitched one of his lead dogs.

"Stamina?" I asked.

He stopped and turned his head to face me. He didn't appear pleased.

Well, I wasn't pleased either.

"Chovis are not used to this kind of intense traveling. If chovis are expected to pull the weight of sleds, they must be allowed time to build strength." He spoke slowly, as if he were speaking a foreign language, and by speaking slowly, I might understand better him.

"Traveling? They've been at it for *an hour*! How tired can they be? You have two sleds, sixteen dogs per sled. How much more strength do they need?" I wanted to pull my hair out. No, I wanted to pull *his* hair out, one braid at a time.

Nu Venia was unhitching the other team. She was a girl around twelve years old, and for some reason, her fur winter suit was several sizes too large for her, which didn't make sense. There was a lot about the colonists that didn't make since, starting with their appearance.

Pegasus Colonists were descendents of humans from Earth who first settled this alien planet, but they didn't appear or act human.

They had one head, two arms and two legs, but their skin was maroon. Some were lighter like Cameron, who was the color of a pink rose. Others were darker like Nu Venia. No one was white, black, or brown only maroon.

But the most odd thing about them—they were all the same height. Well, mostly. What few children I'd seen were different sizes depending on their age. But adults seemed to be two classes of people. The majority were two meters tall. All others were a full head taller, like Cameron, and they braided their hair in many small braids.

Almost all of the colonists had coal black eyes, few had green or hazel eyes, except Nu Venia, whose eyes were bright yellow with green flecks. All the colonists had black hair; Nu Venia's hair as white as snow.

Why was she so different? What was her story?

She saw me staring at her and said, "Chovis are thirsty. They have need of drink and rest. We also have need to conserve energy, Lieutenant. Tea and dried meat will replenish our strength."

I was not going to win this argument.

My original intention in joining WSC Space Force and volunteering for the Akiane Project was to get away from my problems for a few years. I never planned to set foot on this planet. All I wanted was for everyone back on Earth to move on with their lives and forget about me.

Yet, somehow, I'd ended up in the middle of a galactic controversy.

Once WSC appointed me ambassador to the Pegasus Colony, I became a worldwide household name. If I succeeded in reuniting the two worlds, I'd return home to a hero's welcome. If I failed, I'd return shame-faced. Either way, my name would become a permanent fixture in the history books.

No one would have moved on by the time I returned. Instead, they were waiting for me.

Britannia's seven-day layover was up. All hope of retuning with her had vanished. She'd left without me.

I thought my worst-case scenario would be to be stuck in the habitat until the next transport came two years from now. But no! I'm on a stupid religious quest to prove my worth. If I survived, I'd be a hero on *this* planet. If I died, I'll be forgotten like all the others who'd foolishly attempted this feat.

All my life, I'd tried to get my life together, but everything I did turned into a dismal failure. Getting away and resetting my life had been a last ditch effort to get things right. Once again I'd failed.

"Chovis paws are in need of being maintained." Cameron broke into my thoughts. "With more help, work would be sooner finished."

That meant he wanted my help.

It should have been enough that I was under orders and was expected to cooperate with my companions. I knew I should help. But! I didn't want to. My anger was the only part of my life that I had full control over. I wasn't about to give it up, not yet. Not until I absolutely had to.

"I don't like dogs." I folded my arms over my chest and slumped onto a large flat rock. I tried to cross my legs, but gave up. The fur suit got in the way.

The scowl on Cameron's face said he was disappointed but said nothing. He returned to tending his team of dogs.

Every dog wore bright green booties to protect its paws from the cold, rocks, and sharp snow crystals. Nu Venia had placed the booties on the dogs as she picked them for this journey. I knew all about dog teams and booties.

My father had owned a team for his winter sport of dog-sled racing. His dogs also wore booties. But he didn't stop *every hour*. I'm sure he did rest his team, but NOT every hour! He did not converse with each and every single, solitary dog about every little detail. Cameron, on the other hand, did.

He told each dog how beautiful it was, what a great job it was doing, and how glad he was that it had come along. He scratched its head, ears, stomach, and eventually got to its paws. Then he proceeded to tell it how well each paw was doing, *all four of them*, if the paw was in good condition, or if it needed ointment, and why it needed ointment. Once he finished, he set the dogs free to roam at will.

Nu Venia kept her head down as she concentrated on the dogs she was tending. She said very little other than to greet each dog by name. She scratched its head, patted its stomach, and *quietly* tended its paws.

The dog tails on her team didn't wag as vigorously as those on Cameron's team, but I was happier.

"Cameron, must you speak to every one of them?" I asked.

"Each chovis has a need to know the condition of her paws, Lieutenant," he said. "And I must thank each for her service."

"Can't you just say a general thank you over the team? Then tell them about their four paws all at one time instead of telling them about each and every one individually? It would save you a lot of talking, not to mention saving my aggravation."

"That would be impersonal, Lieutenant."

"Cameron, they're dogs for goodness sake!"

"They are chovis," he said, as if that made a difference.

"Nu Venia doesn't carry on anywhere near as much as you, and her dogs are fine."

Cameron studied me, then turned to the dog at hand, finished scratching its head, and said, "Dellows, you have done a fine job."

Aaaaa!

I endured this for all 132 paws.

Nu Venia finished first. Surprise! She lit the stove and put a pot filled with snow to boil, which she refilled as the snow melted.

The habitat Endurance was right *there*. Close enough to walk back to. I was already homesick—domesick. What few friends I had were there.

Jorge was there.

It wouldn't take long for him and Rona to hook up. They were perfect for each other. Both were intelligent, lots in common, lots to talk about. She was beautiful, with dark creamy skin and dark hair. It didn't matter how much I liked him, he deserved better.

I shook my head. *Best not to dwell.*

If I returned to the dome, no one would be able to get me out of it until the next transport came. I turned my back on the habitat.

Which meant, I was going to die out here.

I should just shoot myself and be done with it. Things would be so much easier. Ah, no gun. Don't like pain. Sigh.

Besides, as long as I was alive, there was a chance I might make it. No matter how remote, there was always a chance.

Bottom line—I wanted to live.

Sigh.

At some point, I'd have to cooperate with these people.

Not today.

I stared hopelessly at the snow and rocks.

Jorge would say the scene was pretty. He loved the snow.

To me the landscape was drab white, scattered with ugly brown rocks, and a blue sky without a cloud in sight. The scene would not change until we reached the frozen ocean, when it would be devoid of rocks and everything would be white, one long sheet of ice, with one long endless blue sky.

On the mountains to my left, I could just distinguish little orange figures: Gino, Spago, and their teams. Geologist Larry Gino was collecting rocks. Volcanologist Spago Jorgson was setting up his seismic readers to monitor the mountains. I'd left at an inconvenient time for them, so they had said their goodbyes early and headed out without a backward glance.

Gino had hung around for a bit, but eventually he too left. He at least gave me a goodbye hug and one last wave before he climbed into their land rover hovercraft.

Above the mountains, one of Akiane's two moons shone at half its glory. The other had already slipped behind the mountains.

Not to far away, in front of me, was Jorge's algae patch, the one he had shown me when we first landed. The field stretched out at least 90 meters. It was not continuous, but random patches of red and yellow algae and white snow. He'd told me algae had fine hairs. It was the fine hairs that kept the algae from freezing and made the snow appear different colors.

Had Jorge been out here yet? I'd been so caught up with my leaving that I forgot to ask.

I hoped he'd find the snow ecology he was searching for: spiders and worms and such. Maybe Rona would accompany him and they'd search together.

Worms are his favorite. To him they are fascinating little creatures that can either lengthen or shorten their size. Only one fourth of worms born are male, which means the females can reproduce with or without a partner. According to Jorge, worms prefer partners. I was sure he made that part up.

Because of him, I knew more about worms than I ever cared to know. Including the silly parts.

I already missed him, Rona, and Gino.

And to my surprise, I missed Olivia Zeller, our resident know-it-all oceanographer. She and I always bickered. Now I missed her irritating voice. That was a real surprise. I would have never thought I'd miss anything about her.

But mostly, I missed Jorge. Why dwell? I'd be lucky to ever see any of them again.

Did they miss me? Probably too soon.

With all my heart, I wanted to be on the ship returning to Earth. But Admiral Grossman promised he'd court-martial me for disobeying orders. Would twenty years in the brig be so bad? I'd be alive and warm, and there wouldn't be any dogs.

I had three choices—all bad.

Don't go on this trip, return to Earth, and give up twenty years of my life.

Don't go on this trip and stay on Akiane for the rest of my life. Even that wouldn't work. The admiral would send the military police after me.

The only alternative was to take the journey and hope I survived. A poor choice, perhaps, but unfortunately, it was the best of the lot. So much for getting my life together.

Chapter 3

Jess Hewitt
Alpha Dogs

ONCE CAMERON finished checking paws, he untied a large bag on the sled, dug into it, and threw handfuls of dried fish at the dogs, creating a feeding frenzy. They mercilessly barked and snapped at one another while attacking their meal.

Two dogs grabbed the same fish. They tugged and snarled, each insisting the other let go.

One was Addle, the red and white dog who'd attacked one of the dogs on his team back at the habitat. Great, I was already recognizing the dogs and knew them by name.

This time Addle was picking on Huth, one of the lead dogs from his team. Huth was a husky, all-white dog with ice-blue eyes.

Essal, an all white dog with one red ear, came to her rescue and snapped at Addle's tail. I think he only caught fur. But Addle turned with such ferocity one would have thought blood had been drawn. His gray eyes focused on Essal with murderous intent.

Rona and Lu said they were having trouble finding male dogs. I'd found at least two of them. One was annoying and the other a bully, distinct male personality traits.

Essal dashed off.

Addle started to chase him, but stopped. Remembering the fish, he turned just in time to see Huth snap her head back and toss the fish in the air. She opened her mouth wide. The fish easily dropped in and disappeared. After a few quick chews and one good swallow, she snarled victoriously at Addle.

He howled as if she'd eaten the last piece of fish. With one great leap, Addle lunged at her.

She rose up on her haunches to receive his attack.

Nu Venia started for them.

"They must decide," Cameron said.

She stopped in mid-step.

Back at the habitat, while we were preparing to leave, Cameron had refused to let the dogs fight. Now these two might kill each other and he took no notice. Why? What had changed?

"Do something, Cameron," Nu Venia yelled over the combating dogs.

He remained rooted in place. "They must decide," he repeated.

They weren't fighting over fish; they were fighting for dominance. Addle wanted to be lead dog, but Huth was alpha, she wasn't about to submit.

Essal raced to the fight, but instead of joining in, he yelped at them as if encouraging Huth while reprimanding Addle. Their team stopped eating and intently watched, but did not abandon their fish.

The other team was too busy eating to pay attention or care about the fight. A few pretended to wrestle over their fish, but their disagreements were easily settled.

Addle and Huth tumbled and rolled. Addle rose first to stand over Huth. He tried to sink his teeth into her neck. Huth howled with fury. She twisted out from under his hold, jumped up, slammed into his side, and brought him down.

The fight ended with Huth standing with her teeth at Addle's neck but did not draw blood. He lay on his back with his belly up, a sign of submission.

Cameron threw fish at Huth, hitting her on the side. She jumped in surprise as she released her hold. With one last growl of warning, she picked up her fish and left.

Addle rolled onto his stomach, and wiped his pink nose as if the black spot on it itched. Cameron threw a fish at him. He picked it up, and slunk away to eat in defeat.

With his tongue hanging out, Essal proudly strutted at his contribution to the fight, which had been nothing. Cameron threw a few fish in his direction. Satisfied with how things had turned out, he flopped onto his belly and ate.

Cameron retied the bag and dropped the canvas cover over it.

As suddenly as the frenzy had started, it stopped with startling quiet as if the fury had never happened. All was forgiven. They were once again comrades. All except Huth and Addle. She turned her back on him. He watched her every move.

Akiane dogs made me nervous. They were not just dogs, but savage beasts. If they could turn on each other over a piece of dried fish, what would they do if Cameron ran out of fish? Would they attack him? Nu Venia? Me?

"Do they ever eat red meat?" I asked, afraid they might like the taste of human.

"No, Lieutenant," Cameron said. "Chovis only eat fish."

He pulled a small leather bag from a different place under the canvas covering. In it were three large metal mugs in it. He placed the mugs on a rock near the stove. Then he pulled a small pouch out and poured bits of dried leaves into each mug.

Nu Venia relinquished the watching of the pot to him.

Clear sign who the dominant human was.

He checked the pot and added more snow.

As we waited for tea, the dogs ran free. Most stayed close, wanting affection. Just imagine, thirty-two dogs rubbing against us wanting their ears and bellies scratched. Have I mentioned I don't like dogs?

Soon after my father dragged me from my comfortable home in St. Paul to live in the far north woods of Minnesota, he bought twelve dogs for two sled teams. He thought it was something we could do together.

I wanted my cousins and friends, not dogs. I thought if I rejected them, he would finally understand. Instead he spent a lot of time caring for those dogs and going on sledding trips with them, leaving me behind. Those mangy mutts stole my dad from me.

"On Earth, we tie dogs down so they won't wander off," I said, hoping my suggestion would inspire these people to do something with their animals.

"No need with chovis, Lieutenant," Nu Venia said. She was sitting on a snow bump with one dog laying over her feet, another's head in her lap while one more leaned against her.

Interesting. She didn't give nearly as much attention to the mutts as Cameron did, but they still hung all over her.

Cameron lavished attention on all of them, but only one dog sat at his side. She was deep red with a white belly and three stocking paws. The fourth leg was all red like the rest of her.

That dog followed Cameron's every move as if she were his shadow. She was obviously his favorite.

A mostly red dog jumped up on the rock I was sitting on. His head was level with mine. His tongue hung out, poised to lick. His hot breath exhaled directly in my face. I pushed him off. Confused, he moved to jump back up.

"Don't," I warned.

In the meantime, another dog tried to put his head in my lap. I pushed that one away.

I kicked at another dog trying to sit on my feet.

"NO!" I said as firmly as I could.

Nu Venia scowled as if I were the cruel one.

Red-eared Essal also tried to sit on the rock with me. I shoved him off. He tried to hold on. I was more determined.

He stood and stared at me. I grabbed a handful of snow and threw it at him, hitting him squarely on his pink nose.

"Get. I don't want you near me."

He shook the snow off his muzzle, but didn't move.

Cameron whistled. "Come," he said.

Phyllis Moore

The dog at Cameron's side sat on her haunches with her head held high. She gave no sign that she cared one way or the other if Essal joined them.

That annoying, red-eared mutt just stared at Cameron.

"Essal! Come. Sit here."

Essal jumped as if he were going to obey. Instead, he bounced back and sat just out of reach of my boot.

"Stay there," I warned him with a wag of my finger.

He cocked his head and gave me a half-whine, bark-like noise. Then he lay down, dropped his head on his paws, and watched me. He blended well into the snow. Except, his blue eyes, pink nose, and one red ear stood out against all that white.

Finally—*finally*, now that I was cold, steam rose from the teapot. Water was actually boiling. I thought it was ready, but Cameron scooped up two handfuls of snow and dropped them in. By the time he declared the water was ready for tea, my internal furnace was waning.

Even with all that I was wearing—long johns, a wool hat and a hood, two sets of gloves, three pairs of socks, and over it all, a winter fur suit, the depth of my stomach was icy. It was past time to warm up.

With tealeaves in the mugs, Cameron poured the water and after a few minutes of steeping, handed mugs to Nu Venia and me.

I expected to see tea leaves floating in my drink. To my surprise, the leaves had dissolved. The tea was thick and creamy. Smelled fine. Gingerly, I tasted it. Good. A longer drink.

The first sip was both surprisingly good and hot enough to burn my tongue, but the warmth didn't last long enough to reach my throat. After several more sips, warmth finally made its way to and down my throat. Succeeding drinks reached my chest and eventually the heat spread to my stomach.

Cameron handed us strips of dried meat. He refilled our mugs, then refilled the pot with snow. Just how long was he planning to stay?

As I kept drinking, I became suddenly very warm. I took my fur gloves off, pulled back my hood, and unsnapped my jacket halfway down my chest.

"We have come three kilometers," Cameron happily chirped as if we'd accomplished something meaningful out of the thousands we were expected to cross.

This was going to be a very long trip.

Chapter 4

Jess Hewitt
Bye Again

IT WAS an apparition, a mirage, certainly my imagination.

At the sound of crunching snow, I'd turned to see what it was. My heart leapt. Then turned cold with trepidation. I was positive the vision before me would disappear, but after blinking my eyes several times, it didn't, and I began to trust my sight.

Jorge was indeed walking toward me like a tall, blond god. His orange winter suit was zipped almost to his throat and his hood was pushed back. There was no mistaking who he was.

Why? Was he coming to see me? No, his algae field was nearby. I was no more than a diversion. I hadn't even disappeared from sight and he was already thinking about spiders and worms.

My disappointment melted at the sight of his broad smile.

"Jorge, what are you doing here?" I was too stunned to stand and greet him.

"What are you doing here?" He laughed. I loved his laugh. He dropped his equipment bag on the snow and sat on the rock next to me. "I thought you were on an expedition."

"So did I," I said.

Our shoulders touched. I leaned into him. His smile warmed me far more than a hot drink ever could.

"We're having tea," I said.

One of Jorge's eyebrows lifted above his sunglasses as if to ask, "Tea?"

I handed him my mug. He took a swig.

"Good. A little bitter, but good."

Neither Cameron nor Nu Venia greeted him or acknowledge his existence.

Jorge didn't notice. His eyes were only on me, as if the other two didn't exist. I wish. He took his sunglasses off to get a better look.

I became self-conscious at the way he was scrutinizing me.

"Jorge, what are you staring at?" I softly asked.

"Memorizing every bit of your face, Jessie. I don't want to forget one single thing while you're gone. You have a little scratch on the side of your mouth." The sound of his voice was like listening to a beautiful symphony.

"Do I? I don't remember scratching myself," I said. My hand reached for my mouth.

He took his right glove off and traced the scratch with his index finger from the side of my nose to the edge of my lips. I think he might have traced my mouth but, as he realized what he was doing, he blushed, and put his glove back on.

"So what are you doing here?" I asked again to break the awkwardness.

Pointing to his equipment bag, he said, "Algae. I'm cataloging what kind of algae grows here and what kind of ecology exists around it." He paused and stared at me. "I saw you sitting here." He shrugged. "So I jogged over."

At the mention of algae, Cameron's head popped up. He held still held his mug in one hand. With the other hand, he was kneading an ear of the dog that was constantly at his side.

"Not to worry," Jorge said. "I won't disturb the algae. I just want to study it."

Cameron wasn't pleased.

"Jorge, have you found any fleas?" I asked.

He let out a short chortle, his freckled-nose creased, and his eyes squinted.

"They're not really fleas. That's a laymen's term. They're a member of the species ringtail, classification Collembola."

He would have continued, but upon seeing my face, he stopped.

"I'm sorry," I said. "It's all that technical science stuff. I don't get it."

It wasn't that I didn't care. I didn't understand most of what he was talking about. And that was why he should be with Rona. She was brilliant and could carry on an intelligent conversation about fleas.

Jorge smiled. My heart did that all-too-familiar flip-flop.

"No, I'm sorry," he said. "I get excited and expect everyone else to be just as excited. There is so much that's so very different from anything we know back on Earth." He took his glove off. A finger scratch his eye. "And yet, there are amazing similarities."

"When I get back you can tell me all about it," I said.

Sadness passed over his face, erasing his smile. He put his glasses back on, reached for my hand, and gave it a little squeeze.

Cameron froze as he was bringing his mug to his lips.

Nu Venia was resting her forearms on her knees. Her face was blank, her eyes unfocused, she was somewhere the rest of us were not invited. But when Jorge took my hand, a gasp of surprise escaped her lips, and as she came back to us, her whole body jumped.

Jorge quickly pulled his hand away and said, "I'm sorry."

"Ignore them," I said and didn't bother to hide the anger in my voice. "I plan to."

"You're on an expedition with them."

"I'll manage."

Still holding the mug, Cameron's hand floated back to his knee. He and Nu Venia continued to watch us with genuine concern.

"But I am curious," Jorge asked Cameron, "you have such large algae patches. I've never seen anything like it."

"Do you not cultivate algae on your world?" Cameron asked.

Jorge beamed as he lightly nudged me with his shoulder. "I knew it. They harvest it."

Lifting his mug, Cameron said, "Tea."

"Tea?" Jorge looked in the mug. "Yes, there are some on Earth who also drink algae tea for good health."

"This is not Earth," Cameron said. "Things that seem the same are indeed different."

"Huh." Jorge gave him a blank stare. He wasn't quite sure what that meant. "Vitamin C. Keeps scurvy away," he finally said, as if he did understand.

"You have contaminated our algae harvest," Cameron said.

"Excuse me?" Jorge asked.

"No one will go there now," Cameron said, "because you have been there."

"Oh. I . . . ah." Jorge didn't know what to say. "I . . . didn't realize. I won't go there anymore, if it will help."

"It is too late," Cameron set. "We have another, one you cannot find."

"I promise not to go looking for it," Jorge said with a half smile.

Cameron grunted. It was clear he didn't like Jorge and didn't want him around, one more reason for me not to like him.

Not sure what else to say or do, Jorge extended his arm to Cameron. He took the mug offered. It came back to me, filled with more hot tea.

By the time Nu Venia had re-harnessed the dogs to the sleds and Cameron was finished repacking, which for him was a laborious process, which took far too long, I was again cold.

Cameron started packing by pulling three sets of snowshoes off one of the sleds. Then he placed the tea can, bag of mugs and stove on the sled. For some reason they were not in the correct place. He repositioned each one three different times, then, just when I thought he was ready, he repositioned the stove once more before he tied everything in place, pulled the tarp over, and tied it down.

Nu Venia, who was staring off in another world and seemed not to know what was happening around her, stood just as he finished.

With Jorge nearby, my spirits lifted. He stood with me ready to encourage me on my way.

He held my arm. There was something strange about his attitude. He had the same look when we were with Rona and Olivia back at the habitat, but this time it was more intense.

He took my sunglasses off, then took his off, and stared directly into my eyes. I couldn't glance away. He slowly moved closer. I couldn't move.

My heart. My heart! It wouldn't settle.

He'll hear my beating heart. I feared. *If I can hear it, I know he can.*

He continued to float closer. He bowed his head. I tilted my chin up. Our lips brushed ever so lightly, then separated. He wanted to see how I'd respond.

I was frozen in place. I could neither move closer nor step away, nor could I kiss him back. I stood there, breathless, waiting, fearing I might cry at all the missed opportunities.

After what seemed like an eternal second, his lips came back, pressed in—oh my God! I felt that kiss all the way down to my toes.

He wrapped his arms around me and pulled me in. My arms came up and gripped his back. My fingers dug into his winter suit.

Why hadn't we done this sooner?

I never . . . All I wanted . . . I'd been too scared of rejection.

Rona knew. How many times had she told me Jorge preferred me over her? But I thought *she* was the one who was insecure. It was me all along.

I leaned into him. No, I *melted* into him.

And then he was gone. He pulled away and the kiss was over.

"What a fool I've been, Jessie," he said. "I should have said something sooner. Now you're leaving and I might never see you again. I thought I had time." He pulled me close and bear-hugged me.

I was too stunned to speak, too caught up in the moment, too afraid to say something that would ruin the moment.

"I was hoping you'd fail your mission and you'd have to stay," he continued. "I've been such a fool." He held me more tightly. "I miss you already and you've only been gone for two hours."

"Technically, I haven't left yet," I said.

It felt unbelievably good to be in his arms. I rested my head against his shoulder. Why did I have to leave? Why did he wait until now? Why had I waited?

"Time to go," Cameron said, more harshly than needed.

Reluctantly, we parted.

"Perhaps I can walk with you and have one more mug of tea before you head out," he said.

Hope leaped like a frog out of winter hibernation onto a spring lily pad. Jorge wanted to walk with me, stay with me, as long as possible.

"We are headed into deeper snow," Cameron said. He dropped one pair of snowshoes in front of me, without saying a word. Was he disgusted with us? Why? What had we done?

He abruptly turned and dropped a pair of snowshoes in front of Nu Venia, then took a few steps away before he dropped the last pair at his feet. Stepping into one of the shoes, he knelt on the other knee. "We do not have a fourth pair for your friend, Lieutenant." He adjusted the bindings around his boot until they fit snugly, then locked it in place. He stood and stepped onto the other shoe.

My elation sank back into the muck and mire.

"You don't want him to come along. You know I'll enjoy his company." I wasn't sure I could go on if Jorge wasn't with me.

Cameron strapped the other shoe in place.

"I do not want him along because it will be more difficult for you when he has to stay behind," he said.

"He's right, Jessie," Jorge said. "I don't understand why you have to go, but you do, and I have to stay."

"But..." I didn't want Cameron to be right.

26

"I'll be here when you return." Jorge hugged me tightly. "I love you. I know I should have said something long ago, but I don't know why I didn't. Stupid, I guess. Just plain stupid."

"I should have told you how I felt. " I couldn't say love you. If I did I'd completely lose what little self-control I had left.

Then what? Stay with him and not go? Return to Earth and be court-martialed? We couldn't be together on Earth. I'd be in the brig. Did Jorge love me enough to wait while I served my sentence? Or would he forsake Earth for me so we could spend the rest of our lives on Akiane? Could I forsake Earth? The admiral would send MPs for me.

It was a no-win situation. It was up to me to risk my life so we could be together.

I buried my face in his chest.

"I know," Jorge whispered as he held me close. "I'll be here when you return and we'll get it right then. I promise."

We stared at each other—so much to say—absolutely no time to say any of it.

He kissed me lightly. I think if the kiss had been more serious we might not have parted. I tasted salty tears. They weren't mine but his.

"Here. I'll help you," Jorge knelt to open the straps on the snowshoe. I put a hand on his shoulder for balance and placed my foot in the bindings. This would be the last time I'd touch him for a very long time. He slipped the leather straps over my boot and securely locked them in place.

I placed my other foot in the other snowshoe.

Once finished, he stood. "I'll be here when you return." He sounded confident.

I almost believed him.

"Oh, here." He placed his sunglasses on my face. "You might need these."

"Won't you need them, Jorg?" I asked.

"I brought more than one pair." He took my wool hat off and adjusted the strap behind my head. Then he placed my glasses in my pocket.

Like goggles, they tightly fitted my face completely protecting my eyes from snow, sun glare, and the cold. I'd also packed several pair but these were from Jorge.

"Thanks," I said.

He repositioned my hat, pulled my hood up, and refastened my jacket. His lips lightly brushed mine one last time before he pulled my turtleneck up and over my face and secured it over my nose next to my new glasses.

I was glad for the covering. Jorge couldn't see my chin quivering.

Cameron yelled, "Huk!" which meant, "Go," and the dogs were off.

I *hated* to admit it, but Cameron was right. My heart couldn't have told Jorge goodbye a third time.

Every few meters I stopped and turned back. Each time, he was still there watching me. We waved.

I continued on.

I slowly walked uphill. When I reached the top, I took one final look. I forcibly resisted the urge to skid back down the hill, run to him, and fling myself into his arms. Instead, I turned and started down the other side. For all I knew, that was the last time I'd ever see Jorge again.

The warmth of his kiss had chilled. The comfort of his arms faded. All of it no more than a memory from a lifetime ago.

Chapter 5

Qorow Low
Standing with Adumie

QOROW LOW HAD timidly asked Adumie if she could join him. His custom to was to refuse her requests. This time he had said yes. Now she wished she had not come.

Adumie's fury caused Qorow Low to tremble with fear.

The roof of Endurance was a place to watch night give way to the new day. It offered a magnificent view of the surrounding countryside as Kahair rose from the edge of the caldera as the eastern sky change color from black lava of night to the bright colors of morning.

This day Adumie and Qorow Low had not come for the view but had come to watch Woden quest depart.

They came before first light, and stood with their backs to the eastern sky as they watched the goings on below by the light of blubber lamps.

Several priests stood to one side and prayed for Woden's success.

Fishers examined their nets and played with chovis while they waited for departure of a day of fishing.

These were the ones who believed as Cameron did. Their desire was to welcome off-worlders, or as Adumie had named them, intruders.

Adumie, and many like him, believed those of Earth came to invade and take possession of Akiane and its people.

The fishers and priests who rejected off-worlders had already left for the ocean waters. Some of those priests prayed for Woden's failure.

Qorow Low and Adumie watched as Cameron meticulously packed the sleds. They remained even after the sky had brightened and the night lamps were extinguished. They stayed even as Cameron, Nu Venia, and the Earth priest began Woden.

Priests, fishers, and chovis traveled to open ocean waters.

Off-worlders were on the mountains or at the ocean. All intruders stayed inside Endurance.

Qorow Low and Adumie watched for the first hour as Woden traveled until tea break. It was right to allow chovis to rest and check each animal to see if all were fit for the journey.

The golden haired one, who had contaminated algae fields, joined Woden.

He had been slowly walking to the fields until he saw the Woden quest, then he hurriedly diverted his steps.

Then the unimaginable happened.

Qorow Low covered her mouth to muffle her cry of distress.

Adumie spoke one word as if releasing a steam valve, "Blasphemers."

The Earth priest openly did the inconceivable with the golden-haired one, not caring who saw. They pressed their bodies together as if they might become one.

Qorow Low and Adumie were too far away to see exactly what happened, but what they did see horrified them.

The touching of hands was prohibited, but to touch the entire body to another was immoral, and then to do it in view of others was . . . was . . .! There were no words for such a thing was unmentionable. It was clear that those of Earth had no respect or no shame for public offense.

Adumie shook with rage. "Wicked people. What more proof does Cameron need?" Words could not fully express his indignation.

If anyone asked Qorow Low what had happened, she would be too embarrassed to admit to what she had just witnessed.

"If a priest is so blasphemous, how much more are the others," he fumed. "These are the intruders you and Cameron wish to welcome into our Community?"

Adumie never wanted off-worlders on Akiane or at Endurance. Cameron wished to welcome them and ask for their help to heal the slow-dying sickness, a disease that took weeks, months, sometimes years, to kill.

No one should want help from blasphemers.

Then, repulsion upon disgust, they did it again! The priest and the other pressed bodies a second time.

Adumie turned away. "One should not look upon evil."

"Cameron will not Woden now," Qorow Low said sadly.

She dropped her head and closed her eyes. The reason for Woden was to understand and recognize the other's heart. Cameron, who walked so closely with the Holy One, would not, could not have understanding with a priest such as this. Not when that one's heart was so visibly exposed as wicked.

"Woden does not have God's favor. How can He bless under such conditions?" Adumie demanded.

Qorow Low hated how Community could not come together in agreement over off-worlders.

Decisions were made when all of Community was in agreement. An issue was presented, discussed, given time to consider, more discussion, and finally a solution was agreed upon.

Since the slow-dying sickness, there had been many discussions but no solution. Even prayer had not helped find a cure. Some believed as Adumie that their fate was in the Holy One's hands, even if that meant death for all.

Some believed as Cameron that Holy One had provided an answer to prayer by bringing a cure through those of Earth. But after more discussion, and more prayer, there was still no decision concerning off-worlders.

If only Earth had not abandoned them from the very beginning.

Settlers had come to Akiane with the promise of continual support from Earth, but such promises were deceptions. Those of Earth knew nothing of truth.

If only Holy One gave a clear sign. No matter how much prayer, there was only silence, which caused much speculation and lack of faith.

Woden was suggested by Jecidia, a once-great and holy leader. He had stepped down because of the slow-dying illness, thereby placing Adumie as leader.

Qorow Low knew Adumie was not happy. He was greatly disappointed over the deaths, and angry that Holy One had not granted the request to heal. He now referred to Holy One as "God" as though it was an insult.

As high priest, Adumie should have pronounced the final decision concerning Woden. He would have preferred cancelling the quest, but on Woden Community finally came to an agreement. He had no choice but to allow it.

Qorow Low feared once all learned of this blasphemy, Woden could not proceed. *WSC Britannia* would be recalled to take all off-worlders away.

Through her tears, Qorow Low asked Adumie for confirmation of her thoughts. "Cameron will be returning."

With only a slight nod of his head, Adumie pulled his hood up and turned to leave.

When one works together to survive under harsh conditions, such as Woden, one learns cooperation. From cooperation comes understanding. From understanding comes trust. From trust Community would accept help from off-wolders to cure the slow-dying sickness. If Cameron did not go on Woden now, he never would. There would be no cure.

She watched as Cameron approached the Earth priest with snowshoes in hand.

"Wait," Qorow Low said. "See."

Hurriedly, Adumie returned to her side. He pushed his hood back.

"See." She pointed. "Cameron straps snowshoes on, as do the others."

"Cameron is not reliable. He thinks he knows the will of God better than any one," Adumie said.

They watched as Cameron, Nu Venia and the chovis continued Woden. The Earth priest was the last to follow. The priest repeatedly stopped and turned to wave at the golden-haired one.

That one stood until the quest disappeared from view, then continued to the algae fields.

"*God punishes the wicked and those who follow in the ways of sinners,*" Adumie quoted. "To tamper with God's will is to ask for a greater curse."

Qorow Low's heart became heavy. "But Cameron said Holy One had spoken to him," she reminded him. "Truly, Holy One would have known in advance about the Earth priest." None of this made sense to her.

"Only Cameron says God has spoken. There is none to confirm." After a moment of thoughtful quiet, Adumie continued, "We are a people set apart from all others. Those of Earth bring profanity. God does not want His chosen to be corrupted by such as these. God calls us to Himself for our protection from blasphemers."

"You think the Holy One brings death for our protection?" She could not believe his words.

"There is no other explanation," he said harshly. "I have prayed." He spoke "prayed" as if it were a bad taste in his mouth. "All have prayed. No healing comes. One can only conclude the answer is the death."

Qorow Low suddenly realized how truly disappointed Adumie was in unanswered prayer. She seemed to see him for the first time.

His face was creased with worry. His shoulders were bent from the disquiet in his heart. He appeared much older than his years.

"Woden will fail." His voice sounded both callous and broken. "They will not return." This he spoke with regret not anger.

He left Qorow Low standing by herself.

She did not believe Holy One brought death to save. She believed as Cameron did. Holy One was all-loving, merciful, and forgiving.

She remembered how Cameron was assured Holy One had spoken to him. Perhaps The Holy One had a plan to sanctify the Earth priest and save Woden.

Perhaps hope was not completely lost after all.

Chapter 6

Jessica Hewitt
Chovis

LIKE DOGS of Earth, dogs of Akiane preferred to walk the path of least resistance. That meant we walked in single file in front of them, Cameron first, Nu Venia second. By the time I'd walked the same path, the snow was well packed down. The dogs could easily pull the sled over the snow. Oh, for the life of a canine.

Snowshoeing was no easy task. It was okay for an hour or so, but Cameron planned on us walking until star down. It didn't take long for me to appreciate those hourly tea breaks.

I looked over my shoulder to see how the dogs were doing. To my surprise, both teams moved in perfect formation. These were the same dogs that were just fighting over fish as if it were the only meal of the day. Now they acted as if they'd all passed obedience school with flying colors. Their tails happily curled up swaying with the rhythm of their gait, and focused on us with no thoughts of running off. The over loaded sleds glided effortlessly as if skating over ice.

"Nu Venia, who's the dog with Cameron?" I asked.

"Nella. She is loyal to him."

"What does that mean?"

"All chovis are friendly. Some chovis become loyal to just one. Nella walks at Cameron's side and will warn of danger."

"So, Nella walks point to divert us from something like falling in a snow crevasse," I said.

"We will not fall into snow crevasses, Lieutenant," she promised.

Well, there was one load off my mind.

A snow crevasses is a hollow area covered by snow. If we walked over a weak spot, the snow could give way and we'd fall into a large area of ice and snow cliffs that could be several meters down. Even if we survived the fall, we might never get out.

Which meant, I didn't have to worry about surviving a ten-meter drop, never to be found again. I could reserve all my worry for an ocean of melting ice and the possibility of drowning. What comfort.

"I doubt there are crevasses here," she continued. "But there are hollow places under the snow."

Hollow places? Sounded like crevasses to me, just smaller. Even if a fall was only one or two meters, one could still break a leg—if not a neck.

"Dogs back on Earth are similar. I had a woman friend who used to walk across Colorado's frozen lakes with her Newfoundland." Since she didn't know what a Newfoundland was, I said, "The dog was the size of a small black bear."

I quickly realized that she didn't know what a black bear was. So I explained, "The dog was larger than one of your wheel dogs. Anyway, her dog would push and pull her along the safest parts of the lake. She never fell in, no matter how precarious the ice," I said, but I don't think Nu Venia cared.

She said nothing more.

Neither did I. Why bother? I had nothing to say to her and there was little she had to say that I wanted to hear.

Cameron, on the other hand, did not, could not, *would* not stop talking!

In the unspoiled quiet of the day, the only sounds were the crunch of our snowshoes, the panting of dogs, and Cameron's deep, boisterous, incisive voice.

He rambled on about Scandinavian folklore and how three giant gods created a vast wasteland of ice, a place of nothingness called *Ginnungagap*.

He spoke of *Muspell*, the Land of Fire. In this story, sparks of fire melted ice, formed land, and brought warmth that created the Land of the Living.

It was much the same stories Dad had told me when we went winter camping.

Cameron compared the story with how three great ships came from Earth to the frozen wasteland of Akiane and created a new world. According to him, the ships and their crews were as magnificent as the Scandinavian gods.

He explained how their habitat became heaven for them by protecting them from the cold winter years.

Their ancestors lived in two of those ships while they built the habitat around them and cultivated native gardens inside the habitat. They named it Endurance because they had endured much and had persevered.

On occasion, Nella's head tilted upward as she made doggy noises as if commenting or asking questions.

Cameron spoke of the weather, the sky, the snow, the difference between traveling during the day and at night, what it would be like to cross the top of Akiane to the other side, the wind . . .

"Enough already!" I finally exploded.

"What?" Nu Venia's head popped up.

She seemed surprised by her surroundings as if she'd forgotten where she was.

"Cameron," I said. "Does he never shut up?"

"What?" she asked again.

"Nu Venia, don't you hear him? How could you not hear him?" I asked. "He hasn't shut up since we started walking!"

"We have been together for so long Nu Venia no longer hears unless I speak directly to her." Cameron didn't have to turn his head or speak louder so I could hear him. His voice radiated out of his mouth and carried over the surrounding area to my ears. I wouldn't have been a bit surprised if they could hear him back at the habitat.

"If she doesn't pay attention to you, how does she know when you're speaking to her?" I asked.

"I speak Nu Venia's name," he said. "And that one listens."

"Why do you have to talk so much in the first place?" My voice rose in frustration with each word.

"So, Nella will not become lonely," he said.

"She's a few centimeters from your leg. I can see her fur brushing your pants. I doubt she's lonely. But you're driving me crazy, so shut up already," I said, none too politely.

He was quiet, but I had no doubt that he'd start up again. Those who must speak cannot be silent for long.

The barren land stretched endlessly before us. We walked in and out of ridges and dips. We walked around rock outcrops and between large boulders. We walked around snow mounds the size of a small house, which the wind had blown into interesting free-form abstract sculptures.

Suddenly, Nella barked loudly and leaped at Cameron. She wasn't complaining because he'd stopped talking, or was asking for more stories, she wanted him to stop. He obeyed. She bounded forward, sniffing. We patiently waited as Nella ran up and down rolling mounds of snow for almost ten minutes.

She spoke in dogy language, yelping, yawning, and whining, telling Cameron in great detail what she'd found.

One might have thought those two actually understood each other.

Without question or examining the ground for himself, Cameron followed Nella west, abandoning our northern route. She led us for several meters around the area before she again allowed us to proceed due north.

Except for Nella's paw prints, the snow was unspoiled. I could only imagine what kind of deadly crevasse we could have fallen into.

I shook the thoughts from my head.

"If something happened to Nella, and she wasn't with us any more, can one of the other dogs also detect danger?" I asked. I wanted assurance that we had a backup plan just in case something did happened to our lead dog.

"Nella is with us, Lieutenant," Cameron said.

Well, that didn't answer my question.

Dogs might be aggravating and demand far too much attention, nevertheless, they had their place. Nella would safety guide us, while the others would pull our gear, tent, and food. They did provide a sense of security.

"Nothing better happen to Nella," I said.

"Nothing will happen to Nella," Cameron assure me.

He'd better be right.

Chapter 7

Jessica Hewitt
End of First Day

END OF day was like every other rest stop. Dog necessities came before human needs. After checking paws and feeding them, Cameron started on our dinner. He began by pulling cooking utensils off a sled and set it up.

Nu Venia untied and pulled the tarp off the sled that held our tents and bedding.

I watched both of them and considered not helping, but I wanted to lie down and relax, which I could do only after our tents were pitched. The quicker the tents were up, the quicker I could lie down, so I helped.

First Nu Venia and I pulled several furs off the side. Next we cleared an area of small rocks and smoothed out the snow. We pulled two tents off, placed the smaller one next to the furs, and pulled the larger tent to the cleared area.

Nu Venia stood and stared at it.

"Well?" I asked.

"I am unsure as to how to proceed," she said.

"I don't understand. I thought you and Cameron had been camping before."

"Your captain gave us tents. I think our tents are better, but Cameron did not want to offend," she said

"Ah," I said and leaned down to pull the lever.

There was a hissing sound as air rushed in and the tent inflated.

Nu Venia jumped back in surprise.

The tent flopped and slapped the snow as it unfolded. Poles rose up and snapped in place. Within five minutes we had a fully erect tent.

"Oh my," Nu Venia said. "I have never seen anything such as this before."

"Well, we have one more tent," I said. Having lived with tents like this all my teenage years, I was unimpressed. But I assumed it was much easier than what we might have had to use if not for the captain's generosity. At least, we didn't have to build an igloo.

The smaller tent fit neatly inside the first tent and were much like the layering of clothes. The air trapped between them would provide insulation from the cold night.

We attached a small chimney between the tents to the outside for ventilation.

From there, Nu Venia took over.

We placed several large fur skins with the fur side down on the floor of the smaller tent. They would keep cold from creeping up from the frozen ground and into our sleeping bags. Several more furs were placed on top with the fur side up. The entire tent floor became one large fur carpet. Good thing I wasn't allergic to dog.

Our sleeping blankets were four smaller furs sewn together similar to traditional sleeping bags. Nu Venia placed each against a different wall, leaving the area by the exit door clear.

Cameron had assured me nights were no longer sub-freezing. It would still be far colder than I liked. I remembered Minnesota winters. I hated them. Those same feelings rose up in me again.

As soon as I graduated from college, I'd moved to Baja California, Mexico, where most days were pleasantly hot year round. A year after Dad died, I joined World Space Coalition and moved to WSC Moon Base where I lived in a climate-controlled atmosphere for four years.

For six years and ten months, I lived in a climate-controlled space ship. I hadn't been outside in over a decade.

I was not out of shape physically, but I certainly was not physically prepared to be outside in this cold weather.

So, while it might not have been cold for my companions, it was freezing for me. Okay, I wasn't literally freezing, but I was darn cold. I'd been gone one day, and I already missed warmth. I had no idea when I'd be warm again, or if ever.

No sooner were the tents up and blankets down, than the dogs began to parade in. They sniffed at the blankets, at the floor, at the tent corners, at Nu Venia, and me.

She didn't notice.

Cameron came in and set up his kitchen area between his and Nu Venia's sleeping blankets. He placed the stove on a small platform, then placed a cooking pot on the stove full of fresh meat and frozen vegetables.

To my surprise, the dogs stayed clear of the stove and the cooking area.

I don't like places where people and, in this case, dogs, huddled so closely together. I couldn't move without bumping into, or tripping over one of them. And yet, this was how I would live for who knew how long. My nerves twinged. I needed space—now. I went outside.

Kahair was near setting. Shadows disappeared as the sky darkened. Everything became a dull gray much like my heart.

The dogs became featureless shadows as they sat, milled about, or nuzzled in the snow settling down to sleep.

Without a thought for my feelings, Kahair dragged the last of the light across the landscape into the depths of his nightly retreat. Then as if a switch had been flipped off, everything plunged into complete darkness and Akiane's star had ceased to exist and would never return.

Just as abruptly, the sky lit up with the Milky Way. Just like at home. Some things never change.

Only here, stars were in different positions and were unfamiliar.

Untold loneliness set in and long forgotten memories swept over me.

* * *

Dad loved to take me on a two or three-day winter dogsled trip. I hated camping and I fussed about having to go. But it was the only time I had him all to myself without any interruptions. Well mostly. There was always a team of dogs.

He'd find a small open spot amongst a cluster of low-hanging evergreen trees where it was a few degrees warmer than out in the open. The branches cut the wind. No wind on a winter night was always best.

After dinner, over an open fire we roasted marshmallows with graham crackers and milk chocolate, and made s'mores. Topped off with hot cocoa.

He told me fairytales, old myths, or he'd make up stories. Sometimes, we discussed his next novel. He wrote young adult books about what it was like to live and have adventures in cold weather climates.

I loved discussing his books with him, but I never read any of them. I hated the long hours of writing that kept him away from me.

* * *

I missed him. Guess I always will.

Now trillions of kilometers away, somewhere in all those billions of twinkling stars was home.

I was overcome by homesickness. Why had I left? To get away. From what? Family and friends? Just so I could become isolated from all humankind?

There would be no cocoa or s'mores tonight.

I wanted to be home with my father, and if not him, my cousins and friends. Why had I left them behind? Whatever the reason, it didn't matter now. I wasn't just homesick; my heart ached with loneliness. If I'd known how to cry, I would have.

Which star was mine? I wanted to ask Mother Earth's forgiveness for leaving her. I wanted to say goodnight, and tell her how much I missed her, and if I returned, I'd never, ever leave her again.

Did she even notice my absence?

I'd left the tent to get some space and even though I wasn't one for large crowds, right then, I'd have welcomed a noisy bar with people tightly packed in. They would ease my loneliness. I missed the smell of too much perfume and cologne. Even the smell of sweat, would have been better than the constant smell of dogs.

The horizon was empty. There wasn't the familiar glow, marking the spot of some major metropolis.

During the day, the absence of life made for an unnatural quiet, but at night it was as if nothing existed in the universe but us.

Cold crept into my fur suit, seeped under my long johns, and into my body where icy fingers kneaded at my soul. I was weary, not just from this fruitless quest, but of my very existence.

Dad's death had been hard. I still refuse to think about that day.

But there were so many others who refused to let it go. There was always a good reason for another media story, and just one more interview. There were too many friends and family members who checked in at the most inconvenient times, to consol me. I became frustrated and angry. I wanted everybody to leave me alone and let me grieve in peace.

That was why I'd left Earth, to get away from them and who I'd become. When I returned to Earth, I planned start my life over.

Unfortunately, it was me, who was the real problem. I didn't know how to change or how to leave the old me behind.

A sick realization besieged me. *Things were never going to get better.*

I shook Essal off my leg and retreated back inside the tent for human contact and a diversion from my thoughts.

Chapter 8

Jessica Hewitt
First Night of the Expedition

ESSAL RUSHED ahead of me to jump on my bedroll. I pulled the blankets out from under him and swished it at his face to make him go away, but as soon as my bedroll was back in place, and I was seated, he was back.

I tried to settle in but there were so many dogs.

Nella lay next to Cameron.

Two dogs cozied up to Nu Venia.

One dog stretched out in the middle of the tent at if she owned the place.

Four more snuggled around her. Two of those dogs rested their heads on her back.

Dogs came and went as they pleased.

Every single dog, even those who decided to sleep outside and had already been in the tent, walked through the tent. Each sniffed the fur flooring, checked the corners of the tent, walked behind Cameron, walked around Nu Venia, stepped over the dog sleeping in the middle of the tent, stopped near me, and sniffed, before going outside. They didn't follow the exact path, but they all did the exact same thing as if to make sure they'd made the right decision to stay outside and there was nothing going on inside that they might miss out on.

Those who did stay inside tried to find the best possible place to sleep.

No dog bothered Nella. Evidently, she had a permanent place at Cameron's side. No one bothered the dog stretched out in the middle of the room. Don't know why.

A few tried to displace Essal but he made it clear that he'd staked his claim on me and would not to give it up.

Other dogs were easily nudged aside. The displaced dog would get up so the nudger could take its place.

Displaced dogs went outside, only to come back a few minutes later and begin the sniffing routine all over again as if something might have happened while it was outside. It would find a place to settle, displace that dog, which went outside, only to come back in at a later time.

The dogs grunted and whined and sniffed.

It was like a circus tent.

Noses came dangerously close to my face as they sniffed at me. Pink tongues threatened to lick exposed skin. Wagging tails just missing my face.

And then there was Essal.

He tried to sleep next to me. I moved away. He moved closer. I swatted at him with my boot and yelled, "Go away you stupid dog!"

Nu Venia frowned. Clearly, she felt sorry for Essal even though I was the one who was being accosted. She should have felt sorry for me.

Nella's head rested in Cameron's lap as he kneaded her ears. Her eyes were closed. The very tip of her violet tongue peeked out of her seemingly smiling muzzle. I think she was in heaven.

Cameron watched me with an irritating smile.

"What are you smiling at?" I asked.

"Essal is more patient than you, Lieutenant," he said.

"What's that supposed to mean?"

"It means, Essal will win," he said.

"Uhm." *We'll see about that.*

Cameron's good humor was getting on my nerves. Beneath eyes filled with excitement was a stupid smile of contentment. He was less annoying when he was an impassioned warrior and I was scared of him.

46

"Don't call me Lieutenant. I don't like that rank. I didn't earn it. It was a bribe to get me to do what the admiral wanted," I said.

My companions stopped what they were doing to stare at me. "Your name is not Lieutenant?" Nu Venia asked.

"No, it's not."

"What shall we call you?" Cameron asked.

I considered telling them my last name, but that would also reminded me too much of the military. "It's Jessica."

"Jessica," he repeated and nodded his understanding. It was surprisingly gratifying to be called by my first name.

Until the military, I was always Jessica. On *Britannia*, I was the last of three Jessicas assigned to the bridge and was referred to as Ensign or Hewitt. Off duty, the other two were Jessica or Jessie. Since I was the last to arrive, I became Jess.

The nickname followed me when I moved in with the civilians. Only Olivia and Lu consistently called me Jessica. Jorge called Jessie.

Jess or Jessie didn't feel right. I was Jessica. That was how I referred to myself. It felt good to be finally getting my name back.

Unfortunately, it came from the mouths of aliens.

"Meal is ready, Jessica," Cameron said.

He had thrown fresh pieces of cut meat and frozen vegetables into a deep pan, then dropped snow into it for water and some herbs for seasoning. All of it took a long time to cook over his small stove. As the aroma intensified, my stomach growled in anticipation.

Amazingly, not one dog went near or sniffed the stove.

"Where did you get the meat?" I asked.

"It came with us," he said.

"We have fresh meat?" I asked. "I'd thought all our meat had been dried."

"Just so," he said. "Meet is fresh."

"Won't it go bad when Akiane warms up?" I asked. "Won't it freeze at night and thaw during the day?"

"No," he said, "meat is well cared for."

That was unhelpfully vague.

The stew was warming, filling, and delicious.

On Earth, tupilak was a mythical Inuit sea creature that lives under the ice. On Akiane, tupilak was a real mammal sea creature hunted for its meat.

Cameron's tupilak was less tough than our cooks' back at the habitat. The meat Cameron cooked melted in my mouth. Zhoa and Vong would have liked this recipe.

Unfortunately, the fresh meat would soon run out, and we'd be stuck with dried meat for the rest of the trip.

After dinner, Cameron insisted we strip off our long johns and put fresh ones on. I changed under my blankets with my back to them as I struggled into a fresh set of underwear.

My long johns were military issued. They were soft white wool and very warm. Theirs were thick green silk-like, close-fitting pajamas.

We hung the used ones on the clothesline Cameron had stretched across the inside of our tent. Then we turned our winter suits inside out to let the sweat dry. Finally we were to knead our boots so they would be soft in the morning.

By then I'd had enough and wasn't interested in kneading anything.

"You must," Nu Venia declared.

And when I didn't, she offered to knead them for me, but Cameron wouldn't let her.

I was too exhausted and to care.

I lay on my side with my back to the menagerie in the tent. I thought I'd stay awake all night listening to dogs sniffing and whining, the lights on, and Cameron softly talking to Nella, but . . .

The next thing I knew, it was morning. I was lying on my back. My body ached from long hours of snowshoeing. My back was stiff from sleeping on hard packed snow. I pulled my arms out from under my blankets. Every muscle in my body screamed as I stretched. The fur tickled my nose. A sneeze cut the stretch short.

Oh, that hurt!

Phyllis Moore

As I brought my arms down onto my chest, I noticed Essal was watching me. He was in the exact place as the night before.

I feared Cameron was right. That dog had no intentions of giving up. Well, I had no intentions of surrendering.

I stared up at my long johns hanging overhead and thought of all those nights aboard *Britannia* when Jorge and I could have been together. Now I was stuck with Essal.

How did my life get so messed up? Was I born under a cursed star?

Ever since Mom left, things had been going wrong. No matter how hard I tried, I just couldn't get my life together.

And yet life dragged me forward.

I should never have left Earth. I should never have left Woodlans Village or Dad. He'd still be alive if I had stayed where I belonged.

After breakfast, it was time to move on.

Yesterday's long johns and my winter suit were dry. I'd wear the underwear I'd slept in last night and carefully packed the dry one away.

Because I'd not kneaded my boots the night before, it took all my strength to pull them on. They were as stiff as a piece of wood. They didn't bend or allow my ankles to flex. I couldn't walk heel to toe. I had to walk flat-footed as if marching. Snowshoes make things worse.

It took a couple of hours of walking before they were fully supple again.

For the rest of the trip, every night, before I went to sleep, I gladly changed long johns, turned them and my winter suit inside out, hung them on the clothesline, and kneaded my boots.

Chapter 9

Qorow Low
Blood Vines

QOROW LOW HELD a long Blood Vine in one hand, a knife in the other, and cut the vine close to its roots to free it from the ground.

She quickly dropped the cut end into a large container to hold the sluggish juice from the vine. Then she searched for another vine to cut loose.

Once the container was filled with vines, she took her thin green gloves off, cut a vine in sections, and began to knead each vine with her fingertips, squeezing the liquid into the container. She started in the middle and worked her way to one end then she turned the vine around and squeezed to the other end. Liquid easily flowed out.

The liquid from this container would be poured into a larger container and spices added, then the mixture would ferment into a drink named Lazard.

After she had squeezed all the juice out of the vines, she began to peel each individual thread from the stalks. She dug her fingernail in to loosen a strip, then held it between the tip of her finger and thumb. She gently pulled so she wouldn't break the strip. She carefully placed the threads in a different container. This pile would be spun and woven into cloth.

It was tedious work, but now that there were fewer people, all helped with each chore. Before, when they were many, each family unit had its job.

In the beginning it was a necessity. Akiane was harsh land, brutal, and heartless. To survive, settlers worked as a community. They lived, ate, greeted new births, and put the dead to rest as one larger family.

The first settlers couldn't afford to live as individuals. Their arrival was filled with heartbreak and disappointment. Many died.

WSC *Eagle* exploded while still in space. WSC *Hawk* landed but was overwhelmed by the gravitational storm, which caused giant waves to sweep many on shore out to sea.

Only the WSC *Falcon* landed safely.

It was for this reason the settlers came together as one Community and worked together for the survival of all. In time, each family unit became responsible for one work detail: fishing for chovis, keeping the garden weeded, tending the hydroponics, preparing meals, tending the Blood Vines, and many other tasks.

Qorow Low's family cleaned tupilak hide. It was her family's obligation to the Community. No one thought to complain.

Because of the slow-dying sickness, they were now too few to care for Community, and their habitat Endurance, as they once had. It was now best if all helped with many different duties.

It wasn't until Qorow Low began to learn other tasks that she realized she didn't care for her family's obligation. Tanning hides did not give her the same joy as caring for the gardens. Gardening was her favorite.

Blood Vines gave so much to Community, not just drink to gladden the heart or thread for cloth. The vines also provided nests for their children, milk for nourishment while keeping their cocoons moist.

Qorow Low placed a hand on her stomach. It was time for her to build a nest. The child within was soon coming and would require a nest to mature while in her cocoon.

Mercener came to stand next to Qorow Low. She was one who liked to "swirl the bottle" and cause another distress. This day was no exception.

"You follow Adumie as a chovis follows her master." Mercener spoke with ridicule. "Yet your thoughts do not follow the same path as Adumie."

She was referring to Qorow Low's desire to trust off-worlders. "One only wishes the opportunity of understanding and the possibly of speaking with off-worlders to see if they have the knowledge that heals." Qorow Low did not lift her head as she spoke. She wished to work and for Mercener to leave.

"Such knowledge is not theirs," Mercener said.

Qorow Low longed not to have disagreement. There was already far too much disagreement in the Community. Yet, she could not allow her words to go unheard. "How do you know? Have you spoken with them?"

"This one listens to Adumie. Adumie speaks Holy One's thoughts," Mercener dropped to her knees, so her face was even with Qorow Low.

"They are not evil people," Qorow Low began, but Mercener had not come to listen.

"They are evil. You have seen the blasphemous act of the priest with your own eyes. Yet, you refuse to believe. Perhaps you should live with the off-worlders."

Qorow Low had told no one what she'd seen while watching Woden leave. Adumie would have told no one.

With one swift push of her legs, Qorow Low was on her feet. "Have you again stood in the darkness in secret to learn what one should not know?"

Mercener also stood in defiance. "You watched and did not turn away."

"I did not watch in secret."

"The Earth priest will lead others into evil."

Those working in the Blood Vines stopped and watched. Such disagreement was uncommon.

"You speak without understanding," Qorow Low said. "You do not know. Perhaps off-worlders' ways are different."

"You sound like Cameron," Mercener said. "Perhaps you should have done as Nu Venia and followed after him on a fool's journey."

"You should not be saying such things, Mercener." Qorow Low scolded. "You do not know what Holy One's will is. You might be blaspheming against His will."

Mercener's eyes narrowed, nose flared, mouth curled, her whole face crunched up in hate. "Woden will not return. Holy One will prove Adumie speaks truthfully. Off-worlders will be banished. You will see." She turned to leave.

"Perhaps it is you who snuffles after Adumie and his beliefs," Qorow Low said.

With a growl Mercener stomped off. Suddenly, she redirected her path back to Qorow Low. With one swift kick at the container of Blood Vine milk, all of Qorow Low's work poured out.

The closest vine worker hurried to right the container.

That one called after Mercener, "Such actions dishonor us all."

Mercener gave no response.

"Adumie would not condone such conduct," another called.

Both Adumie and Mercener are single-minded in their thoughts, Qorow reflection. *One does not make clear decisions based upon hatred.*

It was for this reason Qorow Low decided to seek out an off-worlder and learn for her shelf if the possibility of gaining trust was available.

Chapter 10

Larry Gino
So Many Mysteries

LARRY GINO dropped his fork as he watched Rona take the last bit of her second helping.

She smiled at his surprise, then declared, "This was so good. I'm ready to start all over again."

After much experimenting with herbs, cooks Zhoa and Vong, had found in the small hydroponics farm in their assigned quarters, and adding spices they'd brought with them, the cooks were able to find the right mix to turn tupilak into a tender, flavorful, and juicy meal.

The first settlers brought DNA to start their livestock herds. They also brought seeds of every kind of produce from around the world. But there were no farmlands on Akiane; the colonists' produce was grown in a hydroponics facility in water enriched with the planet's minerals. Over time, the mineral nutrients, and ph of Akiane's water, changed the vegetables and fruits so they were completely different. The cooks could only guess at what they were preparing.

"You've already had two helpings," Gino said. "And your second helping was larger than your first. I've never seen you eat so much." He took it as a sign she was doing better.

For a few days, right after Jess left, Rona seemed to have lost her way. She was grieving the loss her best friend and the loss of her genome project.

Larry feared she might be headed for depression.

He was the official team project leader, which made Rona's emotional well-being his responsibility. But he didn't want to step in too quickly, and thought it best to keep an eye on her while she work things out herself.

To his relief, her improved appetite and interaction with others were signs that she was coming around.

"I can't help it, it's all so good." With great effort of willpower, Rona pushed her plate away. "Okay, I'm finished. Let's talk about something other than food." She wiped her mouth with her napkin, placed it along with her fork and knife on her well-cleaned plate, and called, "Bus."

A silver acrylic rectangular container floated over to her. She deposited her dishware, but kept her mug of coffee.

"Finished," Rona said.

The autobus floated back to its hovering location near the kitchen door waiting to be called in use or ordered to the dishwasher.

Lesley Gunn, one of their two doctors, asked, "Gino, have you seen Kahair rise?"

While on *Britannia*, Gino had often enthusiastically declared that he wanted to see the alien star rise and set. It wouldn't be his first extraterrestrial star-rise or star-set. He'd lived on the WSC Moon Base and Mars Colony. Nevertheless, it would be his first interstellar star-rise.

"No," Gino exclaimed loudly.

"Why not?" Lesley asked.

Gino gave him one of his famous, "Are you an idiot?" expressions, though Lesley was anything but.

"There are no streetlights out there, you know," Gino said. "If I had gone wandering in the black of night, I could have fallen and broken a leg or worse, my neck. I could have died. Is that what you're asking me? Did I die? Well I didn't. I'm very much alive." His voice rose in mock indignation as he punctuated his words with the wave of his fork.

Smiles spread around the table. They'd learned well. At the very beginning of their training, the young ones froze in fear of reprimand at the intensity of his voice, but by the time their three-year training was over, they'd learned Gino's rants were rarely serious.

"It's cold out there," he continued to bellow. "It's absurdly freezing." Akiane was warming up and the temperatures already above freezing. "I could have gotten a cold or worse, pneumonia. I'm not dying on this planet. I'm going home— ALIVE." He spoke "alive" as if it were a rare dramatic event.

He liked to yell. It cleared the lungs and his head.

"Oh, my," Rona said.

He couldn't help it. He felt a little glow at the role-playing. It was fun and lightened up so many serious scientific conversations.

"I'm already feeling a flu coming on," he said pathetically, then gave three, *cough, cough, cough*, to emphasize his newfound illness and gain more sympathy.

Instead, he got bursts of laughter.

In mock insult, Larry declared, "No respect for the elderly." Thanks to genetic engineering, at 82 Larry Gino was as spry as a fifty-year-old and was more than able to keep up with 19 to 30 year-olds. "Someone should teach you green-eared brood some manners."

"How are we to know if you're even dead?" Lesley asked.

"What's that supposed to mean?" Gino asked truly taken aback, and he wasn't easily surprised. Did he look dead? He thought he looked pretty good for 82.

"Even if you *were* dead, you wouldn't lie down until in the *mood* to be dead," Lesley explained.

Gino chuckled. Yeah, the good doctor had him there.

"Truer words were never spoken. I did die once, so many years ago I can't remember when. After the viewing and before they closed the casket, I got up and left my coffin behind."

There was a pause and the slightest trace of his childlike grin.

"My beloved wife knew." He took a deep breath and let out a long sigh. "She was at the back door waiting for me." Another pause. He became suddenly sober. "But when she died, I waited for her . . . she never came."

It wasn't funny anymore. The dining area became silent. Gino and his wife Karen had been married for twice as long as any of the others had been alive.

Too many memories came flooding in. Like the first time he saw her.

"More," he said softly. No one knew what that meant, but Karen would have. Whenever she said, "I love you." He'd say, "Love you more." Eventually, the saying was reduced to, "More."

Karen's love had grown his heart by two sizes, but holding his sons for the first time caused his heart to swell to exploding with love.

"She was tired of you," Spago said, breaking into Gino's thoughts. "You're such a cankerous old goat, when she got up, she walked out the front door."

Gino snapped at Spago, "Tired of me?" he roared. "Someone as handsome and charming as ME?" The furrow between his eyebrows deepened. For two whole seconds he held that scowl, but the twinkle in his eye betrayed him.

Spago rolled his eyes. "I can't imagine."

The area filled with joyful laughter. No matter how loud Larry Gino yelled, he was rarely truly angry. Still, only Spago could get away with a comment like that. No one else would have dared to try.

It's best to save the past for times when one is alone and can truly savor the memories, Gino thought.

"So the answer is, 'No,' to the star-rise?" Lesley asked.

In a more serious tone Gino said, "I'm too old for these kinds of subzero temperatures. Besides, I've got nothing to prove." Now that was true. After all he'd been through and all he'd accomplished, Larry Gino thought he deserved the right to do as he pleased. "I go out when it's daylight and warmer."

"Don't let him fool you," Astrophysicist Bonga said. "We set up a floating com to watch the star-rise. We sent the feed to Gino so he can monitor it on his holo-screen from the warmth of his bunk where he's more comfortable than a bear hibernating in his cave." Bonga Sarloin was a tall, thin African of Zulu descent and astrophysics team leader.

All eyes turned to Gino for an explanation. "What? How come you're so privileged?" a voice behind him asked.

"Whoever said life is fair?" Gino said with pride.

"Thanks to Bonga," Spago said, "Gino has a full digital realism image of the star."

Rona gave Gino an indignant expression of horror.

He smiled triumphantly. "I can walk through the star if I want to." He chuckled.

It was good to see the young ones mingling. That was something else he'd taught them. When they first gathered in training, they tended to stay within their research groups. By his suggestion they were not allowed to house together according to their teams. He encouraged them to socialize and worked to bring them closer together as one large family, something they would need once they were far from home.

"Star flares and plasma waves are kicking up and giving us a real show," Bonga said. "We can set something up if any of the rest of you want to watch."

"I'd like that," Rona said.

Several voices agreed.

Gino smiled to himself. It was good to share research and learn from one another. It kept the young ones from becoming stale within their projects. They needed to see how their fields of research fit in with the rest of creation and other points of view. This way they asked questions, debated, and challenged one another. It helped the young ones to gain a better understanding of their field of study when they had to defend their findings. Science did not exist in a vacuum, but created cause and effect. Often a good debate had a great effect on someone's research project.

"Ice is beginning to melt," Olivia said.

"Melt?" Gino asked. "But Akiane's orbit can't be close enough to Kahair yet. At this distance, the star isn't warm enough to melt ice."

"Well," she said with great authority, "the interesting thing is, there are sections of ice that are solid, but there are other places where it's melting."

All the planetary volcanologists and geologists stopped eating. "What?"

"We had the same reaction," Henri said. "We sent a drone under the ice to see what's going on."

"So what is happening?" Gino asked.

"Underwater hydrothermal vents," Henri said. "We found an area of five in one place and four kilometers away we found eight more. The vents running along small faults."

While he spoke, Olivia tapped her wrist computer. A holo-screen of five underwater hydrothermal vents appeared a meter over the table and stretched the length of it.

Black chimney-like funnels rose from the ocean floor emitting billows of smoke. It meant the area was geologically active.

Areas around hydrothermal vents are often biologically productive, creating an environment rich in nutrition for complex marine communities.

"Is that carbon monoxide?" Beth asked.

"No," Olivia said. "It's water. When we first walked the ice, we didn't notice anything different. We sent the drone to see if it was something similar to krill or some other planktonic shrimp."

"The water was 13 Celsius," Henri said.

"That's hot water for an ocean of ice," Beth said.

"That's what we thought," Olivia said. "So we kept watching and searching."

"We followed the heat to the vents," Henri said. "In some places, the water is 48 Celsius."

"Wow," several people said.

"That'll melt ice."

"The hotter water is staying in pockets, but the colder water is leeching the heat and slowly warming," Henri said.

"The ice over the vents is melting fastest. It won't be long before all the ice around both faults are completely melted while other areas of ice remain solid," Olivia said. "Something big is happening under the ocean."

"There have been huge volcanic flows all over the mountains." Spago rested his forearms on the table and leaned in. His eyes matched the excitement of the words that tumbled out of his mouth. "In the past, there must have been multiple catastrophic upheavals."

With the same enthusiasm, Gino said, "Mountains seem to have been taken apart and haphazardly put back together. It's a real mess out there. At one time, those mountains must have been extremely active."

"What's that got to do with ice melting?" Olivia asked.

"According to the seismic readings, the mountains are moderately quiet," Spago said. "But every once in a while, say every five or six hours, there are some intense rumblings. Each new set of rumblings are slightly stronger that the last set."

"We can't feel them," Beth said, "but the seismic readers are recording the activity."

"Soooo?" Olivia impatiently asked.

"Those vents are an indication of fault activity," Spago said. "Submarine volcanoes are either creating small volcanoes or creating hydrothermal vents, geothermal heated water. That's—"

"I know what geological hydrothermal vents are. I'm not a child," Olivia said.

Gino quickly diverted the conversation before Olivia started another argument, one of her favorite sporting events. "There must be a connection between the submarine vents and the mountains."

"It's going to be fun figuring it out," Spago said with an enthusiastic smile.

Chapter 11

Rona Montgomery
New Beginnings

MAYBE RONA should have been more interested in rocks than humans. At least rocks don't object to being examined.

More than once, Rona had wondered why she'd volunteered for the Akiane Project. There didn't seem to be a reason for her to be here except to study dogs. She was terribly homesick and wanted with all her heart to be back on Earth. Dogs and laughing with friends were a distraction, but not enough to satisfy her. She couldn't help feeling there was something missing, a loneliness deep within.

Out of the corner of her eye, she saw Jorge smile. Since Jess had left, he'd not been his usual upbeat self. They rarely talked. She missed his friendship. She got the feeling he was avoiding her.

She missed Jess. Rona had dreams in which she was outside looking for her, but couldn't find her. She worried her friend would never return or was already dead. The worst was not knowing.

Much of Akiane was not what she'd hoped for or expected.

Jorge stood.

"Where you off to?" Gino sounded disappointed that he was leaving just as the conversation was becoming interesting. "Don't you want to hear what we found? I haven't even begun to tell you what I've learned about . . ."

"Maybe later, I'm going for a walk in the gardens." Jorge picked up his dishes. "Bus," he called.

The acrylic tub floated over. He placed his dishes in it.

When it came to Jorge, Rona was tired of getting the short end of the stick. If she wanted things to change, that meant it was up to her to so something.

Quickly, Rona downed the last of her coffee and hurried to bus her mug. "I'll walk with you, Jorge."

"That's okay," he said.

"I don't mind," she said, a little too quickly. It was an automatic response. She immediately wished she'd kept quiet and remained seated. Perhaps this was not the best time to take the bull by the horns. Maybe she should have waited for a time when she didn't have an audience.

She felt the warmth of her face flushing. *I'm acting like a high school girl chasing after this week's crush. Nothing like announcing to the whole world just how I feel about Jorge.*

But she'd started the ball rolling. She might as well see where it lead. Without checking to see who was watching, though she knew they all were, she followed Jorge out of their living quarters.

They walked in awkward silence through the habitat to the lake and gardens. Should she ask about his research? Say something about Jess? No, it would not be good to remind him about her. How was Rona to rekindle their friendship and the hope of a romance with Jess constantly lurking in the background?

Maybe she shouldn't have such thoughts. If he'd only give her a chance, perhaps he'd remember. They were close, once, back on the ship. Rona had thought they were headed toward a more serious direction before Jess.

Then again, maybe not. Perhaps this was just another of Rona's failures.

* * *

On Earth, Rona had been on the fast track, graduating with her PhD at twenty-one and almost immediately recruited into the space program by the World Space Coalition.

62

The day after training, she and the others boarded *WSC Britannia*. She'd wanted to room with Lu so they could get a acquainted but the computer had other plans. Lu got a roommate and Rona got a room to herself.

She'd met Jorge during training and liked him. Everyone did. But it wasn't until they began running on the ship's racetrack together that their relationship developed, and Rona realized just how much she really liked him. He made her feel special. Then just when she thought he was taking a serious interest in her, Jess showed up.

When she first learned of her new roommate, Rona was delighted, until they met.

Upon walking into their room for the first time, Jess threw her things onto her bed and stood, as rigid as a brick.

Rona had half expected her to yell, cry or something, but she seemed to have frozen in place in need of a reboot.

After a few minutes, they went to lunch, where Rona's heart sank like a rock to the bottom of a lake.

For Jorge, it was love at first sight.

Rona's hope for a romantic relationship evaporated like smoke drifting in the wind. In all the time she'd known him, he'd never once looked at her the way he looked at Jess.

* * *

"Mathieu," Jorge called to Mathieu Rutger, one of their two resident doctors and sergeants. He'd eaten earlier and was now admiring the habitat's only lake and surrounding garden.

"Beautiful isn't it?" Mathieu asked.

"Huh?" Jorge said. He glanced at the pond. "Yeah, I guess. Matt, will you do me a favor?"

"Sure, what?"

Jorge hesitated. "I promised to take Rona for a walk in the gardens, but I'm not up to it. Will you walk with her?"

That was a metaphorical slap in the face.

Rona had never received such a rejection like that before. She was half-tempted to physically slap him.

"Um." Mathieu was just as stunned. "Yeah, okay."

"I'll catch up with you later." Jorge gave Rona a quick kiss on the cheek, and walked off without a backward glance.

What's that old saying? *You know who you are by whom you love.*

Well I guess I know who I am, Rona thought. *The fool. What an idiot I've been.* Well, she knew now, didn't she? It was loud and clear he wasn't interested in her, not at all. *If that's the way he wants it, fine. I don't have to talk to him— ever again.*

She slumped onto the nearest rock.

Unsure what to do, Mathieu shifted his weight from one foot to the other and back again. Rona wished he'd follow Jorge. Instead, he tried to say something. "Want . . .?" he began, "I mean . . . "

Rona didn't care what he did as long as he left. She wondered how long before he told the rest of them. How long before they were talking about her? They were a small community with few secrets. How embarrassing! She wanted to crawl under a rock instead of sitting on it.

Mathieu sat on the rock next to her.

Just as he started to turn his head toward Rona, she turned her head so he couldn't see her tears. He placed an arm around her shoulder. She shook it off. Her body completely turned away from him, giving him the message that she was ignoring him.

He removed his arm, but he didn't leave. She felt him turn his body toward her. He was giving her his full attention.

She didn't want his attention. She wanted him to leave.

"I know the two of you are missing Jess," Mathieu said.

"Jess. Yes. I'm . . . I'm . . ." The words didn't come.

"Concerned for Jorge?"

It would have been easy just to nod her head yes and lie.

Instead she said, "It's more than that." *So much more.* She felt like she'd been thrown out with the morning's trash.

When she was younger, she hadn't been interested in a romantic relationship or having children. All she could think of was her career. Despite her youth and little professional experience, WSC had been willing to trust her because, according to them, she had the drive and the brains. She had their full confidence. More than anything, she'd wanted to confirm their faith in her.

Somewhere along the way, love had become important. She'd even begun to consider the possibility of children. On that issue, she'd decided children should wait until she returned to Earth. But love would have been nice. Now she realized that too might have to wait.

She was on Akiane with no love and no project. At least, not the project WSC had commissioned her for.

"Yeah, something's going on and it's not just your research or Jorge." Mathieu's voice was soft and caring. "So what's the real issue?"

Rona wilted. *What difference did it make if she told him or not?* "I feel as naked as a newborn babe."

Mathieu let out a surprised chortle. "I promise not to tell anyone how much you're nothing like a newborn baby, clothed or not."

Rona almost smiled. Then with a sigh, she decided to tell Mathieu everything. "I have to succeed." Her back was still to him.

"Why?" he asked.

"It's difficult for me to admit, even to myself, let alone say it out loud . . . to you . . . or anyone."

Mathieu remained silent.

"It's my family. No one wanted me to leave. Not my sisters, my mother, certainly not my father."

"What? Earth? Coming here? To Akiane?"

"The hydro farm," Rona said. "We, they have a 30-acre hydroponics farm with several six-story buildings."

"That's huge," Mathieu said.

"Yes. They can grow just about anything but corn."

"Why not corn?'

Rona shrugged. "Don't know. Didn't care." She was 32 years old, with nothing to show for her life. "I come from a long line of farmers, even before hydroponics. My sisters and I are all scientists. They studied plants. I studied humans."

"You're different," he said.

"Yeah, but I don't think they ever really thought I'd leave the farm, or at least not Georgia. I could have driven to Atlanta for work."

"But you didn't."

"No, I left Earth." Rona was quiet for a time. Mathieu patiently waited. "All of my sisters are married and have children. Not me. I never wanted love—not then anyway."

She felt the heat of her blush. She hadn't meant to say that.

"Nothing to be embarrassed about," Mathieu said.

"You don't understand."

"Don't I?" Mathieu asked. "It's a love triangle."

A love triangle between her and her two best friends. There was no use hiding it, or lying about it. Rona nodded.

"I was in one of those once. My roommate and my fiancé," he said.

"Oh." Rona slightly turned her head toward him. "That is so much worse."

"Joined the space program because of them. Never even said good-bye. I just packed what I needed and left."

She tilted her head to get a better view of him. "You left everything?"

"Yep, including the bills and rent."

A unexpected snigger escaped Rona's lips. "Bet that showed him." She slightly twisted her body toward him.

"Not really. She moved in with him a week later. My sister sent a message telling me all about it. Soon after that, she was pregnant, and they got married."

"Was she sure it was his?" She shifted again.

His face was thoughtful as he remembered the past. She couldn't tell if he was sad or not.

"Yeah. The bastard named the boy after me. Said it was because I introduced them."

"I'm sorry. That must have hurt."

He dropped his head and laughed softly. "It did at the time, but it's all right now. Sis sent another message just before we landed. They're divorced. Sis says, *she* says giving me up was the worse mistake of her life. Now that's revenge."

"You going back to her?" Rona asked. It would have made for a nice romantic ending.

His lifted his head. A big smile warmed his face. "I've realized that the best thing that ever happened to me was her leaving. Too high maintenance." He chuckled some more. Evidently, there were no bad memories lingering. "So no, when I go back, it will not be to find her. That ship has sailed."

To her surprise, Rona was pleased. Her legs moved in line with the rest of her body. They sat side by side and stared out over the lake.

"How come we never talked like this on the transport?" she asked.

Mathieu's eyebrows raised in wonderment.

"Right." She'd been too busy chasing after a shadow. "Well, my friend, I'm not stepping on that slippery log again," she said sarcastically. "I've fallen off more than once, never again."

"Excellent," he said.

It was good to talk and laugh with him. It was comforting that he understood. She knew she could trust him, and he would not tell the others. So she told him how she was feeling. How she missed Jess, how she felt about Jorge and her guilt.

In all the time she'd known Jorge, he'd never listened to her like that. He would have laughed and would have made some cute comment. Mathieu listened, didn't criticize, or make fun of her.

When she finished, she rested her head on Mathieu's shoulder.

"Thank you for listening," she said.

"Anytime."

Chapter 12

Larry Gino
Amazing Wonders

LARRY GINO sat at his table surrounded by rocks: agates, limestone, granite, and sandstone. They were beaten and battered with gouges and missing pieces.

The team took holo-images of the area they planned to excavate. They'd labeled the most interesting rocks, and marked their positions in the image. They also brought back rocks to examine more closely. Now they were in the process of analyzing what they'd found.

"Whatever happened to you, my diminutive fellow, must have been traumatic," he said to the granite in his hand.

Hovering over his desk was a 3D image from the area of the rock's origin.

Spago and his team had assembled four drones to fly over the mountains, the caldera, and the area between the habitat and the southern coastline, and created maps, then made the data available to everyone.

"Quadrotor helicopter," Gino corrected himself.

More than once Spago had reminded him. A drone usually referred to an aerial vehicle used by the military.

A quadrotor helicopter, or multi-rotor, was for civilian use, or in this case, scientific research. Four rotors made the multi-rotor more maneuverable. It could hover at different heights, which allowed the digital camera to get a broad view of the area or target a smaller, specific area worth studying more closely.

Once that specific area had been identified, a seismic reader would gather specific detail.

Deeper 4D imaging allowed one to feel the roughness of the rock, taste, and even smell it, but Larry liked the real thing, so he'd brought a few rocks back with him.

"Show me P345."

The holo-screen disappeared. A matching image of the rock in his hand appeared.

Digitals in 5D showed the interior of the rock and its mineral, crystal, oxygen, and molecular structures. But he wasn't interested in the interior, not just yet. He was still trying to make sense of the bigger picture.

When magma is trapped just below the ground's crust and does not rise to the surface, it takes a long time to cool. The magma becomes an igneous rock called granite. One usually had to dig for granite, unless a large slab was pushed to the surface with the help of an earthquake.

But this piece of granite was not apart of a slab. It was hand size and by its scars, it had broken off something much larger. So where was the rest of the slab?

The other granites on his table were not from the same geological formation. Their coloring and interior crystals were different.

Underground digital images showed broken bits of granite slabs, which did not fit together.

"Show me the immediate one-meter area around P345."

The holo-screen complied.

Nothing made sense. The base of the mountain was no better organized than construction piles of rubble. Geological formations eluded Gino and his team. Every kind of rock classification seemed unrelated to the rocks surrounding it.

There was the nagging reality that nothing made sense.

"Good." Gino often spoke aloud to himself. He said it was the only intelligent conversation he could have. "Wouldn't want an easy project. I prefer something that's difficult and mysterious." It would produce better results and make for far more interesting reports for the scientific papers and for those back on Moon Base overseeing this project and, of course, articles for scientific journals.

Lu's high-pitched voice leaped out of the gardens interrupting Gino's thoughts. "Hey, come here and see this! It's incredible. You won't believe it. Well maybe Bonga will, but the rest of you will be amazed."

He could still her hear talking as she moved away from the bay door, though her words had become indistinct.

A barrage of questions erupted.

"What did she say?"

"Is she hurt?"

"What does she want?"

One person close to the bay door loudly repeated Lu's words. "Lu's got something for us to investigate."

Being curious by nature, all were interested. Some hurried, some ran, a very few walked leisurely out of the bay door into the garden.

It had been decades since Larry Gino had run.

He sighed heavily. "These youngsters have no sense of patience."

He was the last one to reach the bay door. There was no one in sight.

"Where's the fire?" Larry bellowed.

No one answered.

It was nighttime and the garden was devoid of light. The usual overhead illumination was off.

"Why are the lamps out?" he asked.

Only column lamps faintly glowed. They barely gave enough light for him to see the path. The lamplights in the garden had never been turned off this early before.

Gino looked up. The overhead garden canopy was too thick to see the glass ceiling let alone the sky beyond.

He'd soon grown tired of the overgrown foliage that hindered one's walk along the paths. Branches hung at face level, intent on poking out an eye. Vines were strategically placed to snag shoelaces and purposely tripped an innocent passerby.

Gino had attacked the enemy jungle with a small hatchet.

"Guess it's a good thing I cleared the path," he said. "Otherwise those children would be tripping over foliage and each other in all this darkness. And I'd be flat on my nose."

Now Gino was able to walk unhindered by invading foliage. After several meters, the path divided into two different directions. He stopped and listened for the sound of voices to guide him down the correct path.

From his left came a plop, crunch, plop, and crunch on the basalt path.

Foot steps.

"Who's there?" he called.

"How are you doing, old man?" Spago asked.

"Finer than a frog's hair." Gino gave his usual greeting, then he let out a disapproving humph. "Old man! You should be in as good a shape as me at my age."

"I should live so long to be as old as you," Spago laughed.

"What's all the fuss?" Gino demanded with a shake of his head.

Spago pointed up.

Gino obeyed. There was now a small opening in the overhead canopy, he saw green and red ribbons of lights. "Oh my."

He ran to keep up with Spago.

This should be good, he mused and wished he knew more about astronomy.

Akiane was a light-free environment, in that there were no city lights to interfere with the overhead view. It was fascinating to view the same stars as seen in Earth's sky, but from a different part of the Milky Way.

The young ones were gathered in a small clearing, heads tilted back, staring up in wonder with eyes wide, and mouths agape. Lu and her pigtails stood in the middle of the crowd.

Gino expected a stunning view of the Milky Way. This was more than he'd anticipated. His mouth dropped open in amazement.

The sky was filled with ribbons of white, blue, red, and green lights as they danced and pulsated to a rhythm only they knew.

"Aren't we near the equator?" someone asked.

"Yes," Gino said.

"Then how is this possible?"

"Magnetosphere," Gino said with full conviction.

Auroras on Earth were usually only seen near the North and South Poles. The habitat Endurance was forty kilometers north of the equator and yet, the aurora was as vivid as it was at Earth's poles. Here was another mystery to be solved.

"What does the magnetosphere have to do with the aurora?" Vong asked.

"The star's magnetic activity produces an enormous torrent of energized plasma creating winds which pass over the planet's magnetic field in the upper atmosphere. Charged particles between the two produce the lights," Gino said.

"What?" Vong asked.

Vong and Zhoa were masterful cooks, but unlike his well-read brother, Vong was more physical. He preferred the competition of virtual and physical contact games to reading and understanding scientific jargon.

"Solar flares," Zhoa said.

"Ah." Vong understood.

"We need to map the magnetosphere," Gino said in reverent awe. This was his Holy Grail. He'd come to study rocks, to discover Akiane's mineral composition, to determine the planet's geological age, conduct seismic readings, study digital core samples, and draft contour maps.

But now, at this moment, he became captivated by Akiane's magnetosphere.

"The aurora at the equator." Spago was stunned by the phenomenon.

"I still don't get it," Vong said. "How is this possible?"

"On Earth the magnetosphere is aligned to the North and South Poles. That's why we only see the auroras at the poles, but here the magnetosphere may not be aligned," Gino said. "Anomalies."

"Anomalies?" Vong asked.

"Magnetic patches where the field is strong enough to create an aurora," Spago explained. "Gino seems to think Akiane's magnetosphere isn't aligned, but made up of patches of magnetic fields scattered around the planet, in which case, there would be many auroras not just two like on Earth's poles."

The dam broke; geologists and volcanologists talked all at once.

"The magnetic field could be shifting?"

"Maybe it hasn't settled yet."

"This is a new world."

Gino couldn't help it. He chuckled to himself. *So much speculation. Good.* Such speculation kept their young brains active and kept them from getting stuck in a box. They challenged each other, debated theories, and brainstormed new ideas, which encouraged new lines of thought and new discoveries.

"Yes, it is the magnetosphere but not the way you think," Bonga said. "The star's flares are mammoth and are charging this planet's magnetosphere. That's why we're seeing the aurora this far south."

"Is that possible?" Lu asked. "I mean the flares would have to be huge. Is this normal for Akiane or is it a special event?"

Bonga laughed at her enthusiasm. "Every once in a while the aurora on Earth can be seen in places like Hawaii or Spain because of unusually high energy solar flares."

Star flares would be the easier answer, but Gino hoped Bonga was wrong. How much more complicated and interesting if the magnetosphere anomalies were out of position. Now that would be a fascinating subject to research and write a paper on.

Bonga continued, "Right now plasma eruptions are many times larger than that of our sun back home and are traveling millions of kilometers across the surface of this star in a matter of seconds. Such huge distributions can cause aurora lights this far south. But we need more data to prove it."

"In any case the magnetosphere is part of the equation," Gino said in a disgruntled tone.

"Of course it is, but I don't think it's as interesting as you'd like, Gino," Bong said.

"What could cause such a disturbance?" Zhoa had spent the last six years and ten months of his life with a group of scientists. He could have ignored the intelligence at hand. Instead, he chose to learn from them and was capable of joining in their conversations. "Does the approaching gas planet have anything to do with it?"

"I think it most definitely does," Bonga said.

"What gas planet?" Lesley asked.

Bonga smiled broadly and said, "Tell them."

Zhoa returned his smile and said, "Akiane and a gas planet the size of Jupiter are both on elliptical orbits around Kahair and cross paths once every 11 years."

"We hypothesize that the gravitational pull from the giant gaseous planet passing near Akiane is causing the filament eruptions," Bonga said.

Gino knew the passing of a giant planet would also cause gravitational forces that could greatly affect Akiane. That would explain why the rocks were so mixed up. Akiane quakes could shake the ground with such force that rocks would become confusing. But that would have to be one mighty shake.

"A large enough prominence would also disrupt radio transmissions," Bonga continued.

"That would explain why communications from Akiane to Earth stopped 318 years ago," Mathieu said. "The messages never arrived."

"But what about all the years after that? Shouldn't one of their messages have gotten through?" Vong asked. "Just recently, Jess was able to speak to her admiral."

"At one time large solar flares from our sun did disrupt communications," Bonga said. "But technology has improved. *WSC Britannia* is equipped with the ability to communicate with WSC Moon base no matter how pronounced space electrical disturbances might become."

Bonga adjusted his headphone mouthpiece and said, "Show Kahair two and a half meters in diameter."

The crowd made room for his holo-screen.

Kahair appeared as a blaze of orange fireball.

"You have a satellite?" someone asked.

"A small one, yes," Bonga said. "We assembled it on *Britannia* just before we arrived. The captain launched it once the ship was in orbit."

"But I thought satellites weren't allowed," Olivia complained. She desperately wanted a least one satellite orbiting overhead. She'd placed radio-tags on the fish so she and her team could follow their migration. Without the satellite, she had limited tracking capabilities.

"Well, yes," Bonga said, "WSC thought it best to smooth things over before they started launching satellites around the planet, but they also thought a satellite around their star would not be intrusive."

"Humph." Olivia might have continued to complain if Kahair hadn't decided to give them a show of the star's might.

A giant flare curled up, then exploded outward. It happened so fast, those nearest jumped back with little cries of surprise and laugher. More flares followed.

Plasma waves erupted, making a tidal wave seem like a ripple. They rolled across the surface one after another with such speed that a mere blink of an eye would have missed them.

"This is an extremely active star with solar winds that could easily charge not only the magnetosphere at the poles, but all the way down to the equator as well."

"Wow, who would have thought," Vong said. "Seeing Kahair like this is amazing."

"That's nothing. Watch this." Bonga laughed. He tapped his earpiece. "Show Aurora."

The night sky replaced Kahair as Aurora lights appeared to be rippling through the crowd.

"It's like we're in the sky," Vong exclaimed.

"The Aurora," Gino said with true enchantment. "Most excellent." He felt a slight electric tingling.

The young ones jumped in and out of the ribbons joining in the dance of lights.

"This is better than going outside," Gino said.

In his delight, he shuffled his feet and swayed his hips as he did his rendition of a dance.

Chapter 13

Qorow Low
Decision

WHAT KIND of people are they? Qorow Low wondered if she should be terrified of these off-worlders or amazed. *They call Kahair and he obeys. They call to the skylights and they obey.*

She stood in the thick brush and peered between the leaves. The skylights were amazing. Never in her life would she have believed she could be this close to them.

She had just seen off-worlders call Kahair to stand among them. But the star was angry at being captured. Great flames of fire leapt out in retaliation.

They released Kahair and called the skylights down. Now they celebrated their greatness by dancing among the lights.

How could such deeds be possible? If those of Earth could control Kahair and the skylights, what else was possible for them? They were a people to be feared and honored.

She tuned away for fear of what else she might witness and was startled to find Adumie standing behind her. His eyes were hard. His lips pressed together.

"I did not want to believe words spoken about you," he said.

Mercener had spoken, dirtying Qorow Low's name.

"And yet, you are here silently watching me," she said. "You do not seek my thoughts, but you do listen and believe the one who lays blame on me."

"There are those who will reject you if you continue to walk this path," he said.

"Those? Mercener has already rejected me. Who are the others? Any such as you?"

He did not answer. He did not have to. She knew.

"So I mean nothing to you?" she asked fearful of the truth.

"And what do I mean to you?" he asked accusingly.

Her feelings for him were for too strong. It was wrong, but no matter how hard she tried not to care for him, her feelings grew. She had hoped that he would at least think favorably of her. It was foolish since such relationships were forbidden.

She had seen off-worlders walk side-by-side holding hands. She wanted to walk at Adumie's side and hold his hand.

Blasphemy!

He was high priest and would never compromise himself.

She closed her eyes and shuttered inside.

Why was she so contrary to all that was godly? She had too many thoughts about Adumie, now thoughts of touching him. If that was not horrid enough, there were also thoughts of speaking to off-worlders.

No wonder Adumie wanted nothing to do with her. She was no better than those of Earth.

"Intruders' promises are lies," he said.

That was how he saw off-worlders, as invaders who had come and laid claim to all the Community had built. He did not believe they would to bring friendship or healing.

"They cannot change the path which God has chosen for us, " Adumie spoke forcefully in an effort to persuade her.

He said death was Holy One's way of protecting them from blasphemous intruders.

Qorow Low did not hold to the same convictions.

"Come," he said. "We will leave together. You will *not* return."

She obediently followed.

Chapter 14

Rona Montgomery
Canini Project

WITHOUT AN invitation, Olivia unceremoniously flopped on the floor between Rona and Lu to investigate the progress of their research. They moved to make room for her.

"So you two decided to take my advice and research dogs." There was a hint of amusement in her voice. "Good for you." She adjusted her blouse by pulling on its back tails and then the front down.

She'd come to gloat and take credit; it would do no good to tell her it was Mathieu who had changed Rona's mind or that Lu had begun the research before Olivia's unwanted advice. She didn't care about the truth. She wanted the credit for any accomplishments they might make.

Because all workspaces were in one large area, there was little privacy. It wasn't unusual for someone to stop by and see how another's project was coming along.

Jorge's work area was outside in the algae patch. Few bothered him.

No one bothered the geologists and volcanologists when they were on the mountains.

Geologists brought back rocks they'd collected for their studies. People often stopped to examine the rocks and ask questions.

The volcanologists flew their four multi-rotors outside and digitally film the area, then constructed contour maps, which they shared with all computers. The maps ranged from simple 3D images to in-depth 5D images where one could see the molecular structure of an object.

Everyone took advantage of the digital images.

Oceanographers spent their time on the ice near the ocean. They'd set up three aquaria in the work area, which were a big hit. People enjoyed peacefully watching the marine life, which annoyed Olivia when *she* was trying to study them. Few cared. Olivia was often annoyed about something. Annoying Olivia was becoming a sport.

Engineers were denied all access to the mechanics of the habitat. Out of boredom, they created a 3D role-playing game about Akiane, which anyone could play. The game was another hit.

The only other entertainment was keeping a curious eye on each group project to see who was accomplishing what. It also made for some interesting conversations and debates.

And then there was Olivia.

On this day, she'd decided to grace Rona and Lu with her presence. At times she could be unbearable, but there were other times when she could be the most pleasant person around. Today, she was becoming borderline annoying.

"What do you have?" Olivia leaned closer to see what Lu was doing, even though she could easily see the holo-screen hovering right in front of her.

They make for an odd couple sitting so close like that, Rona mused.

Lu was petite in height and size. She had straight, chin-length black hair. But despite her brilliance, she was a bit insecure.

They were the same height but Olivia was plump with short, curly copper hair. She could be overbearing and thought herself superior to all others.

"We've checked every adult dog that comes into our quarters," Lu said. "They're the friendliest and don't mind us scanning them with the HMS or examining them."

A human naturally carries at least five pounds of bacteria, retrovirus, and fungi within their body, all of which are natural to a healthy person. It was the same for any mammal or in this case alien dogs. A HMS scan would record that which was normal but highlight what was not natural such as diseases or an unusual blood pathology.

When the HMS was placed on the bottom of a paw, it gathered the same information as a blood test: Lipid Reflex to direct LDL Panel, Basic Metabolic Panel, minerals and vitamins, and white blood cell count.

Then all information was sent to the computer to analyze.

The HMS consistently registered an unknown retrovirus, but after the fifteenth dog, it stopped giving an alarm and reset itself. All the dogs had the same retrovirus, but all tests said they were healthy.

Conclusion: the retrovirus was natural to the dogs.

Rona and Lu decided the retrovirus would be their next project, and would take blood samples to properly study it.

"Dogs even like having their pictures taken." Lu giggled.

All dog digital-images (DIs) were synchronized to their identification numbers and HMS data.

Since their computers were synchronized, their holo-screens automatically superimposed as one, when opened at the same time.

"The dogs pose for us." Rona let loose a little chuckle. "All dog DIs," she said in her headphone.

The first image appeared on the holo-screen.

"Scroll images," she said.

One dog after another appeared. A dog was turned sideways and looked up at the ceiling. Another's tongue hung out. Another balanced on her hind legs.

"Fun." Olivia showed genuine interest. She readjusted her blouse, then passed the fingers of both hands through either side of her hair adjusting her curls even though nothing could rearrange those thick copper curls.

"We've also examined dogs who don't hang around us. They're not as cooperative even with the attention we give them. So after a quick check to see if they're female and an even quicker scan with the HMS and photo, we move on," Lu said. "They don't stand still for very long, in which case the scan can sometimes be inconclusive and photos a bit burred. Still, we do get enough data to make the contact worthwhile."

"It's a good thing Lu gets along with dogs," Rona said, "They're more cooperative for her."

Lu smiled sweetly. "They like it when we lavish attention on them and talk to them. They seem to love a good story."

Originally, Lu had wanted to be a veterinarian, but decided to study the human genome instead. This dog project was a dream come true for her.

Dogs freely roamed in the gardens, bay area, and dormitories. Many dogs attached themselves to a favorite scientist, though not all were chosen. There seemed to be no rhyme or reason to whom they picked. Some dogs hung out in the area even though they were not attached to anyone in particular.

There were few dogs that were not at all interested in the newcomers. On occasion, they checked the scientists out, but for the most part those dogs ignored them altogether. Some never returned after just one visit.

Dogs that had officially adopted people followed them everywhere they went, even outside. The dogs slept near or under their bunks.

The one who had attached herself to Olivia lay just outside of the work area watching intently and seemed to be listening.

It took a little effort to convince the dogs to stay away from the research equipment and work areas, but once they understood, all of them obeyed as if they passed the word around so all knew what to do. Even those visiting for the first time knew to stay out.

None of the dogs went near the kitchen or eating areas when food was served.

"And what have you learned so far?" Olivia sat up, straightening her back, her blouse, and her hair.

"So far, from the DNA samples we've processed, we've learned the dogs are descendants of Captain Assetti's Harrie the Spitz," Rona said.

"You're not telling me you actually have DNA from Assetti's dog," Olivia said in surprise.

"As a matter of fact we do," Rona said. "Harrie received a medical examination just like the rest of the crew, and her records are in the database along with everyone else's."

"We have a mitochondria match," Lu said. "Harrie is definitely the mother."

Mitochondria DNA is passed to both male and female children but only the mother passes her mtDNA to her daughter

Rona smiled at Lu's eagerness. She also felt the excitement of the moment. She couldn't help it.

Rona and Lu had followed the mtDNA trail of the first dog to arrive on an alien planet. Now If only they could follow the genetic lineage of the settlers to their ancestral colonists that would be pure joy.

"So, Harrie was in the medical database, who would have guessed?" Olivia mused. "Who's the father?"

"We don't know," Lu said.

"That's the mystery, isn't it," Rona said.

"Isn't the father's DNA also in the database?" Olivia asked.

"According to the records, Harrie was the only dog to come along," Lu said.

Olivia stared at her as if Lu were mentally simple. She could be so condescending.

"But there was another dog on the ship, Lu. There had to be," she said.

"Of course there was, but he's not in the records," Rona said.

"Obviously, you're both missing something." Ah, here came Olivia's unwelcomed side.

"B-b-but, we d-d-didn't," Lu stuttered.

Olivia was making Lu doubt herself.

"Lu, think. Harrie didn't give birth by herself. She had help. So unless there was a dog here when the ships arrived, there had to be one aboard one of the other ships," Olivia insisted.

Rona shook her head. No wonder Olivia had so few friends. She took pleasure in playing devil's advocate.

"Think! These animals didn't just happen. There has to be an explanation." Olivia pushed, as a professor would treat her first-year student. "Find it."

"Don't insult our competence," Rona snapped.

"How do you plan to complete your project if you have gaping holes?" Olivia demanded.

"We've just started, Olivia," Rona said. "Give us time." She refused to buckle under Olivia's overbearing scrutiny. "The settlers had the DNA for livestock. I'm sure there were pets as well. One of those dogs has to be the father. If so, his DNA would not be in the original data base."

"Seems a little weak to me. I mean you can't have just one parent."

Rona and Lu had been doing just fine until Olivia showed up.

"I think it's time for you to go, Olivia."

"You don't have to be snippy, Rona." This from the one who is forever snippy.

"You agreed this research was a good idea," Rona said. "Let us work."

Even with a not-so-subtle hint, Olivia didn't move. "So where are the gentlemen canines hiding?" she asked with a hint of irony.

Lu stared at her. "Where are your gentlemen fish?"

Good for her, Rona thought. *Dish it right back at her.*

"Fine," Olivia conceded. So far she hadn't found one male fish. "How many dogs have you checked?"

"Eighty-three," Lu said.

"How many have you tested?"

"Of those that let us, eighty-three." Lu smirked.

"How are you identifying them?" Olivia asked.

"As we said earlier, we took pictures." Rona pointed to a DI image still hovering in front of them.

"Only adults? No puppies?" Olivia asked.

"Puppies are exactly alike," Lu said. "All of them are white. They change color with age."

"Adults dogs have distinguishing markings," Rona said. "They're easy to tell apart."

"But the puppies, they're all female," Olivia confirmed.

"Of the litters we've checked so far, we've only found thirteen male puppies," Lu said.

"Can you find those puppies again?"

"We have a photo of their mother and a notation that she has a male puppy," Rona said.

"But you have to reexamine all the puppies to find the male?"

"Yes," Lu said with a sigh. "Of the smaller ones we do. But we also have photos of those that are changing colors."

"You don't know what happens to the male dogs after they become adults," Olivia said.

"No, we don't." Rona had a flashback to her college days when she stood under a professor's examination. "They haven't grown up yet," she said irritably.

She didn't appreciate Olivia's examination. They were not her students.

"You need radio tags," Olivia said. "That way, you'll know where they go and what happens to them once they're adults."

"Good idea," Rona said. "But since we weren't planning on tracking humans, we didn't bring radio tags with us."

"I did. We put them on fish and map their movements. If we had a satellite orbiting overhead, we could follow their migrations, but since we don't, we have limited tracking capability. It's not enough, but it's all we're allowed." Olivia's mouth scrunched up as if she'd eaten a sour lemon.

"Bango's got his satellite, but I didn't." Clearly she was not pleased. "He can track his star, but I can't track my fish. I have to wait until the next transport. Only then will I be able to find them. We won't know what path they took, but we'll see where they end up." And without taking a breath, her whole mood changed. "I'll loan you a few tags if you want. I'll even program them to your computers."

"That would be great!" Lu beamed.

"Don't you think we should ask permission first?" Rona asked. The colonists had shown a definite dislike for the scientists. If they found radio tags on their dogs, she doubted they'd be happy about it.

"They're only dogs. What's there to object to?" Olivia said. "We're just doing our job. Besides if you ask for permission, they'll say no."

Rona marveled at how quickly Olivia's moods shifted. One moment she was insulting their work, the next moment, she was volunteering to help gather more information.

This offer of help encouraged Lu. "We're still collecting data, but what we've found so far . . ." she paused for effect. "Peptides are different, the base pairs have one extra protein, and we're having trouble identifying the sex gene. It's a all a jumble, but it's fun unraveling the mystery."

Olivia smiled. "Makes sense, we are on an alien world. We're finding the same things in the fish. And we think we know why these people don't eat fish."

"Why?" Lu asked.

"The fish have a retrovirus, unlike anything we've ever seen," Olivia said.

"The mitochondria is unlike anything we ever seen," Lu blurted.

"Well of course the mitochondria is different, the fish are alien." Olivia wasn't listening, her mind was set on her fish, and if they didn't stop her, she'd spend the rest of the afternoon telling them everything they didn't want to know about alien fish. Their afternoon would be wasted.

"Olivia, Lu just said the dogs' mitochondria is different from Harrie's mitochondria, and if you had allowed her to finish, she would have told you what we learned."

"Sooo." Olivia drew out the word. It was as much of an apology as Lu would get. "What did you learn about the mitochondria?"

"I-i-its ..." Lu began.

"Don't stutter," Olivia reprimanded.

"Olivia!" Rona scolded.

"Rona!" Olivia mimicked. "What?"

86

Lu's dark eyes brightened and she stopped stuttering. "Their mitochondria has mutated."

"Mitochondria doesn't mutate unless there is a problem in the function of body's genetic system," Olivia said slowly. "It can't be altered." She snorted and almost laughed at Lu's ignorance. Nevertheless, her eyes did narrow slightly at the mystery of Lu's words.

Now we have her full attention, Rona thought smugly.

To the holo-screen, Lu said, "Bring up Harrie the Spitz's DNA, specifically the mitochondria, and do the same for canine number . . ." She paused.

The dog's image dissolved and the screen became blank as it waited for further instructions.

"You pick a number, Olivia," Lu said.

"Me?" she said pleasantly surprised, thinking Lu was giving her the honor of picking which mitochondria they would inspect.

But that was not Lu's intention.

"You pick, that way you'll know we're not cheating," Rona said.

Olivia's smile disappeared. She pursed her lips and gave her shoulder a little arrogant shake. "22."

"Computer, continue instructions and bring up the same for Canine 22," Lu said. "Place them one above so we can compare them."

The holo-screen complied.

HARRIE THE SPITZ DNA appeared on the top of the screen with a map of dog's mitochondria. At the same instant, on the bottom of the screen, the name CANINE TWENTY-TWO appeared with a map of that dog's mitochondria.

The mutated genes in CANINE TWENTY-TWO were highlighted.

Olivia leaned in to study the screen. For a long time she was silent. Speechless would be more accurate, a rarity for her.

Rona and Lu stole a glance of satisfaction behind her back.

"That's not possible," Olivia said with genuine awe.

"Yes, we know." Now Lu was the one with a hint of self-satisfaction in her voice.

"Mitochondria does not mutate," Olivia said in awe.

"We know."

"It's not possible."

"We know."

"But . . . But how did this happen?"

"That, Olivia, we *don't* know."

Chapter 15

Jessica Hewitt
Dawn of the Sixteenth Day

IT TOOK us 15 days to reach the end of land and the beginning of landlocked ice. As the days passed, the dogs did indeed become stronger, and we didn't have to stop as often. Maybe they didn't miss the tea stop but I sure did. I refused to complain. Instead, I toughened up, just like the dogs.

Couldn't have mutts outdo me.

We made camp at the edge of land. In the morning we'd step out onto ice. This journey was becoming all too real. As long as we were on land I could remain in denial. There was still the possibility that something would happen and we'd have to turn back. However once we stepped onto the ice, I'd have to face the reality, there'd be no turning back.

At first light, right after breakfast, I took a walk along the edge of land.

A storm often softens ice and if the wind is strong enough, it will break ice into pieces. Storm tossed waters helped waves push broken bits of ice to shore, creating ice shards. Dad and I would go to Duluth and stand on Lake Superior's shoreline and to see its ice shards, but those shards were only a few meters in length.

Akiane's ice shards were more than three times my height. They looked as if someone had stood them in line like dominoes and knocked them over. A mighty storm had tossed them into a jumbled mess and forced the shards against the shoreline. After the storm they'd frozen in place between land and ice.

There are two kinds of sea ice. We were about to step on landlocked ice, meaning it was solid and frozen to the land and would remain in place until another storm, or the power of an ocean current broke it up, or summer came and melted it.

Ocean ice was not solid but huge pieces of ice call ice floes that move with the ocean current. Beyond the current, ice becomes somewhat solid again.

I climbed a good-sized rock and found an opening in the shards. To the east, Kahair's first glow of yellow spread across the ice, giving the appearance that it held the star captive. As the new day began, the lord of the day seemed to burn his way to freedom. Soon he would once again, rule the day and colors would slowly return as if creating Akiane for the very first time.

In the distance, large blackish-green shadows began to take shape against the brightening sky. Slowly the shadows became individual blocks of ice that rose from the frozen ocean.

It would take a long time for all that ice to melt. Spring was coming; Akiane's elliptical orbit was moving the planet closer to Kahair. But even as the star warmed the planet, the ocean waters under all that ice would remain cold. The ice would keep worldwide temperatures cool, which would keep the water frozen.

It would be years before all this melted and Akiane truly warmed up.

I'd never be warm again.

Kahair finally broke free and spilled his light over the ice.

Watching the waking of the new day reminded me that I didn't really hate winter. It did have its appeal.

That day, the sky was yellow, pink, and midnight blue. The same rendering of colors swept over the ice. As Jorge would say, "Beautiful."

Nor did I hate dogs or winter camping. I treasured those times alone with Dad. I never told him. Instead, I gave him a difficult time, just like I was giving Cameron.

The truth was, after Mom left, Dad had never asked me what I wanted. I came home from school one day to find strange men packing up my things. It was then that Dad informed me we were moving.

Those men touched everything I owned. I wasn't even allowed to pack that which was most precious to me, like my dolls and stuffed animals. Those men dropped my best friends in a box, taped it up and shoved them to one side and started on another box.

The same thing happened when I came to Akiane. No one asked what I wanted. I was ordered here, then I was ordered on this expedition. Each time, I was expected to obey.

We were about to leave land and step out onto the ice. It might be locked to the land now, but soon, we'd come to the ocean current and then what? Hopefully Cameron didn't expect us to cross an ocean current filled with ice floes.

The thought turned my stomach.

Ah, but of course that was exactly what Cameron had in mind. We were headed to the northernmost part of this planet, and he expected us to cross the ocean current to get there.

Which meant we'd soon be stepping onto the most dangerous part of the trip—moving ice. It was too easy to miss a step, or for the wind to rise up and toss about blocks of ice the size of a small town like ice cubes in a glass of tea. I could die out there. We could all die.

Just like Dad, there was no changing these people's minds. I could *never* change his mind. He loved living in Northern Minnesota. The more snow there was, the happier he was. It wasn't unusual for him to take the dogs out just after a blizzard when the snow was fresh and soft. He was afraid if he didn't go out immediately he'd miss his window of opportunity.

Dad loved his winter trips.

Ice made me nervous. Early fall and the beginning of spring were the two most dangerous times in Minnesota.

Inevitably, there would some crazy person too impatient to wait for the ice to safely become solid or completely melt.

They would walk across a weak spot in the ice, fall into the frigid water, and die.

That's what we were about to do, traverse a frozen ocean at the beginning of spring. It might take years for all this to completely melt, but it was already starting. There would be weak spots threatening our survival.

Nella was supposed to be our ice navigator, so we should be safe with nothing to worry about.

I learned at an early age, something unexpected could happen in the blink of an eye.

As I contemplated my future, a steady breeze gently pushed at my back, trying to urge me forward. Reluctant to leave land, I remained rooted where I was.

Oceans are full of personality. If Akiane's oceans were like those on Earth, she'd rest peacefully for seemingly forever. Then with little warning and help from brother wind, she'd express her might.

"Olivia says tides, currents, and storms help encourage marine life," I told the ocean. "If you're frozen in place most of the time, what causes you to produce life? What makes you move? Where are your waves?"

She didn't answer.

If I continued to fight Cameron and Nu Venia, Akiane would kill me. If I expected to survive this ordeal, I'd have to change my attitude. This seemed like a good time to relent.

Dad would be proud.

I took a deep breath and said, "This one's for you, Dad."

He taught me how to survive winter wilderness. I might have said I wasn't paying attention, but I was. Maybe some of what he taught me might help me now.

Now after all those years since Dad moved me to Woodlands, I was ready to forgave him. He was dead after all. Being angry with him was a waste of energy.

But I was not ready to forgive the admiral for ordering me to Akiane.

Nor was I ready to forgive Cameron and Nu Venia for dragging me out here, but I would no longer fight them.

Chapter 16

Qorow Low
The Nest

EVEN THOUGH they did not know how, Community knew those of Earth had children differently from them. That was why Adumie told off-worlders not to eat fish. Fish changed the biology of humans.

Fishers and hunters eat small amounts of fish, and only during winter years. There was something in the fish that helped one to endure the sub-freeing cold while fishing and hunting.

The first settlers to land on Akiane ate fish. The change began with those who had been born on Akiane. Their children were born in cocoons.

The change was slow, only five cocoons at first, then normal Earth-like births for the many months. It was thought the change had stopped. When it started again, almost all children came forth in cocoons.

Adumie thought it best not to tell off-worlders how their children were born. They would not understand and it would give them another reason to hate them.

If Qorow Low had consulted Adumie about her birthing a cocoon, he would have said no. So she told no one, but very quietly went to the Blood Vines late at night.

She searched until she found an area suitable, near a lamp. The thick vine jungle would keep her nest warm. It also brought darkness. One could not see the glass ceiling above or the sky beyond. Bright lamps lit the area by day and at night they dimmed to soft lighting for seeing in the dark.

Qorow Low carefully untangled eight sturdy vines and laid them out one at a time. She wove the vines in place to create a stand to hold her nest. One worked barehanded for it was a messy job. The bending of vines released the milky substance within the stalk.

As the vines in the base settled into place, they stopped leaking. Vines bent inward to make the shape of the basket that would hold her cocoon would perpetually leak. It was the milky substance that fed the child inside the cocoon. Thus the vines name were call Blood Vines for they the lifeblood for the child.

Qorow Low sealed the outside of the basket for the milk would not leak out.

Over time, the stalks would grow together as if one. The same would happen to the nest. The vines would fill in the small gaps left during the weaving process. Extra runners would be cut off, leaving only the leaves on top of the basket to cover the child and help keep the cocoon warm and moist.

The basket could be reused until the stalk had gown so tall the basket was no longer easily accessible, and the basket became so large it sagged. Then it would be cut down at the roots.

The milky substance would be completely squeezed out and fermented into Lazard. The stalks would be pulled apart into thin thread-like strands and woven into clothes.

Nothing on Akiane was wasted.

It took several hours for Qorow Low to complete the stalk. She returned the next night to begin the basket.

The eight vines were wrapped in a circle starting at the base and worked out and up to from the basket. She used the runners from the vines to weave the vines in place.

It was easier to weave when there were two or three to help, but there was much fear in bringing forth a child and much discouragement from the others toward any who wished to try.

Phyllis Moore

For many years the slow-dying sickness had been killing both children and adults. No one knew how it started, but most eventually succumbed to the illness. It started with the change in the coloring of one's skin, followed by rapid aging and finally, after much pain, death.

Only a few were not affected. No one knew why.

The illness was not the same for all. Some died after several months. Others died after long agonizing years. When a child was born with the sickness, she did not survive to adulthood. The stress of bringing forth a child hurried death for the life-giver. Now children were dying before they came forth from their cocoons. Live-givers were afraid to bring life forth.

Qorow Low stopped and sat back on her feet to consider what she was doing.

It was said, *Only the most daring still tried to birth a child.*

How many would say, *Only the foolhardy still tried?*

Did she think of herself as daring or a fool? No.

Why was she doing this? She knew the outcome. Her child would die. She should stop, but there was something deep within that urged her to continue. Something she could not define but knew her child had a destiny in the saving of her people.

She hung her head and sighed. Perhaps she was a fool. What difference would one more dead child make? Did she really believe her child would live when all others did not?

Qorow Low almost stood and walked away, leaving her nest unfinished.

Instead she rose to her knees and without another thought, continued to weave.

Chapter 17

Jessica Hewitt
Dog Fight

AS I contemplated my attitude, Essal and Imos sat near by. Essal was always near. Imos was beginning to pick up that bad habit.

Growls pulled my attention from my thoughts.

Addle, who was anything but confused, had been picking on his team's lead dogs, Huth and Tyron. Huth easily put Addle in his place. He no longer bothered her. Tyron used to fight back, but she was weakening. As his aggression worsened, she became more timid.

Cameron had said, "Tyron is good lead dog. Addle wants to lead. Tyron must defend her position."

So philosophical considering they were just dogs.

Addle was again harassing Tyron, only this time he wasn't testing, he was attacking. His barks were demanding. His body was ridge. His held his tail straight behind him. His jaws opened revealing teeth ready to rip into her.

With her tail tucked between her legs, Tyron made a feeble attempt at standing her ground. She hunched down and snarled, but her growls were softer and more pleading than warning.

Addle was loud. Forceful. Confident. He howled his supremacy and snapped at her, letting her know who was alpha. But when he tried to latch onto her, she slithered loose and like a bullet out of a gun, she bolted.

He was faster and ran to block her escape. Tryon slid into a right-hand turn. With one leap, Addle tackled her. She went down hard, letting out a painful woof.

She snarled and snapped. It looked like she meant it as she turned to defend herself.

He became more aggressive.

In a rage of fur and snarling, they wrestled and tore at each other. They pushed and pulled one another across the snow.

Addle's back slammed into an ice shard. It dazed him for a split second.

Tyron broke free.

Blood appeared on the snow. White fur on Tyron's right side turned crimson.

I leaped off the rock and tried to catch her, but she was too fast and easily outmaneuvered me. She didn't realize I was there to help.

The dogs from the same team as the two that were fighting quickly positioned themselves according to whom they supported. Those supporting Addle gathered together to block Tryon's path.

Essal trotted around the fight to sit with Huth. They watched together. Imos stayed at my side, also intently watching.

The other team ignored the fight. It wasn't their concern.

Nu Venia came flying out of the tent, almost tripping over the dogs sitting at the entrance. Without grace, she caught her balance and kept moving. "Ai," she yelled. *Stop.*

She pushed her way through the team of howling dogs as she tried to reach the fight. She grabbed Tyron by the scruff of her neck and began to haul her away. Tyron was willing and seemed relieved to be rescued.

Addle was not so appeased, he bit Tyron's back paw.

More blood.

Nu Venia kicked at Addle to make him back down. She hit him hard in his side.

He stopped cold and turned to face her. He didn't just look at her; he focused on her. The muscles in his back eased then tensed causing his fur to rise. One paw stepped toward her, then the other. In one fluid motion, he advanced on her.

I saw his calculated decision.

His jaw set. He back legs dropped slightly, gathering strength. His front paws left the ice as he lunged.

Nu Venia leapt backward in surprise, released Tyron, and tripped, landing hard on her rump.

Tyron ran off.

I thought Addle was going to land on Nu Venia with his jaws ripping into her. Instead he landed near her feet, then advanced on Nu Venia.

She tried to crawl backwards as quickly as she could.

He kept pace with her. His eyes narrowed. He knew exactly what he was doing. He was enjoying the moment, her fear; his anticipation.

He'd already tasted Tyron's blood. Now he drooled at the prospect of tasting Nu Venia's blood.

I knew these beasts couldn't be trusted, not after the way I witnessed them attacking fish. I knew it wouldn't take much for one of them to attack us. Nu Venia would be the first.

I had to do something fast.

All at once, Huth, Essal, and Imos flew to Nu Venia's rescue, positioning themselves in front of her. They bared their teeth, snarled, barked, and snapped at Addle to back down.

I ran to help Nu Venia to her feet. Together we moved out of the way.

Essal, Imos, and Huth followed us. The team opened a gap to let us out, then quickly closed ranks.

Without another thought for us, Addle's head swiveled from side to side seeking out Tyron.

"Where's Cameron? He'd know how to stop this," I said in desperation.

He was nowhere to be seen.

Every morning and evening, Cameron took a walk to be alone with God. Nu Venia never took that walk. She didn't seem to have as strong a faith as he did. That was why she was in camp and he was not.

Tyron tried to slink into the ice shards, but Addle was on her. His teeth sunk into her back. Blood soaked her coat, splattered across his face, and onto the ice.

With the taste of her blood, he became more savage. With a high-pitched yelp, Tryon twisted out of his hold, scampered to the ice shards, and slipped between a gap. Addle followed close at her heels.

The team jumped on the shards and peered in at either end and from overhead. Their barks echoed off the ice.

Often throughout the fight, Essal would jump to his feet, bark once, and take a step forward; clearly he wanted to come to Tyron's rescue. But each time, his rear slowly dropped back to a sitting position only whined his worry.

Huth seemed frozen in place as she silently watched. Imos lay on her stomach with her head on her paws and whimpered. They appeared to be concerned, but did nothing to help. I think they knew the inevitable.

We all did.

With death on her heels, Tryon flew out the opposite end of the shard leaving a trail of blood behind her. Her wounded leg faltered. She fell on her belly, jumped up, and flipped around snarling as she faced her attacker.

Was she finally ready to fight?

I silently prayed that she was.

Tyron rose on her haunches. Addle rose on his. The dogs wrapped front legs, wrestling. Tyron nipped Addle's nose. He howled as if she'd actually injured him. The muscles on his back rippled in anger. He lurched forward, tripping her.

Addle's jaw snapped onto her injured leg. He dragged and twisted seemingly trying to pull it off.

More blood.

Tryon screeched. Instead of defending herself, she tried to crawl away. He held on. She whimpered and cried, and stopped struggling.

He released her leg.

Tyron rolled over, belly up, a sign of submission. She'd had enough.

Addle didn't claim victory. He went for the kill.

I'd never seen a dog do that. A sign of submission was the time to declare victory. Instinctively, I moved to pull him off. Addle needed to be stopped. Nu Venia grabbed my arm, and held me back.

"No." The pain in her voice and face said she didn't like what was happening, but there was no stopping Addle. "If we interfere, the others will attack us. Huth, Essal, and Imos will come to our rescue. There will be much blood and injury. This way only one dies."

The final kill was swift. Addle straddled Tyron, clamped his jaws onto her throat and held on. She scratched at his belly with her three good legs. Her paws became red with his blood, but he didn't let go.

Then all was quiet. Tyron stopped struggling. A few seconds longer, just to make sure she truly was dead, then Addle released her.

Huth was lead alpha dog, Tyron had been her running partner, and next in line. She was dead. Her replacement stood triumphantly, with his muzzle proudly held high. I could barely see the black spot on his pink noise for Tryon's blood smear. Addle's team stood in support of their new second-in-command.

Some of the dogs from the other team had watched, but remained neutral.

Huth, Essal, and Imos turned to sit with their backs to the group. They did not approve Addle as Huth's running mate.

I feared it would be a long time before I no longer heard Tyron's screams of pain or saw her horrifying death haunting my dreams.

Chapter 18

Rona Montgomery
Canini Project

WHEN OLIVIA gave them thirty tags, Lu complained, "Thirty? That's too many. We'll never find thirty male puppies. We haven't found that many as of yet. Even if we check every litter again, there won't suddenly be thirty male puppies." She paused to take a breath. She gave her head a quick aggravated shake. "All we have are thirteen puppies. There's got to be more puppies around here somewhere. I wonder if the colonists keep the males lock up so we can't get to them, but why would they do that? It's not like we're going to steal them."

At the next breath, Rona jumped in. "You don't know, Lu she said. "We can always give back the tags we don't use. Thirteen is better than not having any to tag. I don't think the colonists are hiding anything. There's no reason. Besides they don't even know about our research."

Once again, Lu wasn't listening, not really. She was in her usual habit of getting lost in her own thoughts.

"Of all these litters, we've only found thirteen. I don't believe it. We *should* have thirty puppies. How can we to come to a conclusion if we only have thirteen? No one will take our research seriously, not with only thirteen puppies. We need thirty more," Lu complained.

As long as their research was complete. If 70% of the dogs exhibit the same behavior, it would be a good result. Lu was a worrier.

"As new litters are born, we'll find more males to tag," Rona assured her.

Lu attached a tag to a small male puppy's pure white ear.

Even though the tag was no larger than a thumbnail and weighed practically nothing, the puppy shook his head in an effort to shake the foreign object off. He shook so hard, he unbalanced himself and fell flat on his face. Whining, he ran to his mother who consoled him by licking his face and wounded ear.

Lu giggled.

She's like a kitten with a ball of twine, Rona thought, *so full of energy. I'm glad she's my teammate. She keeps things interesting.*

Things were by no means dull with Lu around. Instead of brooding over the colonists' rejection, she'd come up with a whole new project. Not one Rona would have thought of, or was originally interested in, but Lu's enthusiasm was contagious. Rona worried less about Jess and sighed less over Jorge, and to her surprise, her thoughts drifted more and more toward Mathieu.

"Lu, thirteen is plenty for us to start with. We also have thirteen HMS scans to process and thirteen files to update."

Lu shook her head and wrinkled her nose. Her hand automatically slipped to the right side of her face and pulled her hair behind her ear.

"Don't worry, we'll find more male puppies," Rona said. "They have to be around here somewhere. They don't just disappear."

"I guess," Lu said.

They'd tagged puppies of various sizes. Two were almost the size of their mothers. Their fur had changed color and was no longer all white. Seven medium size puppies were half the size of their mother. Their fur coats had the hint of changing colors. The four littlest ones were pure white and still youthfully clumsy.

For every mother who didn't mind her litter examined, there were just as many who did. If their brood was very young, they objected with throaty, guttural growls. Mothers with larger puppies were less protective.

So far, they'd not found one adult male and only thirteen male puppies.

Where were the males? Were they, as Lu suggested, somewhere in the habitat? Were the females black widows who killed their males after they mated?

Tagging the puppies should allow them to find answers.

Much to Lu's chagrin, most of the tagged puppies hung around the bay area with their mothers. "What good is it to place tags on them if they never leave? They're always with us. They play and sleep here. The only thing they don't do here is eat."

Twice a day, all the dogs left the area. Olivia said every morning she saw them following the fishermen to the ocean. She was unsure where the fishermen went, but she had heard dogs barking and growling off in the distance. She seriously considered spying on them for Rona and Lu, but was afraid because the dogs sounded ferocious.

"But the dogs return to us all happy and content. Very strange," Olivia said.

Lu immediately wanted to see for herself, but both Rona and Olivia thought it best not to. They had no idea what the colonists might do if they found her watching them.

The Canini Project made Lu impatiently fidget and fuss.

"It's just her youthfulness," Gino had said when Rona consulted him. "She'll learn. Give her time."

So once again, as Lu complained at their lack of data, Rona said, "Give it time, Lu. A watched pot never boils."

"I wonder where they go when they do eat," Lu said. "I wonder if it's in the main buildings."

Lu was caught in her thoughts. Sometimes it was difficult to keep up with her ramblings, but if she kept talking, she often answered her own questions. "They must go to the colonists to be fed. I wonder what they eat. Olivia proved they don't eat meat. So what do they eat?"

One day at lunch, Olivia had thrown bits of meat and vegetables at the dogs. They ignored the meat. They even got up and walked away. But they eat the vegetables.

"Well, Lu, now we can follow them on our holo-screen," Rona said. "We'll see if they do return to the main building. But more importantly, when they grow up and leave their mothers, we'll see the value of the tags and we'll learn something interesting."

"Like what?" Lu asked impatiently.

Rona smiled. "Well, Lu, we'll have to wait and see."

Chapter 19

Jessica Hewitt
Addle

WE LEFT Tyron where she lay. Nu Venia and I sat in stunned silence, emotionally drained, and waited for Cameron's return.

Essal lay next to Tyron with his head resting on her stomach, a sign that he already missed her. Huth sat next to him. Imos sat a little way to the right of them, giving those two time to grieve before she took her turn.

"What just happened?" I asked.

"Addle desired to lead. Tyron was in the way."

"So he killed her?" Who knew dogs were so ambitious. That was why Dad kept his dogs tied to stakes, so they wouldn't fight. But of all the times there was a fight, I'd never seen anything like this. "Why Tyron and not Huth?"

"Huth will not give in. Once Addle established that Tyron was weak, the fight was inevitable," Nu Venia said. "Huth will not be so easily brought down."

When Cameron did finally return, he immediately noted Tryon's dead body. Without asking who was responsible, he walked over to Addle.

The team supporting their newest second-in-command gave way to him.

Addle proudly held his head high showing off his still bloody muzzle and waiting for Cameron's approval. Instead, very uncharacteristically, Cameron backhanded the dog.

To say I was shocked is an understatement. Ever since we'd started this trip, dogs came first, but not this time.

Shamed, Addle dropped to the ground and hid his muzzle in the snow. The rest of his team froze in shock, then they also dropped their heads, tucked their tails between their legs, and slunk away; they knew something was wrong.

Huth and Imos sat with heads held high, vindicated in their disapproval. Essal still lay next to Tyron.

"When Cameron hit Addle; Huth, Imos, and Essal didn't flinch, but the rest of the team cowered. Why?" I asked.

"Huth brought forth Tyron and Essal. Imos is friend. They stand in judgment of Addle. The others wish not to get caught in Cameron's wrath," Nu Venia said.

"If Huth was her mother and Essal her sibling, why didn't they protect Tyron?"

"It is the way of things." Nu Venia seemed tired and sad. "The team decided. Huth, Imos, and Essal must abide or more chovis would have been killed."

"Imos still stands by herself. What's her story?" I asked.

"Imos is a friend."

"So why not sit with Huth and Essal?"

"Huth and Essal are family, Imos is friend."

These dogs had a complicated social structure.

The other team had not been involved. They lay on their sides, gnawed at their tails, scratched their ears, or aimlessly walked around the camp, for them, nothing bad had happened.

But something had. Tyron had died needlessly. More importantly, if Cameron had been in camp, he could have saved her.

"Where were you?" I demanded of him.

"Walking with the Holy One," he said.

"If you had been here, Tyron would not have died," I scolded.

Calmly, Cameron scanned the camp. His eyes hesitated over the bloody snow, then focused on Tyron. He sighed heavily.

"That's it?" I asked, indignantly.

"Some events are inevitable," he said.

"What does that mean?" I asked.

"If not this day, Addle would have found another time when I was not available," he said.

I wasn't angry with Cameron. I was incensed. He'd been off having some mystical experience when he was needed in the real world. He should have saved Tyron.

Why was I so upset? I didn't even like dogs. Tryon's death was senseless, that's why! I didn't like bullies. Addle should have been punished, but Cameron didn't seem inclined to discipline him. A slap in the face and that was it.

If Cameron wasn't present when one of his dogs was in trouble, where will he be when *I* get in trouble? Will he stand over my dead body and sigh regretfully? Then move on because I don't mattered?

"Tyron was leader," Cameron quietly said. "It was up to her to defend her stance. Addle challenged and conquered, and now takes Tyron's place as second to Huth."

"She didn't have to die."

I still heard her bloodcurdling screams of pain. When I closed my eyes, and saw Addle rip into her. I felt guilty that I was helpless and unable to save her.

The same sick feeling of revulsion when my father died swept over me. There was nothing I could have done about that either. Perhaps, I was the worthless one and not Cameron.

Like a dejected, red-furred walrus who had lost his way, Cameron sadly said, "It is the way of chovis."

I had no sympathy for him.

"Tyron submitted to Addle. Instead of letting her up, he killed her in cold blood," I informed him.

"Addle will reap the fruit of such action."

"What does that mean?" I was frustrated that I could not get a straight answer out of him.

"Addle will not run at Huth's side for long."

"What are you talking about?" I demanded. Why couldn't he plainly explain what was going on instead of giving me half-riddles?

"Addle took what is not hers to have. The team sits by her now, but they will soon learn the truth when that one proves her worth."

I had no idea what that meant. For me, Addle had already proved he was worthless. Then I heard Cameron's words "not hers" and "her worth."

"Is Addle male or female?" I asked.

"Addle is female," he said.

So, I was wrong about Addle; he was a she. And she was a bully.

Cameron picked Tyron up and left camp.

"Where's he going?" I asked.

"On Akiane, nothing is wasted."

"What does that mean?"

"Cameron will butcher Tyron," Nu Venia explained.

"What? He's going to cook her?" I couldn't believe it. What was wrong with these people? "Tyron deserves better."

"She will feed us," Nu Venia said surprise at my outburst.

"Will you eat me when I die and declare it the meaning of my life?" I asked.

She said nothing, but it was the way she said nothing that made me suspicious.

And then it dawned on me. I did a quick count of the dogs. I counted twice just to be sure I didn't miss anyone.

"We had thirty-two dogs when we started. Sixteen for each sled." At the time, I thought that was a bit much, but I also thought it was their way.

"With Tryon's death, there are 29," Nu Venia said.

I should have kept my mouth shut, but I had to ask. I had to confirm my suspicions. "What happened to the other dogs?"

"Chovis have met our needs."

I felt suddenly sick. "Sometimes we had dried meat and sometimes we had fresh meat," I said. "Where did we get the dried meat?"

"Tupilak," she said.

"And the fresh meat?"

Phyllis Moore

"What better honor than to provide for our needs?" she asked.

It sounded so innocent, but we were eating dog.

My stomach churned. Revolution spread up my spine. I came close to losing everything I'd eaten since we'd started this trip.

That was why Cameron knew we would not run out of food, we had thirty-two dogs to eat. Was Nella also on the menu? Would he save her for last? I didn't like dogs, but I certainly didn't want to eat them. What happens when we run out of dogs? Who will pull the sleds on the return trip? Was he planning on returning?

I was afraid to ask.

Chapter 20

Qorow Low
Watching, Waiting, Learning

QOROW LOW VALUED the assortment of different work duties, but at the same time it made her feel shamed. The opposite mix of emotions was confusing. The pleasure of variety was the result of the death of so many that she treasured. But beyond the heartbreak of deaths, Endurance demanded upkeep. Thus Qorow Low no longer had to endure the tedious of repetition of only one chore.

It was a relief to wake in the morning and know she would not have to spend the entire day tanning tupilak. But there was also the dread that there would be another death.

Of her new duties, her least favorite was fishing. She did not like the way chovis fought over their meals. It made her nervous to know that such loyal and gentle creatures could become such ferocious eaters.

After chovis were satisfied, the fishers would carry the remaining fish to Endurance, dry them, and save them for the summer years. During the six years of winter, most all of the oceans froze. The only open water circled the equator.

The fish came to the ninety meters of open water at the equator, but as the ocean ice melted, fish disappeared from the nearby waters for long periods of time. They'd return then disappear again.

There were so many, many fish to dry. Yet it was an important task if chovis were to eat. If they were not fed, chovis would jump into the ocean hunting food and drown. It was a great tragedy and waste of chovis.

Chovis were not just friends, but food for when the Community ran out of tupilak, which had been a problem in past summers when there had been many people. No one expected it to be a problem this time round.

After all had died, there would be no one to feed chovis and they would go to the ocean to eat and drown. Everything the first settlers had worked so hard to build would be lost and forgotten.

Some wondered why they should bother since the end was inevitable.

Jecidia rebuked when such thoughts were spoken. "The Holy One will come to our rescue," he insisted. "He loves us and will not let us die. Be patient and believe."

Adumie said nothing but one could see the unbelief on his harden face.

Sometimes, Qorow Low found it difficult to believe herself.

Of the many new jobs she had learned, gardening was her favorite. She had always loved walking in the gardens, now she had an excuse to spend more time in them. She loved to prune and shape. Foliage seemed to speak to her and tell her what to cut and where to trim. She always listened.

Unfortunately, not all the gardens were so cared for. Slowly, one garden at a time was left to nature. Trees and bushes became overgrown. Vines were allowed to grow at will. Now only the pond and surrounding area was cared for.

Yet, the overgrown brush gave Qorow Low a place to hide. She stood in the thickest of the foliage to watch, listen, and learn about off-worlders. She wanted truth of who they were. She had need to know who had better understanding of off-worlders, Adumie or Cameron?

Adumie wished to banish them. Cameron wanted to welcome them into Community. How was Qorow Low had need to know who was correct? So she watched and listened.

But such watching also caused wondering.

She saw how off-worlders controlled the wonders of the sky. They danced among the overhead skylights. If she did not already believe in the Holy One, she might have thought these people were gods.

Within Community, touching was forbidden. That was why all wore green gloves, so there would be no accidental touching and no accidental transference of essence.

Off-worlders held ungloved hands as they walked side by side. When they sat together, shoulders and hips touched or a head rested on a shoulder. They wrapped arms around each other and touched lips.

At first Qorow Low diverted her eyes, but with observing, came the comfort of watching. Not all off-worlders touched. But for the few who did, it seemed natural and loving. They took pleasure in the touching. Those around them seemed to barely notice. The old one often smiled in approval.

Life-givers only touched their children, but as the child became an adult, the child was taught that touching was forbidden. At first they objected, but in time, they understood and complied.

As Qorow Low watched off-worlders, her desires grew.

What would it be like to walk with Adumie while holding his hand? Such thoughts were blasphemy. She cringed in embarrassment.

Slowly, Qorow Low began to doubt and wondered why it was permissible for others to touch but blasphemous for Community. How could such loving actions be wrong?

Of all those she watched, it was the dark-skinned one, who walked with the small one at her side, who most interested Qorow Low.

She and the small one were often together. They seemed to be very interested in chovis. They pointed strange objects at them, but did not harm them. They talked to them as they lavished affection on the animals.

For some strange reason, they were interested in what was under chovis tails, though Qorow Low couldn't imagine what. Adumie would be horrified.

Qorow Low assumed the two off-worlders belonged together as life-giver and child, but they were so different from each other.

The dark one's skin had dark brown hair. The small one's skin was much lighter brown and her hair was black as lava.

The small one often smiled and laughed. She greeted each chovis with great affection. The other did not show the same fondness, yet she was just as interested in them.

The dark one often watched the small one with a smile but not with the affection of a life-giver. Their relationship was confusing.

Qorow Low wanted to know if she should trust the dark one, which also brought shame.

Her heart shook as if breaking into pieces. She did not want to betray Adumie. If he was right about off-worlders, she should not approach them, but if he was wrong, and they did have a cure, her speaking could bring healing.

If off-worlders could dance in the night skylights, why could they not heal?

With all her heart, she prayed that Adumie was wrong.

Almost as much as she wanted her child to live, Qorow Low also wanted Adumie's friendship and approval. If she was wrong and he found out, she would be risking their relationship. But if she did not make contact, her child would die.

She stood conflicted, unable to make a decision. By logic, she should not approach those two and yet . . . And yet, her heart compelled her, pushed her, willed her forward. She desperately wanted there to be knowledge to cure this slow-killing illness.

More than anything, she wanted her child to live. Even if it that meant Adumie would become angry with her and never speak to her again. If contact brought healing for her child, and for so many others, the risk was necessary.

Qorow Low would make contact with off-worlders.

Chapter 21

Jessica Hewitt
Sixteenth Day on Expedition

AS WE moved out onto the landlocked ice, a ray of orange-red light streaked from Kahair pointing straight up, a sign of moisture in the air. With this much ice covering the ocean, Akiane was arid and almost as dry as a desert. The melting of the ice would put moisture back in the air. Without moisture there were no snowstorms. Coming moisture foretold snow storms and blizzards.

Two more beams appeared, extending from either side of the star. The beams stretched out into the sky until their light faded. At the end of the beams, a pale rainbow wrapped up, over, and around Kahair. The sky inside the rainbow was white. The sky out side was pale blue.

"Not a good sign," Cameron said.

"Not a good sign," Nu Venia echoed.

"Where I come from, that's a sign there's moisture in the air," I said. "It's neither a good nor bad omen. It's just a natural phenomenon."

"Snow is coming," Cameron said.

I had to agree; snow was not good. Not while we were over the ocean. A storm has a tendency to warm the ice and turn it into slush.

I scanned the sky. Not so much as a thin wisp of a cloud. I did a 360-degree turn. Not a cloud in sight, although we had picked up a steady wind. Wind was a good indication of a coming storm. If there was one out there, it wasn't revealing itself to us, at least not yet.

"Well, we're not in for a storm a while," I said feeling relatively secure. We had at least a day or two and by then we should have found land to weather out the blizzard.

"All too soon," he said. "We must hurry."

Hurry? Where did he plan to hurry to? We were in the middle of nothing, headed nowhere, but we "must hurry"?

"A steady wind has come to encourage us onward," she said.

"We will attach a mast and sail to each sled," Cameron said.

That was interesting. They planned on turning the sleds into mini sailboats that would be pushed by the wind and pulled by the dogs. We'd make better time and it would be much less stress on our four-legged power.

True to my newfound attitude, and much to my companions' surprise, I helped.

Near the bottom right side of each sled was a set of poles. Each set were untied and screwed together, then attached to the front and end of the sled. On the bottom left side of the sleds were the sails.

As Nu Venia and I secured the sail to the mask, I noticed she'd grown since we'd begun the expedition.

When we first met, Nu Venia was the average height of a twelve-year-old. But now we were the same height. Her facial features seemed more mature. Her cheeks were thinner and her eyes seemed more alert.

On the day we'd left, her fur suit was too large for her. She'd been a child in an adult's winter suit. The pant legs were bunched up over her boots. She'd rolled up her sleeves and the tails of her jacket dragged on the snow.

Her winter suit was still too large but not as much as it had been.

She was an alien teenager. Perhaps she was having a growth spurt. If so, what a spurt! I'd never seen anyone grow so fast. If she kept growing like that, she'd soon be as large as Cameron.

He also noticed her height change.

At his inspection, Nu Venia turned her back on him. "My size is none of your business."

Her size? What did that mean?

"I do not disapprove," he began.

"I have no need for your approval or disapproval."

By the expression of pain, I'd say she cared a lot. I concluded that this was a family disagreement. But what was it about? What different did size make? I had the feeling it was important. But it wasn't about to ask.

Just the day before, Nu Venia hadn't been this tall. I was fairly certain that she'd not been this tall at breakfast. Could she change sizes at will? Now here was something interesting about these people.

"The wind will help chovis pull sleds," Cameron said changing the subject and Nu Venia relaxed.

"Now we will be seeing how fast chovis run." He let out a guttural warrior-like laugh. I imagined him having the same kind of chuckle after a quick beheading. Not inspiring.

I liked him better when he was in a somber mood. His good-humored mood seemed out of place.

"This day we travel far," he said.

I liked the sound of that. It was past time to get this expedition underway and make some headway.

"Chovis have built strength," he continued. "There is no longer need to make frequent stops."

I wasn't sure I liked the sound of that. I'd grown used to those stops.

The dogs seemed to be just as excited at the possibility of a good run. The wind ruffled fur. Tails wagged in excitement. Dogs pranced in anticipation. They knew what was coming.

I'd fought not to go on winter camping trips with Dad and his dogs. He made me go anyway and taught me mushing a dog sled. I'd actually enjoyed it, though I never told him. Another painful reminder; my unforgiveness was part of his punishment for moving us to Woodlands Village.

During the most extreme times of winter, in far northern Minnesota, a dog sled was the only reliable transport. No matter how advanced technology became, there was always the possibility that something could go wrong.

In a time far past, people rode snowmobiles. They would straddle machines with runners that slid over the snow. They had to dress warmly so the cold air didn't freeze ears, noses, toes, or fingers.

Now, only the most daring rode in open air. Those less daring traveled in hover-bubbles. Daredevil jet-mobiles not only zoomed over land but also flew in the air.

Nevertheless, all machines, at one time or another, fail.

They stalled or ran out of energy. Then their riders would have a long, cold walk back. During a spring thaw, someone could travel over the wrong part of the lake and could get stuck in slush or sink through thin ice.

An injured rider would die of hyperthermia.

Dogs rarely freeze or stall. Sleds easily glide over wet snow. Dogs know when the ice is too precarious to travel over. If an injured driver was able to mush the sled, but could crawl onto the sled, the dogs obediently brought him home. If a team returned alone, the village knew to search for its musher.

No one would know to search for us if we were in trouble.

Don't dwell.

Hard not to.

So now, on an alien ice planet, I was glad Dad had taught me the sport of mushing a team. Nu Venia and I would take turns. One of us would ride on the sled while the other stood on the back mushing.

I volunteered to sit first.

Cameron packed me onto the sled with the tent and boat and wrapped me in furs like delicate china. The furs would keep the cold wind from freezing me. Ah, I snuggled in for a nice comfortable, relaxing ride.

Nu Venia stepped onto the back of the sled. It was good that she was larger. It's difficult for a child to handle a sled of this size and weight with a team of fourteen dogs.

Cameron stepped on the back of his sled and yelled, "Huk. Huk." *Go. Go.*

Nu Venia yelled, "Huk. Huk."

The dogs bent their backs and pulled. The winds gripped the sails. The sleds' dead weight moved, slowly at first, but soon the dogs were trotting at an easy gait.

Our adventure was beginning.

The dogs increased their pace to a gentle run.

Cold, winter wind slapped at my face, into my hood and down the back of my neck. I pulled my sunglasses off and put them in my jacket pocket. From the other pocket, I pulled out the visor Cameron had given me. The colonists made it for the harshest effects of winter—like keeping a cold wind out of my face and suit. It easily snapped in place on my hood. I wasn't sure what it was made of but it was porous so I could breathe, and the green tent worked well at protecting my eyes from the bright starlight. I snuggled back into the fur blankets and closed my eyes.

It didn't take long for the dogs to reach a full-out run. They loved it.

I soon regretted it.

Ice isn't as smooth as one might think. There are obstacles. Cameron's team bounded in between and around large bumps of ice. He jumped off his sled, ran alongside as he tilted the sled onto one runner. The dogs pulled the sled around and between the protrusions. As soon as the sled slammed upright, he jumped back on.

Behind me, Nu Venia jumped off. The sled, with me on it, tilted on its one blade as it maneuvered around a half-meter bump. I held tightly to the furs, leaned into the sled, and held my breath, half expecting to slide off. The sled jolted back down, jarring every bone in my body, right up to my teeth.

The sled caught on smaller protrusions, hesitated a moment, but the wind pushed and the team pulled. For one or two brief seconds the sled was airborne, and then it came crashing down onto the ice. Every bone, organ, and fiber in my body objected. Good thing I wasn't a delicate piece of china or I'd have shattered into a thousand irreparable pieces.

I couldn't wait to stop and was extremely thankful when we finally did.

With great effort, I pushed the blankets off. With even more effort, I unfolded myself from the sled. I'd forgotten what it was like *not* to be sore. The furs under me hadn't cushioned the solidness of the packed tent that I'd spent the morning sitting on. My butt hurt. My legs were stiff. My back ached from the pounding. My head throbbed.

I glad that we stopped.

But the dogs were not happy.

They howled their objections and sulked like toddlers. They turned their heads and wouldn't acknowledge Cameron when he checked their paws. Their tails lay quietly in the snow as he praised them. They did the same to Nu Venia, even though stopping was not her decision.

All that sulking even though they were the reason we'd stopped in the first place. Cameron wanted to give them time to rest.

All was forgiven when he threw dried fish at them. I say "threw at them" because he didn't gently toss fish; he *threw* fish as if throwing missiles.

The dogs did not tenderly eat—they attacked. They fought and ate as if that might be their last bite of fish for the rest of their lives.

Despite the hostile snarling and growling, no blood was drawn.

You'd think after watching the same ferocious feeding twice a day, every day, I'd be used to the aggressive meal. I wasn't. I knew no one would be hurt, but still, it was a violent scene.

Once finished, the ferocious dogs suddenly become placid. They gathered together in groups of three or four, nudged each other like long time friends, licked the other's face, and slept one on top of the other.

Every one of them reminded me of Dr. Jekyll and Mr. Hyde. They made me nervous. How was I to trust them with my life after a meal like that?

After their nap, the dogs were again hitched to the sleds, I happily volunteered to mush and let Nu Venia sit.

Standing wasn't any easier.

I had to run behind the sled to help get it going and alongside when needed. The sled flew off small protrusions and landed hard. Several times I came close to falling off. By the next stop, my legs could no longer hold me, my back was even more sore, and my head throbbed from the noise.

Noise?

Akiane's unnatural silence was being shattered by low moans and grinding that assaulted us from every direction.

"What is that noise?" I shouted over it.

The ice shivered as if *it* were cold. I jumped back afraid it was about to break off. "Why is the ice vibrating?"

"Sea ice moves with the current and scrapes against the landlocked ice," Nu Venia yelled back.

"I can't see the edge," I said. "Where is it?"

"We are at least two kilometers away," Cameron said.

"If it's that far away, why is the noise so loud *here*?" I asked.

"It will become louder," Nu Venia promised.

"We camp here," Cameron said. "In the morning, we cross onto sea ice."

It sounded like a demolition derby tournament. If it was this loud at two kilometers, what would it be like when we reached the edge where ice was actually pulverizing itself?

Ice shifted, vibrated, dipped, and rose, the moving never stopped. Neither did the noise.

Once camp was set and I sat waiting for my dinner, my thoughts wandered to my childhood. *A winter outing on an alien planet is a far cry from those days,* I thought.

Growing up in Woodlands Village, after a day of playing in the snow with friends, we'd go to one of our homes to warm up by a fireplace with a hot cup of cocoa. We played games or watched digital vids of children's adventures.

Those stories helped to develop the desire for my own adventure. I wanted to be a heroine with a story of my own.

What's that saying? *"Be careful what you wish for."* If only I'd known my future. I'd never have left home, Dad might still be alive, I'd never have joined the space program, and I'd be at home with him.

Instead of a warm fire, I sat in a cold tent with a small burner stove and a small cooking flame, which offered little heat and took forever to warm our food. Instead of hot chocolate, we drank milky tea. Instead of games and laughter, we sat in silence.

I had little to say to these people. Sometimes they tried, or rather, Cameron tried to make conversation, but neither Nu Venia nor I were interested.

It didn't matter. Most of the time, I had no idea what they were talking about anyway. We were from two different worlds, from opposite sides of the universe, and though it sounded like we spoke the same common language of English, we in fact, often spoke different languages.

Nu Venia usually stared off into space with her eyes glazed-over. I couldn't tell if her brain had turned off or if she was in another world where Cameron and I were not invited.

When the stew was finally ready, Cameron handed me a bowl. I hated the idea of eating Tryon, but what choice did I have? It was too long a trip to refuse nourishment. I could continue to complain, not eat, and starve.

Starving wasn't an option.

"Don't mess up or this could be you," I told Essal and showed him my bowl.

His head cocked to one side and his one red ear turned toward me as if he didn't understand, but he did. He wasn't as dumb as he pretended to be, or as annoying.

He'd stopped trying to sit in my lap and incessantly lick my face. Instead, he lay sprawled out quietly watching me. I wondered what he thought of Cameron cooking his sister. Did he understand the concept that nothing on Akiane was wasted? Did he accept our eating one of his own was a result of death? What would he think if he knew it was not normal—at least not on Earth.

Every other dog, except Nella and Essal, went through their nightly ritual. They walked around the tent, checked every corner, and sniffed our bedrolls. No matter where I was, I was in the way.

It didn't take long before every floor space was taken and became a living carpet of dog. The nightly routine of one dog displacing another and dogs parading in and out of the tent continued.

As a matter of survival, I was adjusting and had learned when to duck as a tail swished my way and lean away from a sniff. But most importantly, I'd learned to tuned out the nightly commotion, rolled over, and went to sleep.

Chapter 22

Rona Montgomery
Puppies

IT WAS Rona's turn to check the puppies. With a command, her holo-screen appeared, with the 3D map Spago had downloaded to her system.

For security reasons, computers were linked according to team projects but Spago made the area maps available to everyone.

Rona and Lu would have loved it if one of Spago's multi-rotors could have flown inside the habitat and inside the two main buildings so they could have digital images of the those areas. Of course, the colonists would never have allowed it.

Of the fifty-two puppies they'd checked so far, Rona and Lu had only found fifteen males. Three male puppies were inside the habitat's interior.

Two were in the bay area. One was in the men's dorm. Another played a few meters from Rona with his sisters. His mother had adopted Tech Terzo the computer technician.

Terzo was presently studying something on his holo-screen.

As long as all computers were in good working order, there was little for Terzo to do. To keep him from becoming bored, Lu had found a project for him.

Rona purposely stayed out of it, she didn't even ask what they were doing for fear of being dragged into it. Puppies were more than enough for her right then.

One puppy was on the mountainside with the geologists and volcanologists.

Evidently, the cold bothered neither the puppies nor their mothers because where the mothers went, puppies were sure to follow.

The seven remaining puppies were playing just outside the habitat.

Radio tags also monitored heart rate. But since the male puppies only followed their mothers around, their heartbeats usually remained constant, except when they wrestled with each other. Even then their heart rates rose only slightly.

Rona checked each puppy individually. The heart rate of one of the puppies outside seemed unusually high and was rapidly rising. She quickly checked the rest of his vital signs. Everything normal.

What was he doing?

This doesn't make sense, she thought. *I must be doing something wrong.*

Once the heart rate peaked, it became steady. While she studied the screen, a neighboring puppy's heart rate also slowly began to rise. As far as Rona could tell, both puppies remained stationary. They weren't wrestling or chasing each other.

Rona labeled the first high-heart-rate puppy, P1 and the second puppy, whose heart rate was just beginning to increase, P2.

The screen began to flash a warning that something was wrong with P1.

What was happening? Were the dogs having a heart attack? Were they dying?

If so, that would explain why there were so few males—they died young—but that didn't make sense either. If all the males died, how did they breed?

Rona quickly checked the other puppies. Everything was normal. Even the male puppies on the mountain didn't show signs of stress as they romped up and down the slopes.

P1's heart rate had been high for almost ten minutes. Something else was happening. Something physiological? Probably. But what?

She and Lu needed to go outside and check in person and see for themselves what was happening. It would only take a matter of minutes to dress in their winter suits and find the dogs.

Puppies P1 and P2 were in the shadows between the tunnel entrances on the south side of the habitat. They were no longer all white. P1's fur looked as if he'd been splattered with a can of red paint and it spilled down his sides. His head, belly, and paws were still pure white.

P2 sported deep red fur with lighter apricot tufts.

Rona now understood why P1's high heart rate was so high.

He was mating.

Even so, it was close to double his normal heart rate.

She had feared he might be dying and was surprised that he wasn't stretched out in the snow already dead.

As soon as he was finished with one bitch, he mounted another. In the seven minutes they'd been watching P1 had already mated with two bitches, with only a couple of minutes rest in between. There were eight more females waiting their turn.

"Where does he get that kind of stamina?" Lu asked.

Rona touched her earpiece and spoke, "Record." She and Lu could study the recording later. She also called up her holo-screen. P1's medical file had adjusted itself. The new rapid rate was now normal.

Lu tried to scan him, but the HMS went crazy.

"Information is too fractured," she said.

Rona leaned in closer to the holo-screen. Bits of information flashed in and out of view, too fast for her to read.

Lu scanned P2, the puppy that was quietly sitting. The HMS locked on. It registered his heart rate. It was still rising and would soon be as high as P1. All other readings said he was normal. Yet the dog panted heavily as if he'd just run around the habitat.

"These puppies are no longer puppies," Rona said. "They're the size of an adult dog. Not to mention P1's breeding more than one bitch. I'll bet P2 is getting ready to also start breeding."

"I don't believe it," Lu said. "I mean . . .P1. How can he keep it up like that?"

"I don't understand it either," Rona said.

There were now eighteen females milling around the red-splattered dog waiting their turn to mate, some were more patient than others.

"They can't all be in heat at the same time," Lu said.

One female snapped at two of the bitches in front of her as she tried to force her way past them. Instead of complying, they joined forces and turned on her. The aggressor hunched ready to attack. The two in her way pounced first and easily brought her down.

After a short scuffle, she rolled over, exposing her belly, in submission. The victors backed off. When the defeated bitch rose to her feet, she tried to slink to the back of the group to wait her turn. The victors had other plans. They charged her. She turned and ran.

The champion bitches took their turns next.

P1 didn't stop or pay attention as to who was next. When a new female presented herself, he mounted.

"He's been at it for the last twenty-three minutes since I first started to monitor him. Who knows how many times he's mated before we got out here," Rona said.

"He won't mate with all of them," Lu said. "He can't. No dog has that kind of energy, even if he is alien. He's descended from an Earth dog. An Earth dog can't do this. I don't think any animal on Earth can do this. I know he's alien, but this is not possible. It's only been three centuries. That's not long enough for this kind of evolutionary change. He'd have to be truly alien with little of his original genetic makeup left."

"We saw changes in his DNA," Rona reminded her. "Maybe if we understand those changes, we'll understand what's happening here."

"He can't do it. Not mate all of them. His sperm motility rate will plummet. He should not be able to do more than five or seven in a day, certainly not the twelve he's done so far."

"Well, if there are only a few male dogs on Akiane, maybe their sperm count is higher than anything we've encountered on Earth. And if the dogs are going to propagate with so few males available, the males would have to have unusually high sperm motility."

"That would explain why there are so many puppies running around," Lu said. "As soon as they become mature they breed with every bitch in sight. But they can't all be in heat. If only we could do more than just scan them."

"You mean like cut them open and see what's inside?" Rona asked.

"A bit drastic, but yes, that and far more tests," Lu said. "Scanning is just not enough." A mischievous grin suddenly appeared.

"What?" Rona asked. She feared Lu had thought of a way to secretly autopsy a dog's corpse.

"Imagine the surprise of the medical community," Lu said. "We might just get that Nobel Prize yet."

Rona laughed. "I'm not sure this is the research WSC expected when they contracted with us."

P1 didn't mate all the bitches. P2 joined in.

Rona and Lu watched and recorded all of it. When the women grew tired of standing, they stooped. Eventually, they sat in the snow.

P1 stopped and refused any more females. He barked once at his male counterpart, then walked out of the area. He sat with his back to the crowd and waited until his companion finished.

Once mated, the females left the area. Word must have spread, because now there were thirty-six females waiting their turn.

After thirty-eight minutes, P2 decided he'd had enough and joined his comrade. Together, they headed southward.

The last of the females stood and watched. One gave a high-pitched howl. Several more joined in. The males ignored them.

Lu checked the data on the P1. "His hear rate is still high but considerably lower than when you first noticed him."

"How long was he mating?" Rona asked.

"Thirty-three minutes."

"How often did he mate?"

"Average of five minutes each including a short respite inbetween."

"Six bitches in 30 minutes," Rona said.

"Know any man who has that kind of endurance?" Lu asked with a giggle.

"I know a few who wished they did." Rona smiled.

"Some guys are really loaded," Lu said.

Rona was shocked. "And how would you know?"

Lu blushed.

The women snickered.

"Hm." Lu was thinking.

"What?" Rona asked.

"A hippopotamus can mate for a half hour, then seek out another female," Lu said. "Butterflies mate for an hour."

"So this isn't that unusual?" Rona asked.

"I guess not," Lu said. "Think the colonists would mind if we inserted a nano-cam in a puppy and watched his sperm motility?"

"I think if we do something like that, we have to do it secret," Rona said.

"Doesn't matter anyway, we don't have a nano-cam." Then Lu had an after thought, laughed, and asked, "Maybe Olivia has one?"

"You think she planned on counting fish sperm?" Rona asked.

Lu chuckled. "I don't think she's found a male fish yet."

"Well, we're ahead of her on that one. We've not only found fifteen males, we've seen two of them in action. Good thing we recorded this. Otherwise, no one would ever believe it." Rona laughed.

"If I didn't know better, I'd think they stopped because they were bored," Lu said in awe. "I guess there's a limit to how much sex one can enjoy at a time."

"Good thing Jorge isn't here to hear you say that. He'd adamantly disagree," Rona said.

Rona couldn't remember the last time she'd thought of Jorge.

"The dogs are getting away." Lu jumped to her feet. "Let's follow them."

"Lu, no."

She was already hurrying after the dogs. Reluctantly, Rona followed. They had to run to keep up with the males, which wasn't easy in heavy winter boots. But the dogs weren't in a hurry, so the women easily caught up with them.

A half an hour later, Rona stopped. "This is far enough. I don't think it's a good idea for us to be out here alone. We're on the path leading us out of the caldera."

"Olivia's been out here." Lu kept moving, though more slowly. She turned to face Rona as she continued to walk backwards.

"But she's out here with her team and they have a hovercraft," Rona said. "It's kilometers to the ocean. No one knows we're out here."

Lu stopped disappointed and unconvinced.

Rona continued, "We didn't tell anyone what we were doing. If we get in trouble, no one will know where we are."

"We'll tell Larry later. We'll tell him it was in the name of science, he'll understand." Looking from Rona to the dogs, Lu said, "We'll lose them. They're headed to the ocean anyway. We'll get a ride back with Olivia."

"They're probably just going to play somewhere along the way. Why would they be going to the ocean? We'll keep an eye on their transmitters." Rona made the final decision. "We'll catch up with them when they return to the habitat. Come on, we're going back."

"No." Lu took a few more tentative steps. "I want to see where they go. Following them on a holo-screen isn't enough.

I want to record them. They might do more than just play. We'll need the recording for our files."

"I'm not leaving you out here alone," Rona said. "We're going back. Together!"

Lu took another step, then stopped. She was having difficulty deciding what to do. She took two steps toward Rona. Then whipped around in time to see the dogs race off.

"You can't keep up with them anyway. Now they're running. Even if you had your running shoes, you couldn't keep up," Rona said. "Come back now. If I have to go back alone, I'll radio Olivia and have her drag you back."

"Olivia won't come. She's working. You know there's nothing that will take her from her work. Not even if one of us was injured. We'd have to wait until she was ready to come and get us."

"You know very well she would. She wouldn't be happy about it. She'll make everyone else miserable, and they'll be upset with you for causing Olivia to go on one of her rants." Rona laid it on a little thick.

Olivia probably wouldn't come. She'd send one her teammates, then make such a fuss, Lu would be mortified.

With a sigh, Lu complied. "All right."

But by the time they'd returned to the habitat, the dogs had wandered out on to the ice and into the ocean beyond. Soon there after, both radio tags stopped transmitting.

Chapter 23

Rona Montgomery
Puppies

OLIVIA BENT over Lu, grabbed her arm, yanked her off the floor where she'd been working, hauled her to an empty dining table, and sat next to her in a huff.

Lu's face turned crimson.

Stunned at Olivia's response to their request for help, Rona stared open-mouthed at them. "Didn't mean to ruffle your feathers," she sarcastically called after Olivia, which grabbed the attention of everyone who was in the room.

Lu ducked her head and hunched her shoulders trying to make herself smaller.

Why did Olivia have to fly off the handle like that? Rona and Lu had made a simple request to see if the tags were working correctly.

As more puppies became adult male dogs, they also disappeared from radar. They'd lost five so far. Rona and Lu thought they were doing something wrong and had asked Olivia to help them fix the problem.

But she'd acted as if they'd asked her to perform brain surgery and was overwhelmed by the gargantuan nature of the task.

Rona hadn't wanted to bother Olivia. She'd wanted to ask someone else.

Lu thought Olivia would be insulted if they'd asked someone else for help since she was the one who had set the program up in the first place. Evidently, she didn't been wrong.

"I don't know why you two insist on sitting on the floor." Olivia's loud voice vaulted off the walls. She relished the spotlight, but today she was insulted when all eyes turned toward her. "Mind your own business."

Heads turned away.

"We gave up our tables so you could have a place to sit at meal time." Rona spoke just as loud, but she didn't need to reprimand those listening.

They smiled and nodded their approval.

"You don't have to be so snippy about it," Olivia said.

With a shake of her head, Rona stood. *Olivia could make a preacher curse.*

When Olivia dragged Lu off the floor, her computer abruptly disconnected from Rona's, which turned both screens off.

Olivia forcefully grabbed Lu's wrist and spoke into her computer. "Open." In her fury, she forgot a computer only responded to the voice command of its owner. "Grrr."

Slowly, and in forced calm, Rona join them.

Leaning forward, Lu spoke to the band computer on her forearm, "Open."

The screen appeared. Olivia released Lu's wrist, leaving red finger marks behind.

Rona swung at the back of Olivia's head. *Lu and I don't need your bull.* She fumed.

In horror, Lu adamantly shook her head.

Rona had intentionally missed. She wouldn't actually hit Olivia. It wasn't in her nature but, at that moment, she wished it were. That woman deserved a good slap.

Several people laughed softly. If she had hit Olivia, no one would have objected. Her sour nature was not popular, not even with her teammates.

With a soft growl, Rona dropped in the chair on the other side of Olivia, leaned back, and crossed her arms over her chest.

What's her problem? In her head, Rona heard Jess answer, *Nothing. She's the goddess of her world. When things don't go her way, she makes everyone pay.*

"Evidently," Rona said softly, then asked, "Why are you so angry?"

Lu gave Rona a quick glance of dismay.

"When I loaned you the tags, I didn't think I'd have to babysit them and you. I have my own project to tend to," Olivia snipped.

"Gutting fish?" Rona asked. "Do tell."

Olivia sneered nastily.

"The tags were your idea," Rona reminded her.

"Well, pardon me for trying to help."

"R-Ro-Rona, it's ok-k-kay Just let Oli-i-ivia f-f-fix it. Then s-s-she can b-be ab-b-bout her bu-b-business," Lu said.

Olivia brought all Lu's insecurities to the surface, which meant Lu would not stop stuttering until the wicked witch was gone.

"We really don't need to put you out like this. We could ask someone else if you'd prefer." Rona didn't bother to hide the irritation in her voice.

Olivia made a move to get up.

"B-B-but Ol-l-via set it up and we as-s-sked her." Lu seemed to shrink inside herself. She hated confrontation.

"Stop that stuttering," Olivia snapped. "It's annoying."

Rona unfolded her arms, straightened, and reprimanded Olivia, "Don't yell at Lu."

The stuttering was annoying, but it was part of Lu's personality and as long as she remained calm, it wasn't a problem. Rona wasn't about to let Olivia's bad temper make things worse for Lu.

"Do you want me to fix this or not?" Olivia demanded.

"Yes," Lu said before Rona had time to say no. "We want your help." Lu sat straight-backed in her chair and seemed to have gained control of herself.

"Do go on, Olivia." Rona spoke her name as an insult.

Olivia understood. With one last glare at Rona, she turned her attention back to the screen and aggressively jabbed at it with her fingers. It responded accordingly.

Shaking her head, Lu pleaded with Rona to please let it go. Then she glanced around the room. It made Lu even more nervous when she became the center of attention. She really wanted this to be over and done with.

For Lu's sake, Rona decided to keep her mouth shut. She again leaned back in her chair, folded her arms over her chest, and looked away. She was met the sympathetic stares and smiles of encouragement.

Olivia continued to poke at the screen.

Images on the floating holo-screen appeared for less than a second, then disappeared to be replaced with a diagnostic system. "As far as I can tell, the tags are working just fine but the tags are out of range," Olivia said.

A map of the surrounding area and shoreline appeared on the screen.

Pointing to the shoreline, Olivia said, "Here is where they left land and headed out over the ice."

"Why would they go out on the ice?" Lu asked.

"I don't know," Olivia said. "Maybe they went for a swim."

"They're in the water?" Lu asked.

And just like that, an internal switch flipped and Olivia became as docile as a kitten.

If Rona didn't know her better she might have thought her psychotic. She wasn't. Olivia was literally the most annoyingly, self-centered person on this side of the galaxy.

If she didn't get things exactly her way, which was most of the time, she'd bite off the nearest head. Ah but, when she was in a good mood, butter wouldn't melt in her mouth.

"I don't know." Caught up in the moment, Olivia's tone softened. "But I'll find out." She continued to tap the screen. Then she spoke to her own computer on her wrist. "Open."

"What are you doing?" Lu asked.

"Calling up my maps. They extend into the ocean. Yours don't."

Olivia upgraded the maps on Lu's screen, which meant the new maps were now also on Rona's computer.

"I didn't expect the dogs to go this far out so I didn't give you full maps. You might have lost contact because the dogs are beyond your original map's range," Olivia said.

Curious, Rona dropped her arms and leaned forward.

"I'll reset your tags to also include the ocean." In a much softer voice, Olivia spoke to her computer.

The map on Lu screen changed and became smaller as it included the mountains, the caldera, the ice, and the ocean.

"Computer, adjust," Lu said. The screen disappeared then reappeared a third larger than before.

With a touch of her fingers, Olivia moved the map to cover the dogs' paths, then zoomed in on the area. She pointed to the screen. "See these lines? They belong to your the dogs." The lines traveled over land, over ice and into the water. "As far as I can tell, all of them are in the ocean."

"Evidently, they can swim. I had no idea. The dogs with us don't go near the water." Olivia's fingers expertly tapped the holo-screen. The map widened to include the ocean.

"See there?" She again pointed. "That's where they played on land for a bit before they moved on." The lines meandered over the ice, circled, and crossed each other before they headed northwest where they entered the water and finally disappeared at the northern edge of the map.

Olivia tapped more keys. "Sorry." She straightened her blouse, leaned back in her chair, and pulled at one of her copper curls while she thought. "If we had a satellite orbiting overhead, we could find them. If I can't find them, I can't reset the tags. You've lost them. They're gone."

"How were you planning to track fish? You didn't expect then to hang around here in their old stomping grounds," Rona said.

"No. We knew they'd move out of range. I've requested the use of a shuttle when the next transport arrives. A few quick flyovers and we'll pick up their radio signals. We might not be able to see where they've been, but we will be able to see where they migrated. We'll put whatever data we find in the computer and analyze it," Olivia said.

"The dogs must be on shore somewhere," Rona said. "They didn't just swim out into the ocean and drown."

"Where would they come back on land?" Lu asked Olivia expectantly.

"I don't know," Olivia said with her usual arrogant shrug.

"Other side of the mountains, maybe?" Lu asked. "They could have swum around for a while and then come back on shore someplace north of here."

"Lu, I don't know," Olivia said. "Spago's multi-rotors didn't fly that far."

"Will the computer pick up the tags' radio signals if the dogs returned to the habitat?" Rona asked. She thought it logical that they would return home at some point.

"Yes, of course," Olivia said.

"Perhaps the dogs came back on shore beyond the mountains," Lu decided. "That has to be right. They're not here and they can't stay in the ocean. They must be on the other side of the mountains. We'll have to ask Spago to fly his multi-rotor over the mountains and find them. It's the only way we'll ever know what happened to them. We can't complete our research if we don't have all the answers."

This project was not going well, Rona thought. *If we don't learn where the dogs went, what next?*

Rona certainly wasn't going to search frozen mountains or a thawing ocean to find those dogs.

"I'll ask Spago to fly his multi-rotors farther along shore to the other side of the mountains and see what's beyond," Lu said with wide-eyed hopefulness.

"No," Olivia said, "The multi-rotors are too small. They were only meant to fly in the immediate area. Going into the mountain range, even along shore, is too far.

"The only reason he has maps of the ocean is because of my multi-rotors," Olivia said. "I don't think Spago is planning to scale the mountain range just yet. Maybe after he finishes his research here, but not now." She fussed with her blouse, then resettled in her chair.

"Does that mean we have to wait until the next transport before we find where the adult males went?" Lu was both disappointed and frustrated.

"'Fraid so," Rona said. "We have to settle for what we find right here."

Lu moaned.

"I doubt all the dogs will go for a swim. We'll see what the next generation does," Rona said.

"According to what we know so far, they do go in the ocean. Five have already done it. What if they all do it? What then? Do you think they drowned?" Lu asked.

"No," Olivia said cutting Lu off. "If they had drowned near shore, the tags would still be transmitting."

"Even at the bottom of the ocean?"

"Yes, Lu, even at the bottom of the ocean. The tags were designed to be on fish, remember?" Olivia said impatiently. Then her face crunched into surprise. "You said you were missing five dogs?"

"Yes."

Olivia pointed to the screen. "Well according to this, eight dogs have gone into the ocean. All had a spike in their heart rate." Perplexed, she tapped her upper lip thoughtfully. "All their radio signals are also out of range."

"How is that possible?" Rona asked. "They become adults, mate, then go to the ocean? That doesn't make sense."

"I don't know." Olivia pointed to a red flickering light. "But you might want to get outside and check on this one. According to his vitals, he's having a heart attack."

Chapter 24

Jessica Hewitt
Seventeenth Day on Expedition

WE STOOD at the edge of the landlocked ice as the eastward ocean current moved past us. The current was strong enough to break up both landlocked and sea ice in to huge ice floes, and carry them away. We needed to cross the current so we could continue our journey north.

Some of the ice floes were the size of small houses while others were the size of a small town. When they slammed into each other, water sprayed like small geysers from between them. Often a piece of moving ice would grind along landlocked ice and pulverize it.

All the grinding and slamming was one explosion after another. Then there'd be a boom like a jet passing through the sound barrier. I was sure my ears would never get over the intrusion.

I asked or rather, screamed, "Why don't we just go around it?" I did not relish the thought of crossing moving water.

"Akiane's current flows for many days in either direction," Cameron said. "We must cross at some point if we are to continue northward."

"You expect us to travel north while the current pushes us east?" I said.

"Just so," he said.

"How wide is the current?" I asked.

"We should cross before end of day."

End of day? If it takes all day to cross, just how wide was this current?

I asked again, though more precisely, "How many kilometers do we have to cross before we reach the other side of the current?"

"No more than a day's journey," he repeated.

I wanted to ask, *Was that a slow walking day or a chovis running day?* But didn't bother.

Just so I know what to expect once we crossed the ocean current, I asked, "What is the ice like on the other side?"

"Solid."

"How solid?"

"It will not melt before we have finished out journey."

"Promise?"

Cameron's mind churned as he tried to decide whether I was serious or not. Without answering me, he walked to his sled.

Not a good sign.

At that moment, the current gathered the ice together like puzzle pieces with little open water between them. If everything remained the same, it would be an easy crossing.

But things never stay the same and things are never easy. Change is *always* inevitable, as was the unexpected. Life was just that unfair.

The team of dogs couldn't walk straight across from one piece of moving ice to another. The ice would pull the first few dogs out of step with the rest of the team. The weight of the sled would drag the wheel dogs more out of step. Dogs could get hurt.

So the team ran along the edge of the ice pacing with the new floe. Then with the grace of a ballerina shifting her balance from one foot to another, the team and sled slipped onto the new ice floe.

I admired the skill of the crossing, but I had a terrible thought. What would happen if the new floe suddenly decided to move, leaving an open gap of water just as the team crossed over? Answer: We'd tumble into the water and drown.

Apprehension—no—*panic* set in. One missed step and we'd be lost forever. I couldn't wait to reach the other side of the current, one day away. This would be one very long, nerve-racking day.

Then I remembered the blizzard Cameron had said was coming. As my sled came alongside his, I asked, "Cameron, what if a storm hits while we're out here in the current?"

"One should not worry about the future and its many possibilities," he said.

"You said a snow storm was coming." I insisted.

"Just so, but it will not arrive until after we have crossed the current."

"How can you be so sure?"

"I am familiar with storms of Akiane. We will cross the current in time."

"Where I come from, both are unpredictable."

"Then it is good that we are not on Earth."

We crossed one ice floe at a time, traveling to the northern edge where we waited for the next ice floe to come alongside. Then we'd cross over and continue to the northern end of that floe where we waited.

We did a lot of waiting.

We could only travel as far as the edge of the ice floe we were on. When we reached open water, and there was no place to go, we had to wait until another floe came alongside.

Sometimes we waited as little as twenty minutes. Other times, we waited as long as two hours. It was the waiting that made the crossing last all day. In the meantime, we slowly floated eastward. It was difficult to judge how far the current took us or how far we'd crossed.

The current moved chunks of ice several kilometers long and wide as if they were mere slivers of ice. Blocks bumped, bounced, and slammed into each other, turning ocean water to spray. Ice shivered, tilted, and occasionally changed directions.

We'd just crossed an ice floe several kilometers long, and were almost to the northernmost edge, when another floe rammed into us from the southwestern side. In a matter of minutes our floe had completely turned around. We were now on the southernmost end—again. We turned around and crossed the entire length a second time.

There were times when we sat and stared at open water for what felt like days. During one of those times, Cameron decided to go fishing. He wanted to save the dried fish for when fish were not readily available.

He stood at the edge of the ice, with his fishing net in hand, and stared into the clear, frigid water. His shadow, Nella, stood at his side. Together, they watched and waited for a school of fish cruising in the current.

With one great expert swing of his muscular arms, the net flew, stretching out to its full width and length before delicately landing on the surface. The weights tied to the net quickly sank the net. With one swift and powerful tug, Cameron closed the net around the unsuspecting fish.

Stepping back, he began the laborious task of hauling the fish out of the water.

Nu Venia ran to help.

Yes, I also helped.

The dogs were an essential part of our survival. It was important that they were well fed. So, I joined them in pulling the net onto the ice.

Cameron didn't check paws. That would take too long. He didn't even unhitch the dogs from the sleds. He wanted them ready at a moment's notice. They seemed content until they saw the fish, then they howled like a pack of wolves baying at the moon.

One more survey of the situation, no ice floes. Cameron set the dogs free.

As always, they ate with the same ferocity. Once finished, they were again harnessed in place. They quietly napped on full bellies.

Cameron again threw the net. We hauled in another catch.

Nu Venia placed one of the sled's canvas coverings on the ice. We threw fish on it so they could dry off. If they'd been stored in a bag still wet, they'd freeze into one large lump. This way they dried off and began the freezing process. Then the fish were placed in a leather bag and stored on the sled.

I found shiny round manmade objects attached to some of the fish. I took the little tabs off and pocketed them. Later, I'd place them in a container and give them to Olivia. She'd be angry that I took them off, but it had to be better than letting the dogs digest them and leave them along the way. No telling how many they'd already eaten today.

As soon as we reached another floe, we immediately crossed over and continued our journey north.

We walked in silence, ate in silence. Not just because there was nothing to say, but the constant noise from crashing and grinding, even of distant ice floes, made it impossible to carry on a decent conversation.

If the rest of the trip was going to be like this, I didn't have to worry about starving or drowning, or even freezing to death. I was going to go stark raving mad.

Right then, I promised myself as soon as I returned to Earth—if I returned to Earth—I was going to knock Admiral Grossman's block off. I didn't care if it cost me that important job he'd promised or the pay.

Then again.

Maybe I'd retire first, collect my pay, secure it, and then march into his office. When he stood and extended his fat pasty hand to congratulate me for a job well done, I'd slug him.

Admiral Grossman with his fake smile ordered me to come on this quest. He'd also ordered me to keep an eye out for signs of aggressive alien life. What a fool.

Thank You Note to Grossman:
So, I'm out here in the middle of nowhere, just wanted to say, Thank you.
I could have had a life, but now I'm going to die.

You sent me out here because of your stupid public relations.

That's supposed to be your department. If anyone should be out here with the threat of dying—it should be you!

But you're safe at home, drinking your wine and enjoying your family.

The thank you note came to an abrupt halt.

If I died out here, I determined my spirit would return to Earth and, for the rest of that miserable little man's life, I'd haunt him.

Chapter 25

Jessica Hewitt
Late Afternoon of Day Seventeen

STANDING ON the back of the sled ignited warm, forgotten memories, and nagging guilt. A lot of that guilt was for how poorly I'd treated my father.

As I matured into my late teens, I'd let Dad teach me about the dogs. I even took a team out on my own a couple times. I preferred going with him. But just like here, dogs always came first. Maybe that's the real reason I dislike them so much. I came after dogs.

Dad and I shared a lot—the loss of Mom, the warmth of a good fire, a good story.

Spring was a time when snow and ice melted leaving behind standing water, creating long tracks of mud, which held puddles of water that became mosquito-breeding pools. Mosquitoes were an important part of the ecological food chain for creatures like birds and frogs.

Mosquitoes no longer carried diseases dangerous to humans, but they still swarmed and sucked blood one drop at a time, driving their victims crazy. Late spring in Woodlands was a good time to stay indoors.

When summer came, breeding pools dried, decreasing the mosquitoes to a tolerable level, Dad and I went summer camping, hiking, and canoeing.

Summer nights were similar to winter trips. We sat around the campfire, told each other stories, and discussed his next novel.

Those were the very best times, when Dad left his dogs at home and the two of us were completely alone and we didn't fight. We talked about hopes, our dreams, and ourselves.

I told him how I wanted to go on an adventure and explore places no one had gone before. Dad said there were no such places left on Earth; everything had been explored.

"Well then, I'll leave Earth and explore other planets," I said.

He just laughed. We both thought I was a foolish little girl. I'd grow up and find a more mature profession.

Unhappy times seem to have overshadowed the good memories. It took going to an alien planet to remember them.

As soon as I was old enough, I left Woodlans for my migration south. It didn't take long for me to forget what I liked about Minnesota: cool summers, northern lights, story time—mostly Dad. I only remembered what I hated: below zero temperatures, droves of mosquitoes, isolation from everything and everyone I loved, and the arguments.

I wish I'd forgiven Dad while he was still alive.

Maybe, if I continued to remember the good times, I'd finally forgive him. He'd like that. So would I.

Kahair slipped behind a thin veil of very light gray clouds and became a diffused white ball. The sky and ice became a drab gray. The water turned threateningly inky black. It rose and fell and slapped against the ice.

Our ice floe swayed and rocked with the water's movement. A few of the dogs lost their footing and stumbled. The sled bounced with such force that my left foot slipped off the sled, hit the ice, and twisted. The sled kept moving, but the ice held my foot in place. Though it held me for no more than a second, it almost pulled me off the sled. I gripped the handles and, with great effort, regained my foothold.

Cameron stopped his sled. My team pulled alongside, so we could assess the situation.

Nu Venia, who had been bundled in furs on my sled jumped off.

We were on a floe less than a kilometer long and half as wide. We had been on a larger floe. Unfortunately, the only way to the next large slab of ice was to cross this little one.

Just a moment ago, the waters were quiet. The ocean current had gently granted us save passage, but as the water became restless, ice floes instantly rearranged themselves. The slab we'd been headed for was gone, leaving a long stretch of open water.

Ice floes bobbed and slammed into each other. Such ramming made little difference to ice the size of a small country, but we were on a much smaller piece of ice. It quaked and rumbled. I feared it might shatter.

A smaller floe forced its way under and lifted our stern, tilting us forward. Our floe slipped off that piece and dropped several centimeters into the ocean. Water sloshed up and over the sides.

With a dizzying swish, we popped back up. The turbulent ocean swayed us from side to side, and up and down like a piece of Styrofoam. The small floe couldn't handle the pressure. Behind us, a huge chunk of broke off.

Dogs howled.

I could barely hear them over the grinding, screeching, and cracking ice. The noise penetrated my head and rattled my brain against my skull. My bones and joints felt it. My stomach and heart collided. This was it. We were going down.

At lightning speed a large crack appeared in front of us.

A wave swept up heading toward us. The fracture broke off. We stood in the exact center of what was left of our ice floe with no escape. Water lapped all around us.

The dogs frantically pranced in fear of wet paws freezing to the ice. They knocked into and snapped at each other. If we didn't get moving fast, they'd start fighting and become tangled in their harnesses.

We'd be stuck with nowhere to run.

I had a terrifying vision of our floe shattering, and us dropping into the ocean. In this churning and subfreezing water, dressed in bulky furs, we'd sink like bricks.

With an intense jolt, a third floe slid alongside us to our right. It was much larger and more stable. Nu Venia ran to Cameron's point dogs and pulled them toward it. She yelled at my point dogs, Huth and Addle, to follow. Cameron's team responded and headed to the new floe.

I yelled, "Huk. Huk."

Cameron and Nu Venia did not look back. They were concentrating on getting their team to safety and assumed my team would obediently follow.

That was what they were supposed to do. They'd always followed Cameron's team before.

Not this time.

Huth tried, but Addle froze. This was no time for her to lose her nerve.

"Don't just stand there. You know what to do, follow them," I yelled, hysterically.

If they heard me, they didn't respond. Only Essal turned to ask what I'd said.

Cameron and Nu Venia were leaving me behind. Why didn't Nu Venia come back for me? Doesn't she know how stupid dogs are? No, she thought Akiane dogs were brilliant. Well, this proved they weren't.

"Follow Cameron, you stupid mutts!" I shouted.

Nothing.

I started to step off the sled with the intention of pulling the team after Cameron. Before my foot hit ice, Huth leaped and turned left.

"What?!"

Addle hesitated then moved to her side.

The team eagerly followed. We were heading in the wrong direction.

"No, you stupid dogs, follow Cameron."

He was now safely on the other ice floe—a nice, large safe floe, but the ice between us had crumbled. Water frothed and sprayed upward. Bits of ice bounced as if being ground in a blender. It was no longer safe to follow the other team. We were headed away from the dangerous water, which was a good thing, but we were also heading away from Cameron.

Strong winds shoved ice floes forcefully jamming them together. Our tiny ice floe might shatter under the impact.

My team was headed for a large floe to the north of us. They were taking me to safety. I breathed a sigh of relief. Once we were clear of all this mess, we'd hook up with Cameron and Nu Venia.

Huth tried to turn Addle so the team and sled would run alongside the edges of the two floes. Addle would have none of it. She ran straight for the edges. She wanted off this crumbing ice as quickly as possible. I didn't blame her.

But it was dangerous to run straight at the new ice floe. Too many things could go wrong.

Huth rammed her right shoulder into Addle and pushed, Addle wouldn't change course.

Then the sled came to a sudden halt.

Without warning a small gap of water appeared between the two floes. Addle came to a sudden stop, tripping Huth. She very nearly landed on her nose. She turned her head just in time and hit the ice with her shoulder. She came up snarling and snapping.

I feared there'd be another dogfight and I wouldn't be able to stop it.

But Huth knew better and didn't attack.

Addle dropped to her belly and whined.

Huth turned and made direct eye contact with me. What was I supposed to do?

The gap was small enough for the team to easily jump over, but Addle was hunched over with her tail wrapped around her body. She was terrified of the water.

Huth tried to pull Addle onward. She refused.

If Addle was still running next to Essal, the team would have dragged her along, but she was in the front of the line. She didn't move; the team didn't move.

Small hairline cracks were forming underfoot. Our ice floe was crumpling. We had no choice. Despite the dangers, we had to cross here.

Huth was right; it *was* up to me.

Quickly jumping off the sled, I headed for Addle.

Huth nipped at her. The two dogs behind them excitedly jumped—demons of death were chasing them. The wheel dogs pranced, ready to dash forward. Essal and his new partner, Imos, seemed unnaturally calm. The rest of the team was in various stages of fright or unwillingness to obey my command. If only they'd listened, and followed Cameron.

Desperately, I grabbed Addle around her stomach and tried to lift her to her feet. She slumped back down into a cowering ball. I wanted to kick her.

Our floe eased against the larger ice with a gentle bump. Now was our chance. If we waited too long, anything could happen.

I managed to drag Addle across. As soon as her feet hit the new floe, she shook herself from a deep daze of fear and ran in pace with Huth.

The next two dogs quickly followed. I encouraged the team onward as they passed me. I didn't think they could hear with all the noise, even so, they obediently obeyed.

Essal and Imos hopped over and literally hit the ground running. The next two followed.

In what seemed like an eternity, the wheel dogs finally crossed over, but the sled tilted upward as the edge of the ice slab began to rise. The weight of the sled slowed the team.

The floe behind us had just come to our rescue and had gently pushed us to the larger ice seemed to have changed its mind. It was moving on top of our old floe and tilting the edge upward as if to stand vertically in the water.

If the sled slipped backwards, it would drag the team into the ocean. The front of the sled hung over the edge into empty space. I leaped onto the sled, hoping my extra weight would help the wheel dogs haul it the rest of the way.

"You can do it," I encouraged.

The wheel dogs bent their backs and heaved with every bit of power they could manage. The rest of the team pulled in an effort to give the wheel dogs the extra strength they needed. The sled teetered forward, then came free. I didn't hear it hit, but I felt the jolt as it threw me backwards onto my rear. Now the sled was moving—without me.

Scrambling to my feet, I ran after it and managed to grab one handle. The sled pulled. I almost lost my grip. My other hand grabbed hold.

Dad's training came rolling back to me. *"Don't let go. Run and catch up."* A few more good steps and my feet found their place. I was on.

Sneaking a quick peek over my shoulder, I saw the vertical piece of ice continue to move up before it came crashing down. It cracked, splintered, and was no more.

The team ran at full speed.

Luckily this ice floe was large enough to withstand the beating it got from the smaller floe. It didn't crumble. This floe stretched for a good distance. I couldn't tell how large it was, the diffused light had erased the horizon.

I let out a sigh of relief. We were safe. The team would stop and we'd wait for everything to calm down and rejoin Cameron and Nu Venia.

They didn't stop. The team kept running.

If we got too far away, how would we find the others?

Time to panic.

"AI. AI."

They kept going.

"That means stop, you stupid dogs! AI, AI, AI!" I yelled with everything in me.

Not even Huth showed signs of stopping.

Terrified of being left alone in the middle of nowhere, I held on.

Chapter 26

Jessica Hewitt
Whiteout

THICK FORMLESS clouds completely covered the sky and Kahair, turning everything around me white. It wasn't a pristine white, but a drab, lifeless white eliminating all shadows and shading. The world disappeared, taking away all perspective. I couldn't tell up from down.

The team, sled, and I seemed to be flying in nothingness. Repeatedly, the sled bounced, sprang up, and slammed down. A foot slipped. A hand almost released its grip. On one jolt, I bit my tongue. But the hardness of the ice was an illusion. In reality, I was traveling in a cottony world.

The mist thickened. One by one, the dogs and most of the sled disappeared until all I could see was the sled just beyond the handlebars. Everything else melted away and ceased to exist.

It took all my energy and strength to stay on the sled. If I let go, I'd float away, never to be found again. Fear oozed like sweat seeping out of every pore in my body.

I'm not sure how long we floated like that. My hands cramped. My legs and lower back became weak from fatigue. The cold latched onto my sweat-soaked long johns. I began to shiver. I wasn't sure how much longer I could hold on.

The sled came to an abrupt stop.

I waited for the team to continue. The sled didn't move. I expected to see the dogs floating overhead. Nothing. Not under my feet either. Everything had been swallowed up by the white. Maybe, the white had eaten them and they no longer existed. Only I existed—alone, by myself.

Don't think like that.

"Essal?" I called.

Bark.

At least he hadn't deserted me.

More barks. It sounded like they were all there. They'd not left me behind. Cameron said chovis were loyal. Right again.

I was so tired. I slumped over the sled and slept.

It was some time before I lifted my head. It took a moment longer to remember where I was.

The shivering had stopped. I couldn't tell if I was cold or dead.

Everything was still white and, as far as I knew, we hadn't moved. Gingerly, I took a step backwards, half surprised at the solidness in the soft white world engulfing me.

Other foot followed. My first steps staggered.

I used the sled to keep upright, then I touched each dog's back, head, or ear as I passed. When I reached Huth and Addle, I could clearly see the lead dogs. The second pair behind them were no more than shadows. There was nothing behind them.

Giggle.

For some reason, it was funny that the sled and most of the team were missing. I didn't know why.

"No matter, they'll come back," I said. "Chovis are loyal. They won't leave me."

My brain shifted and my reality faltered. The past and present collided.

I was lost just outside my home in Woodlands Village. My cat wasn't in the house. I'd checked. She was outside in an all-day blizzard.

The snow was thick and dense. I couldn't see the fence at the edge of our yard. I was thirteen, an age when one does not always think before acting. I'd run outside without telling

Dad or dressing in my snowsuit. I ran with the intention of saving my cat from certain death.

When I turned around, my house was gone, swallowed up by falling snow. A cold dread swept over me. I was still in my yard. I know I was. Yet the house was gone. The entire village was all gone. I was the only one left.

The thought came that I was floating inside a snowflake. It was fun to think one could be small enough to fit inside a snowflake and float at the whim of the wind, but the next thought terrified me.

There were so many snowflakes. How would Dad find me? I'd be lost forever.

I'd hysterically run around my yard hoping to find my house.

I smacked into something hard enough to knock me off my feet. I realized this wasn't my house; it was a solid piece of ice.

Even nose-to-nose with it, like everything else it looked soft, cottony white. I ran my hands over its rugged, hard, cold surface.

Just like that, I returned to Minnesota.

My house! I found the house. "I have not been left behind. Where's the door?" Frantically I felt for the doorframe, the door handle. I couldn't find either. Not even a window.

"Dad?"

I couldn't find the door! Why couldn't I find the door?

"Daddy?" I banged on the wall with the flat of my hand. But my hand didn't slam, bam, bam against the wall. It sluggishly patted it.

"Let me in. I can't find the door."

I was having trouble concentrating. My brain was cold.

Why wasn't Daddy answering me?

"Daddy?" He doesn't know I'm outside.

In my mind I frantically screamed "Daddy!!!!" But it came out as a whisper.

A dog barked.

Another bark. More barks. Frightful howls.

My cat. Where was my cat? The dogs were after my cat. I have to find my cat.

Wait! A voice in my head shouted.

Reality came rocketing back. There was no cat. I wasn't in Minnesota. I was on an alien planet. My forehead ached. With great force I pulled my head up. Why I was leaning my head against a gigantic piece of ice? I'd been hallucinating about the past. I'd forgotten where I was. Now I remembered. I was lost on an alien planet. My only companions were a team of dogs.

Awkwardly, I made my way back to the sound of the barking dogs. I didn't want to be in this nothingness by myself. Too terrifying. Too confusing. So cold.

I sat in the middle of the team, hoping to find some warmth.

I closed my eyes and was again thirteen years old, back in the blizzard.

Dad found the front door opened, and knew I'd gone outside. He quickly dressed in his snowsuit and boots, tied a rope to the house, then around his waist, and methodically searched the yard.

The reality of my situation hits me. Dad had found me then in Minnesota, he'll find me now on Akiane. As a little girl, I'd curled up in a ball. I waited for Daddy to find me. I'll wait for him.

Essal jumped onto my lap, followed by Imos. Huth rested her head on Imos' neck. Addle was at my back. All the dogs nuzzled in as close as they could, fourteen dogs protecting me. Or was I protecting them? It was difficult to tell. We were all scared.

I closed my eyes and folded over Essal for warmth. I'd take a nap and wait for Daddy to find me.

Phyllis Moore

The wind came—from everywhere—all at once. I pulled my hood tighter. The wind was relentless. I forgot that I had a visor to protect my face. The wind forced its way into my hood, around my neck and swept down my back.

The house moved. It was closing in! I could feel it. The ground vibrated. I heard the house creeping—moving closer.

Too much wind. I couldn't breathe. Hot. I sat up and open my jacket.

Can't breath. No air. Need air.

I hadn't asked for this—to be out here! This was the admiral's fault. I'm going to die of hypothermia all because of him. I'll haunt that wretched bastard for the rest of his life.

Something groaned. I forced myself to listen. There it was again. It wasn't one of the team. It came from out of the whiteness. It wasn't the house moving. It was something else.

There was something out there. But my eyes wouldn't focus. They wanted to close and stay closed. My head started to drop.

Just like the wind, the groaning came from all around. I was surrounded by monsters waiting for me to fall a sleep, so they could pounce. I forced myself to stay awake.

The whiteness called my name, "Jessica."

"Daddy? Is that you?"

The ice shivered. Or was it me? I couldn't tell.

"Daddy, I'm hot."

The wind swooshed past my face, taking the air with it.

The hood cut of my air supply. Pull it off. Didn't help. Can't catch my breath. My chest was constrained, begging for air.

Mama's disapproving glare came into focus.

It was the first day of kindergarten. She sat behind the steering wheel and told me to get out of the car. I did.

"Shut the car door and go inside," she said.

I closed the back door and walked to the passenger window.

"Mommy, don't leave me," I pleaded.

She didn't look back to see if I was all right or wave good-bye. She faded into the mist and was gone.

Daddy loved her best. If not for me, she would have stayed. She would never have left him.

I stood on the kindergarten steps—alone.

"Jessica."

I was alone on Akiane, lost in a whiteout, with no hope of ever being found. Dad was dead. He'd never find me now.

My life was over. What had I accomplished? Nothing.

I was in the middle of nowhere. No one knew were I was. Jorge and Rona might hold a memorial service when I didn't return. Then I'd be forgotten. In my entire life, I'd never done anything significant.

"I'm hot."

Took my gloves off.

"Daddy? Where are you? Mama left? Daddy?"

I smelled him, his aftershave. I smelled his sweat after a hard game of hockey.

Essal's head popped up followed by Imos'.

I heard a man's voice. It was thin and far away. "Jessica."

I strained to listen but I imagined it.

No, there it was again, a bit louder. "Jessica." Coming closer.

I heard it. I know I did.

"Daddy? Is that you?"

Daddy's coming.

Huth's head appeared. She was breathing my air! I tried to push her away. She let out a yelp in my ear. Ouch!

That yelp brought me back. I'm on Akiane—not in Minnesota. I'm twenty-eight, not thirteen.

Was there really a voice or did I imagine it?

Something was coming, but it wasn't Dad. I heard it grunting, panting.

The dogs stood, barking furiously. They were warning me to get away, but I didn't have anywhere to go. I couldn't find the door to get in the house.

Phyllis Moore

I clearly heard scraping and crunching. Something was coming. Aiming toward me. I strained to see into the white. A formless shadow appeared, faint at first, but as it came closer, it darkened. Not a man, it moved on all fours, running.

It knew I was here and was coming for me. As it came closer, it grew in size.

Out of the white, the monster leaped at me. Its eyes were bright with anticipation, its ears laid back, its tongue hanging out of its mouth. The tongue disappeared. It opened its mouth full of sharp teeth coming directly at me, ready to rip into me.

The team barked louder.

I crossed my arms over my face and doubled over trying to protect myself. It knocked me back, pinned me down. I tried to push the monster off. It was relentless.

The whole team was barking, whining, howling, ready to defend me. But they were in their harnesses with limited mobility. I should have loosed them; now it was too late. Hot foul breath filled my nostrils. Drool splattered on my cheek. It was going to eat me alive, starting with my face.

It would have been less horrifying if I'd drowned or frozen to death. But to be eaten alive!

The monster forced past my arms and hands to . . . to . . . lick me?

It's tasting me?

"Ai." A man's voice yelled.

"Dad!?!" Daddy found me. I'm safe. He'll protect me.

"Nella, no." The monster stopped.

Daddy! He will carry me into the house and lay me on the fur bear rug in front of the fire where it's warm.

Already, he's wrapping me in warm blankets.

"Her coat is open." A woman's voice. "She is like ice."

"Mama? You came back?"

"Yes." Her smile was so beautiful. She was relieved to see me. She missed me. I thought she hated me. But she came back. She didn't hate me after all.

"How? How did you find me?" I my voice speak just above a whisper.

"Chovis find chovis," Mama said.

Mama's back. She and Daddy found me. Chovis helped.

"Don't leave me." I heard the words in my head, but I didn't know if they came out of my mouth or not. I couldn't tell.

A lantern spontaneously lit. It moved to sit near my feet. Several more lights came alive. A large furry bulk moved in and out of the light. It reminded me of the monster a had once lived under my bed.

I floated between soft diffuse lights. Nothing made sense. The Void closed in, pressed against me. Couldn't focus. Where was I?

The monster from under my bed stood in front of me. It spoke. It had never spoken before. I saw its lips move, but sound didn't come. Waited for the words to unfreeze. They didn't.

The monster picked up a lantern. He and the four-legged creature walked away swallowed by the Void. Only his light remained. Then the darkness swallowed the light.

The light at my feet fell. I watched it fall. Disappearing into the darkness. I fell after it. I tried to stop. Couldn't. Kept falling, falling, the Void engulfed me.

I ceased to exist.

Chapter 27

Qorow Low
Day of Coming forth

IT HAD been difficult for Qorow Low to keep her happiness held within. People noticed as her mind wandered back to her child and her possible future. Friends asked what she was thinking about.

At first she bowed her head and tried not to smile, but hope would not be contained. When she finally decided to explain her mysterious grin, there was shock and disappoint.

Her Community took a slight step away from her. There were no encouraging smiles. No shared joy. Only worry for her and her child.

She did not blame them. How could she, when the same worry constantly gnawed at her heart.

There were no secrets within Community. If one person knew, all knew.

Qorow Low froze when next she saw Adumie.

By the way his eyes focused on her, he knew.

His eyes did not leave her face as he approached.

"It is said that you have brought forth a child." His words were not accusing. They were a statement of truth.

Yet his words hit Qorow Low in her. She knew he disapproved. "I . . ."

"I know. You innocently hope for the best," he said.

She nodded.

"I fear much disappointment for you."

She sniffed.

"This is the reason you wish to trust off-worlders." Now his words held a hit of anger.

"I want . . . Not just for me." She looked up at him pleadingly. "I want all children to be healthy."

His face-hardened. "Healing is not for Community. You act foolishly."

Qorow Low nodded. "My child has already come and is in her cocoon."

"She will die." His statement of truth was a slap in the face.

"But if . . ." she began.

"There is no *if*," Adumie said with much frustration. "There is no *hope*. You are not a child, yet you act like one hoping for the impossible when you know the inevitable. Your actions will bring much heartache to you and the Community."

She didn't understand why he spoke to her like this. She was not the only one with a cocoon.

Her heart was already heavy. His disapproval made her heart hurt more.

"This will not turn out well," he said and walked away.

He was right, but when she stood over her cocoon, love overruled her reasoning.

Every day, Qorow Low spoke to her child. It was by the life-giver's voice that the child was knowing of her life-giver. It was by speaking to the child that the child learned to speak.

Every day, she rolled her cocoon in the milky liquid so the porous membrane would remain moist.

The joy of giving birth was giving way to uncertainty. What if she was wrong? She feared it was more probable that her child would be stillborn.

Could she survive such heartbreak?

She had been filled with youthful excitement of one day becoming a life-giver. How old was that dream? Too old.

Despite the enormous risk, she could wait no longer and had chosen to give birth.

Now, no matter the consequences, it was time.

It took an average of ninety days for the cocoon to mature and the child to come forth. Forty-seven days had passed. Forty-three more days of waiting.

And yet, her child's cocoon was hardening. This was not a good sign. Her child was coming too soon.

Despite his disappointment, Adumie was with Qorow Low for the coming forth of her child.

With much tenderness, he knelt before her. She sat on the birthing stool with the cocoon on her lap. His face was more serious than she'd ever seen it before, but his eyes had softened.

"I do hope all goes well," he whispered.

The oblong cocoon was too small for one ready to come-forth; it should have been almost the length as Qorow Low's arm, but this one was only the length of her forearm.

Nevertheless, the outer membrane had hardened.

The moment a life-giver holds her cocoon for the first time after birth, she wonders who is inside. Who will the child become? What will her smile be like? What will her voice sound like?

The thrill of a child recognizing her life-giver was indescribable. Then there's the joy of the child taking her first step.

Because of the slow lingering death, birthing no longer held such elation. Now a life-giver wondered if her child would live long enough to come forth from her cocoon let alone live long enough to become an adult.

A moment of panic swept through Qorow Low and collided with her heart.

The nagging question, *What if I am wrong?* shouted at her. What if she had condemned her child to a life of pain that only death could ease?

In spite of all that had happened, in spite of all her fears, deep down in the depths of her heart, Qorow Low knew this child was meant for more than coming forth and dying.

But she was coming too early.

Do not fear, she told herself. *I must hold on. This child has a destiny. The Holy One has promised.* How many times had she repeated those words in an effort to stay strong? Yet, doubt lingered.

No one welcomed her child alone. The welcoming of new life should have been a time of celebration. But on this day, the usual chatter of excitement was missing. Even so, there was a spark of warmth that Community stood with Qorow Low no matter the outcome, if not to rejoice, then to comfort in time of sorrow.

No one died alone. Even on the deathbed, many gathered to speak words of encouragement or sit and wait.

In birth, one or two closest friends helped with the delivery of the cocoon. The soft almost clear membrane allowed the mother's the first sight of their child. Then the cocoon became cloudy giving the child privacy to grow. When the child was ready to come forth, the cocoon became brittle, making it easy for the child to break free.

When Community numbered in the thousands, only those of the same family unit attended the Day of Coming Forth. The rest of Community waited in the gardens to be introduced to the new little one.

Now that Community was only a few hundred, no one wanted to miss a Day of Coming Forth. There might be a chance of success.

Adumie scanned the scene around them.

Qorow Low followed his eyes and saw a sea of worried faces.

"The cocoon has turned opaque and the outer casing has hardened," Adumie whispered. His fearful voice pulled Qorow Low's attention back to the moment.

A healthy child could easily kick and break free from the cocoon.

Her child was not kicking. There were no sounds of a child fighting to be set free.

If they waited too long the child would suffocate. Then when opened, they would find the child stillborn. For fear of what one might see, the cocoon was never opened. The child was declared dead, wrapped in the yellow funeral cloth and placed in the ocean for its final rest.

Adumie rested his hand on the cocoon. He had never looked at her so intently before. He had never openly acknowledged a relationship between them.

"What is your decision?" he asked.

He not only acknowledged their friendship, but tenderly acknowledged her fears. Her hopes reflected in his face. He understood. For the first time, she knew he truly was her friend.

Qorow Low showed little emotion except for the tears that silently slipped down her face. Perhaps it would be best if the child were dead.

Then it would be over, she thought. *Why make the child endure a life if she was destined to die?*

She desperately wanted to hold her child and love her, even if for a moment. At the same time, she could not bear to see her child dead. That would be her only memory. But to place her child at rest . . . never having seen her . . .

Qorow Low's heart would break either way. She was unable to decided.

"I am in need of a knife." Adumie had decided for her.

A fisher placed a knife made of tupilak leg bone in his outstretched hand.

She watched as the tip of the point inserted and moved the length of the cocoon. The casing cracked. Pieces fell way.

Qorow Low took several deep breaths, but could not breathe deeply enough to settle her nerves.

The silent was so extreme one would have thought Adumie and she were alone. She sat perfectly still, staring only at him. Not daring to look at her child.

She felt Community lean closer and heard soft whispers, "Can you see?"

"Is the child . . .?"

No one dared say "dead" or "alive."

Then they knew. Adumie knew. He steadied himself with a beep breath and nodded.

Very slowly Qorow Low lowered her eyes. Her heart melted. Her heart pounded. Her breathing became quick and shallow.

It was the terror that this perfect little person, her baby, would never turn her head to look at Qorow Low. She might never hear her child's voice or see her first awkward steps. Never hear her laugh as she played with a chovis pup. Or would she grow to become an adult and have a cocoon of her own.

Qorow Low's child was neither the pink of life nor blue of death, but gray. She could not tell if her child was dead or alive. She lay with one arm over her chest. The other arm lay at her side. Her hips turned sideways with her legs partly bent at the knees.

Gently, Adumie pulled the crumbling cocoon away and reached inside.

"She is not warm or cold." He carefully folded both arms over the tiny chest then slipped one hand under her head, back and legs.

Qorow Low couldn't be sure, but she thought the child moved.

Adumie lifted the limp body. "She is as light as snow."

The child's arms fell to her sides to rest in Adumie's palm. Her legs seemed to twitch. He cradled her body and placed his free hand over her chest, and froze.

"She lives," he said. "I can feel her heart beating."

All cheered.

Qorow Low sobbed with joy.

Chapter 28

Jessica Hewitt
Mid-Afternoon Eighteenth Day

NEXT MORNING, I was *not* at home wrapped in my father's love. I was on an alien planet wrapped in dog furs, staring up at the tent ceiling.

I was pissed. My teeth gnashed of their own accord and refused to relax. Last night, I'd almost died!

How many times was that going to happen to me? I didn't want to die. I wanted to go home and live a very, very, very long and productive life. I didn't understand why I was out here in the first pace, or why I couldn't go back to the habitat, back to Earth, back home to Woodlands.

Cameron and Nu Venia were already up and making breakfast. Dog meat. I wanted bacon and eggs. I wanted a real breakfast. Not dog food.

Essal's head immediately popped up, blocking my view. I reached out and pushed his head away.

Like all Akiane priests, Cameron had a head full of small braids. Sometimes, like now, he secured his braids at the nape of his neck to keep them out of the way.

The light from the overhead lamps spilled over him, creating shadows under his eyes, nose, and chin. He looked like a warlock sitting over his cauldron.

Cameron lifted the lid off the cooking pot and stirred the contents with a bone spoon. As he replaced the lid, he absent-mindedly patted Nella, who lay peacefully sleeping at his side.

The same lamplight turned Nu Venia's white hair pale yellow. In contrast, her bright yellow eyes stared vacantly out of her shadowed face. As usual, she was somewhere in her private world. Often when she stirred from that world, she'd look around confused at first then disappointed. What did she think about when she was away from us? Where did she go?

The constant smell of dog and damp fur overwhelmed the aroma of stew. Even so, when the odor of food did reach my nose it quickly awakened my stomach. I was ravenous.

Essal's tail beat the fur carpet. His excitement for attention alerted the others that I was awake.

Nu Venia returned from her faraway place and smiled. Was that the same smile I'd seen when she found me last night? Was it only last night? I remembered her smile being beautiful. My mind must have been playing tricks on me.

"How are you feeling?" she cheerfully asked me.

How could she ask me that after what had just happened the night before?

"Ready to go home to Earth," I said, grumpily. "You've made your point. We can survive extreme cold. It's time to go back and warm up."

Cameron said nothing, but he was dissatisfied with me. I didn't care. I was frustrated with him for dragging me out here in the first place.

"I could have died," I forcefully declared.

Nu Venia turned away. "But you didn't. You were saved."

"Saved?" I fought my blankets in my effort to sit up.

Essal jumped to his feet, his tail happily wagged the rest of him. Imos was lying next to him and also raised her head seemingly pleased to see me awake.

I ignored them.

"So, what, I should thank you? If it weren't for the two of you I wouldn't be out here in the first place. I wouldn't *need* saving. I should be on the transport *Britannia* on my way back to Earth."

They turned their heads away.

I didn't care.

"Hallucinated. That's what I did. I thought I was thirteen years old. I thought I saw my mother. I thought my father had come for me. My father's dead. I thought I was dying and he'd come for me."

"Well, you did not die," Nu Venia scolded me.

She'd never so much as raised her voice in the slightest before. Not at me. Not at Cameron. Not at the dogs. She never complained. In fact she was so compliant, I thought she was part dead inside.

"You were saved." She glared at me for a whole second. "You should be grateful," she said as if I *should* be glad.

"I am not grateful," I declared. "I want to go back to Earth. I don't want to be out here. I *never* wanted to be out here."

"Then why did you come?" she asked.

"Because you tricked me. Because my stupid admiral made me. But be assured, I did not come of my own accord. I don't understand why we're out here in the first place," I yelled.

"We are here to prove ourselves," Cameron calmly said, "and to become Community."

He said as if Community was the name of their people group, and he wanted me to become a member of his Community.

I'd never become one of his people. I was unable to be part of any group. I never fit in anywhere—ever.

In my frustrated, I wanted to shake him until his head came off and he came to his senses. I hated his calmness, I wanted a good knockdown yelling match, but he was so damn calm. Aaah!

"We couldn't prove ourselves by walking around the habitat?" I asked.

"No."

"How about going outside the habitat?"

He shook his head no.

"Even if we did it at night and included the mountains?" I insisted. The intensity of my anger was subsiding with the ridiculousness of my questions.

Cameron smiled. "It is the perseverance of Woden that proves one's character."

I flopped on my back.

Essal and Imos lay back down still keeping a close eye on me.

"Well, my character was certainly proved last night." I stared up at the tent ceiling. "How long was I asleep?"

"It is the afternoon of the next day," Cameron said.

"What? That's some 20 hours." I propped up on my elbow.

Essal and Imos jumped to their feet came toward me.

"No one sleeps for 20 hours," I declared, swishing the dogs out of my face.

"You did." Nu Venia was back to staring at the floor. "We thought we had lost you."

"Soon, things will get better for you," Cameron said.

"I don't want things to get better. I want things back the way they were on Earth." I threw my blanket aside and sat up. I must have sounded like a five-year-old having a fit. I felt like one and didn't care.

"When you release your fears, you will be ready to return," Cameron said.

As much as I hated to admit it, I did have a lot of fears and it would be nice to be free of them. But I didn't know how.

"If I told you I'm no longer afraid, could we go back now?"

He shook his head. He knew I hadn't changed.

"What will it take for me to get over my fears?" I asked.

"That will depend on you," he said.

That didn't sound good. If it truly depended on me, we'd head back right now. Ah, but that wasn't what he meant.

Cameron wanted some sort of wisdom from me, a sign that I'd matured. If I'd known what it was, I'd have given it to him right then and there.

In reality, I was in a lot of trouble. Life was one traumatic event after another, which I had no control over. How does one get over *that* fear?

"You're hoping for a miracle," I said unhappily.

"We are walking in Assetti and Striken's footsteps," Cameron said.

"So? What is that supposed to mean?"

"Like them, we wish to be victorious."

I watched him for a moment. "I don't understand."

He took a deep breath. "If we are victorious, we will have the ear of our people. Some are unwilling to be convinced of Earth's willingness to help us. Some are too frightened to make a decision. Once we return, all will listen and hear."

Sounded like a lot to accomplish.

"But why Assetti and Striken? What did they do?" I asked.

"They brought back life and hope."

"You are expecting a miracle," I confirmed.

Cameron didn't speak but watched me intently.

"I know your people are sick," I said, pressing the issue.

Nu Venia had once again left us for her inner thoughts. But at my last statement, she came back to us. I expected her to say something. She didn't.

So I kept speaking, remembering Rona's diagnosis of the colonists. "Their skin is splotchy. They're losing hair. Their eyes are watery."

"My people are dying," Cameron said in a flat voice, but his worry expressed told his true feelings. "That is why we are on this quest. At one time, we were many, more that 2,000. Now we are only 235."

"Why are they dying?" I asked.

"We do not know. Without knowledge, we are able to find a cure." He shook his head.

He had asked for my moment of truth, instead here was his moment of truth.

"Why are we out here?" I asked.

He closed his eyes.

I patiently waited for him to speak.

With a heavy sigh, he opened his eyes and said, "My desire is your help. But my people will not accept it. When we return victorious, I will speak. My people will listen. I will tell them you are worthy of trust. They will believe. You will find a cure and we will again be healthy."

"It's sounding more and more like you want a miracle," I said.

"Indeed." He smiled. "Perhaps so."

"What will it take to for us to be victorious so we can go back?" I asked.

Again, Cameron closed his eyes and ran his hand over his face. Perhaps he thought we'd already failed.

"The three of us must make Community," Cameron began.

Nu Venia wasn't happy with that answer. She let out a low moan, which got me to thinking.

I asked, "Are the two of you in Community?"

They frowned. As I suspected, all was not paradise.

"I'll take that as a no," I said. "So what does it take to be in Community?"

"Understanding," Nu Venia had never spoken with such feeling before. "Something Cameron does not value."

Clearly, those two did indeed have trust issues.

"Nu Venia must realize Nu Venia's worth," Cameron said. He lifted the lid off his cooking pot and stirred the stew, which I now knew was not breakfast, but dinner.

"What does that mean?" I asked.

That was not the right thing to ask.

Cameron froze in mid stir. "That is for Nu Venia to say."

She went rigid. Like hot air seeping from a steamer, she muttered under her breath. Her jaw clenched. Her eyes narrowed. She shrunk in size, literally shrunk in size. Her face distorted with misery.

I'd not seen her so forlorn before. I feared she might burst into tears from a broken heart.

"Nu Venia?" I spoke softly.

She shook her head and wouldn't speak.

Cameron filled a bowl with stew and handed it to her. But she'd already retreated back into her private world. He gently touched her shoulder with the bowl. She took it without rejoining us.

Next, Cameron filled a bowl for me, then for himself.

"Is there dog in this?" I examined the stew suspiciously.

"There is no chovis," Cameron assured me.

"Good. I don't like dog." I lied. In actuality, it reminded me of tupilak. I liked tupilak.

I didn't understand how he could show such loving affection, then kill, gut, cook, and eat the same animal. So far we'd eaten three dogs, two from my team and one from his. In between we'd also eaten dried tupilak. I wasn't about to tell Cameron that I liked his stews or that I felt a little guilty about eating dog.

There seem to be a collection of things I refused to tell him. *So much for trust.*

It reminded me of the many things I regretted not telling Dad. He tried to get me to share my thoughts. He'd love it if I opened up to Cameron.

Not a chance. Even though I was having serious thoughts of forgiving Dad, I wasn't in any mood to forgive Cameron. Nor was I about to start telling him everything about me. Whatever I was thinking or feeling was none of his business.

I was more parched than hungry so I drank the broth, then ate the rest.

"This tastes different from the other stews you've made," I said. "What's in it?"

With a guilty look, Cameron didn't answer right away.

He was hiding something. These people had too many secrets. If they'd plainly talk to me like a normal human being, we might make some headway in our understanding of each other.

But if they started tell me their secrets, I might be obliged to tell them mine.

Not interested.

I decided not to press the issue.

As I ate, the cold was expelled from my body. I hadn't even realized I how cold I was. It wasn't as intense as last night. It was more like a chill. Either way, it was nice to be warm again.

The warmth started in my chest, moved to my stomach, and ran down my limbs to my digits. Chovis stew never did that to me.

Nu Venia seemed to inhale her meal. As soon as she finished, she leaped to her feet, grabbed her jacket, and went outside.

"What's with her?" I asked.

"It is not good to remind Nu Venia of her lack," Cameron said. He reached for her bowl, then mine. "I will clean these. Then we must hurry."

The longer I stayed with these people, the less I understood them. I pulled my fur pants, jacket, and boots on, and I went outside.

It was a cloudy mid-afternoon. The clouds were less thick than the night before, but the light was still diffuse.

Kahair was a white ball in the mid-afternoon sky. Thankfully, shadows had returned as had up and down.

You'd think these people could wait until morning to start out again, but I guess not. Why would we sit around doing nothing when we were on the hunt for a miracle?

Nu Venia was hitching Cameron's team.

"Addle has deserted," she said.

"Cameron was right. She proved her worth yesterday as a coward," I said. "Well, good riddance." It sounded strange to refer to Addle as a she after all the time I'd thought she was a he.

"There are some Chovis that choose not to be loyal and leave us," she said.

"How will she survive out here by herself?" I asked. Did I really care?

"Those who leave us are never seen again. Some think tupilak eat them. It is unknown what truly happens to them," she said.

Addle was more trouble than she was worth, but I wasn't so cold-hearted as to want her out there alone starving to death or being eaten alive.

Even if we did search for her, where would we start? In reality, there was nothing we could do. Addle had made her choice; it was up to her to live with it.

In the far distant western sky, ominous dark gray clouds billowed, the blizzard Cameron had foretold was coming.

Though the misty sky, a sliver of a black disk rose above the clouds. I knew exactly what it was.

While on *Britannia*, when my orders changed from being a communications expert to WSC negotiator to the colony, I was also ordered to read all reports about the colony and their planet.

Once every eleven years, Akiane and a giant gas planet crossed paths. They both have an elliptical orbit around their star. Since Akiane was closer to Kahair, she moved faster, which made the gas planet appear to rise in the western sky.

That's what was rising above the winter storm clouds, a giant gas planet passing Akiane.

There were no signs of Akiane's twin moons. When we started this trip they followed each other, but each night the smaller one was catching with the larger one. If they did eclipse each other, it would be at full their moons.

Nu Venia knelt to hitch the dogs to our sled. They were already sitting in their assigned places. Instead of the usual excitement of continuing the journey, every one of them quietly sat and stared at the western horizon.

I wondered if our hurry to leave had something to do with the gas planet.

Nu Venia made only one change. She promoted Imos to run at Huth's side. Huth licked Imos' face in approval.

Cameron exited the tents with an arm full of supplies and practically dropped all of it on one of the sleds, before hurrying back in the tent, not his usual manner of packing. He was always meticulously. It sometimes took him a couple hours to get everything just right. But today everything stayed where he placed it.

"What's wrong?" I asked.

"Here ice is melting," Nu Venia said.

"I don't understand," I said.

"On ocean bottom, small volcanoes are erupting," she said. "In those areas, ice is melting."

"Is it common for underwater volcanoes to erupt like that?"

She shook her head. "They erupt because of Loki."

"Loki?" I asked. "Who's Loki?"
She pointed to the gas planet.
"We must hurry and find land or we will drown."

Chapter 29

Larry Gino
Vigilance

GINO STOOD with shoulders hunched and hands clasped to his chest.

"We should do something," Rona said.

Gino cringed at her words.

Rona knew there was nothing anyone could do. It was the waiting and not knowing that ate at her, at all of them.

What's that saying, *a watched pot never boils*. Wait was *all* anyone could do.

There was a raging blizzard outside. Spago and his team were in it.

Everyone's attention was centered on the tunnel entrance, fearful of what they might not see.

"What are we supposed to do?" Gino asked.

"Go find them." Rona pleaded, coming to his side. "We shouldn't just stand here and do nothing. We should be out there." She pointed down the tunnel to the blizzard outside.

Gino knew she was merely venting her worries. "Then we'd be just as lost," he said. For the first time in his life, he felt his age. All 82 years. "It's safer to wait for them in here." He wanted to be out there searching, but how many would be lost in the effort? No, he couldn't risk it.

Spago and his team should have been back an hour ago. It was maddening.

Gino wasn't sure what he'd do if they were lost or dead.

Still, he knew it was best to be patient and wait, even though waiting wasn't working. They were all scared and worried.

"How do you know they'll find their way back?" Rona asked.

Gino didn't reply. He took halting breaths. He was having trouble breathing. Anxiety. Rona was making *his* fears worse.

She placed a hand on his shoulder. He panicked fearing she would become more adamant. She didn't. With a heavy sigh, Rona moved away.

The howling wind echoed up the tunnel. Swirling snow formed a drift at the far end. With the amount of snow falling, the entrance would soon be completely blocked. Spago and his team might never find it.

The geologists and volcanologist had been on the mountain, but Gino and his team returned in the land hovercraft before first snowfall. Spago promised once his team had finished they'd return as soon as the hovercraft came for them. They just needed a little more time.

When Olivia and her team returned in their amphibious hovercraft, she loudly complained how quickly the snowstorm had intensified. They'd barely made it back in time.

Now all were gathered at the exit near their living quarters, holding vigil.

"They should have returned with you, Gino," Lu said. She stood, every muscle tense. She lightly shifted her weight from one foot to the other as if preparing to sprint down the tunnel. Her fingers clasped and unclasped nervous fists.

"There's something wrong with the seismic instruments. They wanted to finish checking them before they left," Gino said. "That's why they were out there in the first place." He should have told them to wait. He and his team should have stayed to help them. Then they'd all be back by now.

Rona was beside herself. "It couldn't have waited for a more opportune time?"

Gino took a deep breath. "It was sunny when we started out, but the clouds came in so fast. We arrived here just as the flurries started." He took several more breaths. "If I had known, I'd have insisted they come back with us. I never thought . . ." His heart beat too fast. He'd been in a situation just like this once before, when he'd been caught in a dust storm and was positive he was going to die.

* * *

He had been much younger and just starting his career of planetary geology. His first assignment was to study a territory of land on Mars, labeled Mars Chart 5 (MC5), known as Ismenius Lacus Quadrangle. The quadrangle was located in the northwestern portion of Mars' eastern hemisphere. It covered a large area of Mars' landmass, 4.9 million square km. He'd come to study Lyot Crater and its many channels, determine their origins and to learn if they'd been formed by running water or something else.

The team was already on their way back to the Northern Plains Research Laboratory when a dust storm rose up and overtook them more quickly than they'd expected. They weren't going to make it back in time.

Marshall.

There was a name Gino would never forget. It was said if a research team became lost in a dust storm on Mars and wanted to live, they'd better have Marshall at the helm.

Their rover almost stalled as its energy faltered. Marshall didn't force the vehicle like most would have. He eased up on the power to give the rover time to reboot itself. Once the engine had settled, he charged forward.

When the directional instruments got confused, Marshall didn't. He was like a hound dog on the scent of his next meal and wasn't about to be distracted by the all-consuming dust storm, Marshall drove straight for Davies' door.

Charley Davies was the other man Gino would never forget.

The scientists, who came to study and live on Mars, brought their families. Children needed schools; wives and husbands of scientists needed jobs. All of them needed entertainment. The research center grew to the size of a small city.

There were 25 bay doors in and out of the city. There were delivery doors and doors for tour rovers. Seven doors were designated for strict use by the research center.

Bay door seventeen was Davies' door, and no one knew Marshall as well as he did.

Minutes past the absolute last second for all doors to be locked down for the safety of the center—Davies' Door #17 remained opened. He knew Marshall was on his way, and Marshall knew Davies was waiting for him. Neither was about to let the other down.

On that day, young Larry Gino had only known how he felt sitting in that rover. He knew what Marshal was doing. He was thankful beyond words for Davies standing at the door and waiting. But it never occurred to Gino what Davies must have felt. Now he did.

* * *

Davies was helpless to do anything but wait. Which was what Gino was having trouble doing, waiting.

"I'm sure if Spago had known how fast the weather was going to change, he'd have held off on his tests until the blizzard passed," Jorge said. "On Earth snowstorms can be unpredictable. I'm sure here on Akiane they are even more so."

"Maybe they're planning on taking cover on the mountain and waiting out the snowstorm," Vong suggested.

"No," Gino said, though with all his heart, he wished it were true. "The mountain is too rugged. And there aren't any caves. Not where we were anyway."

"They'd be buried," Jorge said. "With this much snow, we'll never find them. We'll have to wait for the snow to melt before we can find their frozen bodies."

"Jorge!" Olivia exclaimed. She'd been nervously pacing, but had stopped to glare at him reproachfully.

"I'm just saying." Jorge lifted his hands in an apologetic gesture.

Gino took another deep breath. Today he was Davies waiting for Spago and his team, but there was no Marshall on the hovercraft with them. If the craft died, they wouldn't know what to do. If they got out of the craft and tried to walk back, they'd be lost, and like Jorge had said, they wouldn't be found until snow melt.

Lu turned white as a sheet as stepped back from the exit and let out a sharp squeak.

Rona took a step closer to see what had upset Lu. She too gasped.

Gino held his breath.

Two dogs, one all white, the other apricot with red and white tufts, casually trotted out of the blizzard as if they on a morning stroll. They stopped just inside the entrance and shook the snow off their backs. The storm meant nothing to them.

Those who had been sitting jumped to their feet. Those pacing froze.

They were two of the dogs with Spago's team.

All eyes focused on the tunnel and waited in hopeful expectation.

Gino's stomach tightened. What if none of the team was with them? What if the dogs had returned alone.

Before the dogs had time to finish shaking the snow off, someone kicked his way through the snowdrift and stepped out of the shrieking storm. He pulled back his fur hood. It was Avil, one of Spago's team members, and the hovercraft's driver.

Applause of unbelievable delight rose from the crowd.

Another dog, followed by six puppies the size of Shelties followed him in. Two more team members, Beth and Artemis. Finally Spago appeared. The team had safely returned.

Gino took several calming deep breaths.

Lu jumped into Spago's arms almost knocking him over.

Her enthusiasm surprised Gino.

Spago also seemed pleasantly surprised and leaned in— for what? A kiss? He quickly glanced around and stopped. Was there a hint of disappointment? If those two had been alone would there have been a kiss? What was going on between them that Gino didn't know about?

Each team member was enveloped by hugs and pats on the back.

"Had I known I'd get this kind of a reception, I'd have come back sooner." An embarrassed grin of pleasure spread across Spago's face.

As Lu released him, Gino stepped forward.

Smiling broadly, Spago asked, "How are you, old man?"

"Now that you're back, finer than a frog's hair." Gino smothered him with a bear-hug. He bear-hugged each member of the team. It had been a long time since he'd been that scared and this relieved. He'd lived so long that those kinds of scares didn't always end well. But today, he was beside himself with delight.

"We were so afraid we'd lost you." Rona took her turn at hugging each member.

"We would have been lost if it weren't for the dogs," Avil said. "The hovercraft stalled. I don't think it likes all this snow. But the dogs didn't falter once. They walked straight here, herding us like naive pups, so we wouldn't get lost along the way. I don't know how they did it. We couldn't see the entrance until we were close enough to touch it." He let out a little chortle of relief.

"When we started back, I thought we'd have time. I never expected the snowstorm to turn so quickly," Spago said. "One minute it was soft flurries, then suddenly the snow was so thick we could barely see what we were doing." He reached for Lu and lovingly squeezed her closer.

Gino dropped to his knees and bear hugged the nearest dog. Evidently there was more than one Marshall with the team after all.

Just like Mars, kismet had once again smiled upon them.

"Spago, why didn't you come back at first snowfall?" Lu scolded.

He must have momentarily forgotten they were not alone. Spago's emotions took over and he kissed her.

They weren't just friends any more. That kiss was noteworthy. It wasn't just a peck from a friend. It lingered.

Ah but just like a woman, the kiss didn't ease Lu's frustration. "Why were you even out there?" she said the instant he released her mouth.

"The mountains are doing something," Spago said to Lu, then turned his attention to Gino. "Something significant."

"What?" Now that all were safe, Gino's interest rolled back over to the mountains.

"They're not dormant after all. They're beginning to release gas, hydrogen sulfide. I was afraid we might be overcome," Spago said with real concern.

Gino took a couple of steps toward him. "How are you feeling? Having trouble breathing, headaches? Should the doctors examine you?"

"No we're all fine." Spago did a check of his team.

"No ill affects," Avil said. "But the smell was bad."

Lu pulled away from Spago. "So you stayed in a deadly blizzard, on a live volcano that's about to explode?" She hit him in the chest. "For what?"

He smiled, wrapped both arms around her, and tightly held her, almost burying her in his orange jacket. She let out a little angry growl followed by a giggle of relief.

To Gino, he said, "We wanted the equipment set up properly so we could monitor the mountain from here." Spago chuckled. "Didn't want to miss anything just because of a little snowstorm."

"So everything is all right?" Gino asked.

Here Spago's face fell as if he'd just remembered he's left someone behind on the mountain. He released Lu and shook his head. "Not really."

"Out with it, son." Gino became concerned.

"We checked every one of our seismic readers. All of them have been smashed."

"What?" Gino felt sick to his stomach.

"Why do you need seismic readers," Lu asked. "You have drones."

"Multi-rotors," he corrected, "move too fast, they pick up an amazing amount of information, but they only give us an overview. Seismic readers do the real work and gives us specific time data."

"So what happened?" Gino asked.

"Sabotage," Spago said. "We'll get no information on what's happening under those mountains now. We have to start over. And if we can't get back on the mountains, we'll have to use the multi-rotors and get what we get." He shrugged.

"What does that mean?" Olivia asked. "Is the habitat in any danger?"

All eyes turned to her.

"What?" she demanded. "Spago just said something's going on. He also said those mountains were built on an old volcano cone, he thought was inactive." Olivia barely took a breath before she continued. She pointed a finger at Spago. "He also said this caldera was created by a massive explosion. So I ask again," Olivia was on the verge of hysteria. "Are we safe?"

All heads turned to Spago.

"I don't believe there will be a super volcanic explosion."

"How can you be certain?" Olivia demanded.

"I'm fairly certain the first super volcanic eruption was hundred thousand years ago," Spago said. "We need more data to be absolutely certain of the time."

"So? What does that mean?" Olivia cut in.

"This is just an hypothesis," Spago spoke directly to Olivia.

"Yes?" she demanded.

"We know the gas planet's path nears Akiane every eleven years. The gravity from that planet and the star will pull on Akiane, causing tectonic plates to shift, which will produce earthquakes," Spago said. "The gravitational pull will also have an effect on pools of magna, which will become active. There will be volcanic eruptions."

"Won't that produce a super volcano?" Olivia's usual grave voice raised two octaves.

"I don't think so," Gino said. "Because this gravitational storm happens every eleven years. That means every eleven years magma pressure is released through volcanic eruptions. If there's never a build up of pressure, there will never be another super volcanic explosion."

"So why was there one in the first place?" Olivia asked.

"I can guess, but it's only a guess, mind you," Spago said.

Gino knew full well how a scientist hated to guess. Their minds do not follow guessing, they wanted facts. But even a hypothesis was a supposition based on fact.

"Out with it!" Olivia ordered.

"The first super volcano happened when the two planets first crossed paths," Spago said.

That seemed to ease Olivia's fears.

A big grin spread across Spago's face. He turned to Gino.

"Just as we called the multi-rotors back, we think one of them found a lava coulée."

"A dome flow," Gino said in awe.

But before they could continue, Olivia cut them off. "So we're safe."

Spago's face fell.

After a moment of silence, he shook his head. "I think so, but with a volcano, one is never completely positive." He scanned the overgrown garden then looked down the tunnel.

"I hope the ventilation in this place is secure. If that gas becomes too thick and manages to drift in here, it won't matter what the volcano does. We'll be so sick, we'll wish we were dead.

"Or worse, the gas could be so bad it could easily overwhelm us and kill us all. And then there's the ash from the volcanic eruption." His gaze returned to Olivia. "Things might get bad."

Chapter 30

Jessica Hewitt
Nineteenth Day on Expedition

IT CAME gently at first. Flurries of snow swirled and quietly floated about me. It's amazing that snowfall with no wind, lightning or thunder, so silent and pretty, was considered a storm. Snow landed on my nose and immediately melted. I tilted my head back and, like a little girl, stuck my tongue out. Snow floated into my mouth. It reminded me of good times with my friends at Woodlands Village, downhill sledding, digging forts out of mounds of snow and snowball fights.

It reminded me of Dad. Too much reminded me of him these days, oh how I missed him. Since his death, I'd spent too many years trying to forget. In the process, I'd forgotten too much about him, like when he and I used to go outside at first snow and play in the snow. We'd lie in the snow and make snow angles. We built snowmen and dressed them up. And of course, we'd have snow fights.

A snowball fight would be good right about now. It'd be fun to see Cameron's reaction when I hit him in the back of the head. But he was almost twice my size. The force of his snowball could knock me out. I smiled. Cameron throwing a snowball back at me? Not a chance. If I did hit him, he'd turn and ask what I was doing. The man was devoid of fun. He thinks Woden is entertaining.

For two days, we'd watched as storm clouds tracked us. Cameron pushed us hard as if we could outrun the thing. Rest stops became even more infrequent. We camped at twilight and were on our way before daybreak.

But the storm out ran us.

Within an hour, the winds came, the snow thickened, and the snowstorm became a blizzard. Snow drifted onto my forehead, in my eyes, up my nose, and into my jacket. It melted down my neck, back, and chest.

I attached my visor to the hood of my jacket. It didn't take long for that stuffy feeling to rise up, but at least I wasn't cold and damp from melting snow.

Why didn't Cameron stop? He, Nu Venia, and their dog team faded in and out of sight, engulfed by the snow, leaving my team and me to battle the blizzard alone.

The cold fear of being left behind again swept over me. Ever since I'd come to Akiane, my life had been out of my control. Not that I'd ever had much control before. At least *before* I could pretend. On Akiane, there were no illusions.

"Cameron," I shouted, the next time he came into view. "Shouldn't we stop and make camp?"

He disappeared again.

From out of the blizzard, I heard, "Ai." *Stop.*

Finally.

My team pulled alongside Cameron.

"Stopping is agreeable," he said.

Nu Venia shook a mound of snow off her but didn't dismount the sled.

"Can we make camp here?" I asked.

Cameron said, "Snowfall is too heavy. It will cover us up while we sleep. We might not be able to dig our way out of the snowfall."

His logic was sound. But I wasn't sure how much more of this I could take. Back in Woodlands, a really bad storm could last for days. How long could a blizzard last here?

"Don't we have to pack the snow down for the dogs?" I asked.

"In an ideal situation. Now is not possible."

"I don't understand."

"The snow is unending." Pointing to where we'd just traveled, he said, "Already our trail is covered."

He was right. The snow was immaculate.

Cameron walked along the teams, quickly checking each dog. I followed him. Essal had lain down. Cameron knelt to check him. He patted Essal's head and rubbed his hand over his back and under belly.

"We have no choice," he said. "We must make camp."

Cameron knelt to unhitch the lead dog on his team, but she pulled away and stepped around him. Her team moved forward.

He called, "Ai."

They didn't stop.

My team didn't move.

From on the sled, Nu Venia echoed Cameron, "Ai."

They didn't obey her either.

Cameron tried to hold one of the turn dogs by the scruff of his neck. She snapped at him. A wheel dog also snapped as he attempted to grab hold of that one.

The dogs had never reacted like that before. They always obeyed Cameron without question. Addle was the only one who'd ever given him any real trouble.

Cameron stepped back, and, as the sled passed him, he jumped on and was soon lost in the snowfall.

"We move on," his voice came back to me.

I couldn't believe it. What was wrong with his dogs? Didn't they know it was snowing? Couldn't they tell how difficult it was for them to pull the sled? Why won't they stop?

Hurriedly, I jumped on my sled, fully expecting my team to follow. They didn't.

"Huk," I yelled. Nothing. "HUK." *Go.*

Cameron was getting too far ahead. Once again, I was being left alone.

No, not again.

Perhaps the dogs couldn't hear me through the visor. I unsnapped it and yelled with all my strength, "HUK!"

Nothing.

Re-snapping the visor, I trudged forward to confront Huth.

"What's your problem?"

186

She opened her mouth and spoke in half backs and whines, which I didn't understand.

"What is the matter with you, you stupid dog? Cameron is leaving us behind. We'll get lost again and won't be able to find him. We have to keep moving."

Tears of frustration welled up but didn't come. Somewhere in my childhood, I'd forgotten how. I sure wanted to cry now.

Imos barked at me.

"Oh shut up."

More dogs howled.

"What?" I yelled at them. "What is your problem?"

They whined and barked.

"I don't understand. Why didn't you say something when Cameron was here?"

All the team barked at me.

What was their problem?

I walked along the team, checking each dog. They were fine. When I almost tripped over a mound in the snow, the dogs stopped barking.

Was this what they were upset about? I knelt and brushed the snow way and found one red ear. Essal was lying on his side breathing heavily.

"Essal. What's the matter with you?"

He moaned.

"Get up."

His eyes were closed. He moaned in pain.

"What's the matter with you? Get up. Cameron is leaving us behind."

I tried to get him to his feet. He slumped back down.

Cameron wasn't here to help. I didn't know what to do. The team wouldn't let me go on without Essal, and to tell the truth, I didn't want to leave him behind either.

I stuffed my fur gloves in my jacket pocket, unhitched him from his harness, and picked him up. As soon as I placed him on top of the sled, the team moved forward. I jumped on the back of the sled and quickly replaced my gloves.

"Please find Cameron," I prayed. I couldn't stand the thought of being lost out here all alone again. "He says chovis find chovis, please let him be right."

Chapter 31

Jessica Hewitt
The Blizzard

I'VE BEEN in this blinding blizzard, for days, weeks, years. Okay, hours, but it felt like years. Would this Woden ever end? Would I ever see Earth again? I had my doubts.

Akiane continually reminded me that I was no more significant than a flea on a grizzly bear's back. My life depended on dogs. I couldn't survive without Cameron and Nu Venia.

Why did Nu Venia have to settle on Cameron's sled? I wouldn't be so forlorn if she were here with me. We'd be in this together. And I wouldn't be alone again, lost in a blizzard.

The far end of the sled dissolved into the snow. I assumed the team was still attached since we kept moving.

I leaned over Essal for warmth. I felt his shallow breathing. I hoped we'd find Cameron in time. I'd grown used to this stupid mutt and didn't want to continue this journey without him.

Dogs were such a bother. If only they'd let us make camp. Essal would be in a reasonably warm tent recuperating from whatever ailed him. I'd be snuggled in my warm bedding. Cameron would be cooking dog stew. Nu Venia would be staring off in her private world. Things would be as they should.

But no!

Once again my life was dependent on a pack of animals. I was lost in another whiteout with no hope of finding Cameron. His team would roam Akiane's ice pack until the blizzard ended. If Cameron found me, I'd be on the sled, doubled over, frozen to Essal. Pleasant thought.

Jorge won't get the samples of algae I picked for him. Gino won't get his rocks. Olivia won't get her fish radio tags. The admiral was going to be angry because I hadn't found his aliens. Ha. At least he wouldn't be able to throw me in the brig. I'd be here with Essal.

Wonder how they bury people on Akiane. Cameron says nothing is ever wasted. Wonder if that included me.

No, don't think like that, I reprimanded myself.

I needed to be positive and remember these dogs had some sort of sixth sense, which enables them to find each other.

Cameron's team had found me when my team ran like crazed cowards from the danger of drowning. Now my team would find Cameron.

I have to believe.

I battled despair. Sometimes, I wholeheartedly believed I was doomed. Just get off the sled, find a nice place to lie down and go to sleep. It would soon be all over.

Then I'd reprimand myself for such thoughts. In my head, Cameron's voice said, *Chovis find chovis.* I repeated his words out loud like a chant. "Chovis find chovis. Chovis find chovis."

In my heart, I wanted to believe we were just behind the other team. I couldn't see them through the thick snowfall, but Cameron and Nu Venia were there.

My heart knew they weren't there. I was alone. All the times I wanted to be by myself, to get just away. This was not what I meant.

Watch what you wish for.

Time stopped. Once again, I drifted in the white of nothingness. But this time I was determined to keep my sanity and not fall into another hallucination. I refused to drift back to my past. Then just when I thought I might lose the battle, the sled stopped.

Bark. Bark. Whine. The dogs were again upset about something, but what? Was another dog in trouble?

Laboriously, I pulled myself off Essal and off the sled. I was cold and stiff.

The last time they acted like this, Essal was in trouble and was covered with snow. Another other dog was in trouble. I had to find it.

Bark. Bark. Whine.

"I know, I know, keep looking," I wearily answered them.

I got down on my hands and knees. *Find the dog.* They wouldn't move on until I did. We needed to keep going or we'd never find Cameron. I couldn't find the dog it was buried in the snow.

Two sets of hands grabbed my arms and lifted me to my feet.

"I can't find the dog," I said. "There's an injured dog. Huth wants me to pick him up. I can't find him."

"It is unnecessary to be anxious," Cameron said. "We will take care of everything."

The hands helping me belonged to my companions.

"Where did you come from?" But I knew. *Chovis find chovis.* They'd found the other team. We were all together again.

God bless chovis.

Nu Venia took me by the arm. I thought she was taking me to the tents, but no, she led me to a small, sloped entrance. I had to bend over to enter, but stood once inside.

I blinked several times. We were in a cave. The dogs had found land and we were safely out of the blizzard.

Lamps lit the lopsided grotto. Rocks piled against the wall suggested that Cameron and Nu Venia had cleared them in preparation of laying furs on the floor. Furs were packed on my sled along with the tents, but we weren't going to need the tents only the furs.

Cameron led my team into the cave and had them park the sled next to the other one.

There was enough room for us, dogs, and sleds.

This time I came before the dogs. Cameron and Nu Venia quickly untied and removed the tarp from my sled and pulled the furs off. While Cameron lay the flooring down, Nu Venia helped me out of my fur suit and wrapped me my fur bedding.

The dogs patiently waited to be unhitched and fed. But they didn't go into their usual eating frenzy when fed. Instead they were surprisingly docile.

Everything in me shivered. I was cold inside and out. My arms and legs were numb. I couldn't feel my toes and fingers. My rear end was as cold as an iceberg. My inside furnace was flickering off. I wanted to be warm and never be cold again.

"What happened?" Nu Venia moved to the cooking fire to pour me a bowl of hot stew. Instead, she handed me a bowl of broth. The bowl was warm in my hands.

"Huth and the team wouldn't leave without Essal." I took a drink of the brought. "He's not feeling well."

Cameron carried Essal in his arms. He gently placed him at my side.

Essal settled on the fur flooring next to my bedding where Cameron hand fed him bits of fish.

I realized we'd both be dead if wasn't for my team of dogs.

"I don't understand. How are the dogs able to find each other even in a blizzard?" I asked.

"It is the way of chovis, Jessica," Cameron said.

Translation: he didn't know either.

Nu Venia handed Cameron a bowl of stew, which he fed to Essal. Chovis don't eat meat. So what was in the stew? Not chovis, that was certain.

I took a long drink and chewed the morsels floating in the broth. Soon a spark of warmth stirred deep in my stomach. The warmth seeped slowly from my inner core into my back, down my legs and arms, into my fingers and toes. Even my brain thawed. My nose stopped running. I felt the glow from the inside out from with the satisfaction of being warm. The same thing happened the last time I was this cold.

From under my fur beddings, I changed into new long johns, hung my old pair over a large rock turned my snowsuit inside out and kneaded my boots and wrapped fur blankets around me.

I sat next to Essal and ran my hand over his head and down his muzzle. "You're not going to die on me are you?"

He said something in doganese.

Essal wasn't a bad dog, when he wasn't being obnoxious.

"You lie there. Cameron will take good care of you. You'll see. You'll be up and around in no time."

I felt peachy, as if I'd not just been lost in a blizzard. I was as comfy as if I'd been sitting in front of a warm fire all afternoon. I'd felt he same feeling of warmth the day after I almost died of hyperthermia, which made me wonder . . .

"What's different about this stew?" I asked.

Very slightly, they seemed to turn away from me.

"What's in the stew?" I asked.

Neither spoke.

"Well?" I pressed.

"Fish," Nu Venia finally said.

"Fish?" That didn't sound too bad. "I thought you don't eat fish."

She took a deep breath.

"Weeelllll?" I drew *well* out for emphasis.

"Fish warms," Nu Venia said. She refused to look directly at me. She rarely did, but this was different.

"Warms? What do you mean? I thought you said only chovis eat fish."

She bit her lip.

"What?" I asked. They were scaring me.

"You will not eat enough to make a difference," Cameron said.

I pressed the issue. "When my friends and I first arrived on Akiane, Adumie made it perfectly clear that we were not to eat fish. Now you're giving me fish? Why? What's going on?"

Cameron looked directly at me. "When the first settlers to come to Akiane they ate fish and changes occurred."

"What changes?"

His eyes flickered away, then back to me, but he didn't really see me. He appeared distraught. Why?

"What?" I softly asked.

He focused on me, shook his head, and turned away.

"Is this the first time I've eaten fish?" I asked.

"No," Nu Venia said, reluctantly. "We gave you fish when we found you in the whiteout."

"Why?" I asked.

"You were so cold. We feared you might die," she said.

"I don't understand. How could fish save my life?" I asked.

Nu Venia sighed. "There is something in the fish that warms. It keeps the cold away."

"What do you mean 'keeps the cold away'?"

For some reason, it was difficult for her to speak. Thoughts flashed across her face as she tried to decide how best to tell me.

I was unusually patient as I allowed her to gather her thoughts.

But it was Cameron who spoke, "The eating of fish is necessary to survive Akiane's six years of winter."

"That's why the dogs are never cold," I said, "because they eat fish."

Both nodded their heads. Evidently, there was something else about fish they weren't telling me. Did I want to know? It might be best not to ask too many questions. I might not like the answers.

Chapter 32

Qorow Low
Closing the Door

QOROW LOW watched as Adumie's eyes focused on the condition of the off-worlders' living area. Tables near the kitchen were placed in two long rows with chairs neatly pushed under them, whereas the tables across the room were cluttered with strange Earth equipment.

Adumie stood with his hands at his side staring, taking it all in.

One table had a collection of rocks. On the floor nearby, were small containers filled with what, algae? There were three oversized glass containers, sitting on strangely made tables, full of seawater and fish.

"Fish, water, algae, rocks," Adumie said, "is there nothing these intruders will not steal?"

They do nothing right. Everything they do angers him, Qorow Low thought.

"Go," he commanded.

Adumie refused to enter the off-worlders' living area. He said they were impure.

Qorow Low felt no such qualms. She did not perceive off-worlders as unclean, but different, maybe even misguided in their rudeness. She wanted to learn as much as she could about them. This was a perfect opportunity. She would never have come into their living area otherwise. Adumie would have forbidden it. But he'd ordered her in, so she took the time to observe.

Her daughter squirmed in the scarf that wrapped around their bodies and physically secured her close to Qorow low's heart. Did she also object to these people or did she know the hope to her living might come from the knowledge of those from Earth.

Off-worlders slept like those of the Community, each in their cot, all in neat rows. Under the cots were containers of secret possessions. What would she learn about these people if she examined those containers?

What surprised her was the way chovis cowered under the bunks. They knew what was coming and had pressed in against the containers for protection. Why had they not returned to the main building? Because they were loyal unto death.

Qorow Low softly whistled. Chovis heads popped up. She whistled again. The sound of a whistle had meaning. "Come."

They might have become loyal to off-worlders, but they still knew who their masters were.

"Return to the main building," she softly said.

Chovis immediately obeyed.

There were too few off-worlders. Where were the others? She saw chovis also answering her call coming from a door farther down the wall.

She investigated.

The room was exactly the same, cots in neat rows with only one sleeping occupant and containers under the cots. Why so many containers? Why two rooms? Perhaps they were two different families.

Now she had more questions about whom these people were and no chance of obtaining answers.

Qorow Low followed the last chovis back to Adumie.

One by one, chovis glanced fearfully at Adumie. They knew his disapproval of their attachment to off-worlders.

Even though she held great affection for Adumie, Qorow Low also feared to displease him.

At first, he became annoyed at her continually being at his side. He stiffened when he saw her coming, spoke roughly to her, and eyed her critically. She tried to stay away, but there was something in her that would not let her. Despite his animosity, she wanted to be near him. There was happiness with his presence.

Over time Adumie seemed to become tolerant of her presence. His words became less harsh. She even imagined she saw a faint smile when he saw her coming toward him. But that was only her imagination.

She tried not to speak so many words when they were together, but her tongue would not remain quiet. Now her constant chattering no longer seemed to aggravate him. At times he added his words to hers.

As long as Adumie and Qorow Low did not touch, no harm would come.

"These are the last chovis," she said as she returned to his side.

"Are you sure?" he asked.

"Yes. None are left," she said. "Chovis sense the coming of The Storm. Many were curled up, hiding their muzzles in their paws. Their tails wrapped around them in protection."

"Once the door is closed, chovis would have become trapped." Adumie said. "They might have become attached to off-worlders, but it is the Community who feeds and cares for them. It would not be wise to leave them with no food or water."

"For some reason off-worlders sleep separately," Qorow Low said. "There is a wall that divides them."

"They are strange indeed." Adumie snorted.

"And yet, there is goodness in them." She knew this would upset him, yet the words tumbled out anyway.

Even though he did not answer, she felt his anger. He did not like it when she spoke well of them.

"Should off-worlders not be informed as to why we lock them in?" she asked.

"This way is best. It is unnecessary to waste time by speaking to them. What if they objected? What then? Argue with them until they listen? Force them by spear to remain in their living quarters while we close the door?" Adumie shook his head. "If we leave the door open, they might go outside. I would prefer the mountain to come down on them, but what would World Space Coalition say or do?"

"I do not know," Qorow Low said. She could not imagine their response.

"I do. It is their way to retaliate," he said. "No, this is best. Do it while they sleep, so they will remain save."

The small, black-haired one came out of the sleeping area. "Oh," she said. "I couldn't sleep. When I got up, I noticed all the chovis were gone. Why are you here? Is something wrong?"

Adumie hit the bay door button with the heel of his hand. Slowly, the door slid downward.

The small black-haired one hurried toward them. The door was already half way down by the time she reached them. The off-worlder knelt as the door and asked, "What are you doing?"

Qorow Low held her child close to her chest as she also bent over to answer the small one. "It is for your safety. The Storm is coming. You must stay inside," she said.

"Wait . . ." the black-haired one tried to object.

The bay door sealed closed.

Chapter 33

Larry Gino
Speculations

"THEY SAID we are to stay inside where it's safe," Lu said.

She'd sounded the alarm. They'd hastily dressed or wore bathrobes. Now all were gathered at the bay door.

"Safe from what?" Gino didn't bother to hide his exasperation. These people were unreasonable. They'd rejected Earth's hand of friendship. They wouldn't consider allowing Rona and Lu's offer to research their disease. Now the colonists had locked them up under the pretense of safety.

"Something about a storm coming," Lu said.

"What could be so bad that we had to be locked up for our protection?" Rona asked.

Lu shrugged. "You know how they are about details."

Olivia pushed her way through the crowd. "What is this? How are we supposed to get any work done?" She was the last to arrive.

Of course she's the only one who's fully dressed. Gino shook his head. *She'd miss her own party, then complain that we hadn't waited for her, but she'd be properly dressed for the occasion.*

Olivia beat on the door with the palm of her hand. "Hey, anyone out there?" She placed an ear to the door.

"Hear anything?" Jorge asked.

She vigorously shook her head, bouncing her orange curls. She stood back, straightened her blouse and adjusted the waistband of her pants. Then crossed her arms over her chest, clearly frustrated that she was the only one being inconvenienced.

Gino ran his hand over the door as he examined the outer perimeter. "No latch. I don't think there's anything we can do until they decide to release us." *Most frustrating.*

"And just when will that be?" Olivia demanded.

Gino stood with his hands on his hips, still examining the door and said, "Well, since they didn't confer with me first, I don't know. Let's just hope it's when this storm they speak of passes." He too was annoyed. It had been a long time since he'd been a child and needed to be sent to his room. Even then, he'd never been locked up.

"Think it will be worse than the blizzard?" Rona asked.

"Can't imagine a storm worse than that," Avil said.

"Unless it's a volcanic eruption. The mountain is doing something, remember?" Beth's nose crunched in disgust. "I can still smell the hydrogen sulfide."

"But no one can predict the exact time of an eruption." Gino tuned the conversation over to Spago.

"Scientific research has come close. I've never heard of predicting the exact time. There are signs that indicate something is happening, Warnings saying 'sometime soon.' And those can be accurate within days, months, or a year of an event," Spago said. "Since we don't have data of what is presently happening with the mountains' activities, we can't conclusively say what's happening now. We don't even have historical information to hypothesize on." He shrugged his shoulders. "We just don't know."

"I doubt the colonists can predict an eruption with such accuracy," Avil said. "There must be something else going on."

"What if they know something is coming and are preparing for it?" Beth asked. "Who knows how long we could be locked up like this?"

"How long? You mean we could be in here for months or a year?" Olivia exclaimed. "Let me out." She banged and kicked at the door.

This conversation was becoming unnerving.

"Settle down," Gino said in a disciplinary tone.

"Don't tell me what to do," Olivia yelled at Gino.

If only Olivia had gone on the expedition instead of Jess. Unfortunately, it wasn't up to Gino who should go and who should have stayed.

Rona reached for Olivia's arm in an effort to comfort her.

Olivia whipped her arm away.

Rona stepped back in fear Olivia might slap her.

Before Gino had time to react, Jorge stepped between them.

"Where would you rather be during an emergency, Olivia? Outside, on the ocean, or here with us where it's safe?" he asked.

"I don't want to be locked up in here for a year," she yelled at Jorge.

"No one said we would be here that long," Spago corrected.

"But you don't know." Olivia rounded on him.

He stepped back in surprise.

Olivia may have been little, but she was fierce and ready to make her opinion heard.

The group of scientists murmured their concern. They were already upset enough as it was without Olivia making things worse. She needed to settle down before she became hysterical.

Gino stepped in and try to speak, "Olivia . . ."

But she wasn't listening.

"What if they leave us here to rot?" she screeched.

"They'll have to let us out when the next transport comes. Won't they?" someone asked.

"That's not for another two years. Do we have enough food if they do leave us here that long?" Beth asked.

"Please, this speculation isn't helping," Gino said.

"We will not starve," Zhoa said. "We have the a ton of dried and smoked meat, and the hydroponics. We can easily last for a year or more,"

Murmurs quieted down.

Gino knew even if there was enough food for "a year or more" it wasn't enough to ease the tension in the room. Something bad was about to happen. Not knowing what it was only exacerbated things.

"Let's have breakfast," Zhoa said.

Instead of receiving an enthusiastic, "Yes." He received stunned silence.

Gino almost smiled. *God bless Zhoa. Get their minds off the problem. Give them something to eat. Brilliant.*

"What are you talking about?" Olivia exploded.

Olivia. Gino shook his head.

But Zhoa was not to be deterred. "Come on, you can stand here and beat on the door and theorize all you want. The door's not going to budge until they open it from the outside" he said. "In the meantime, Vong and I will make you a spectacular breakfast." He waved both arms up to indicate how large and wonderful the meal would be.

"What happened to your hand?" Rona asked. "Last we talked you had a little rash of red bumps. Now your entire hand is bandaged. What happened?"

Zhoa's hand was bandaged with gauze and tape, not the usual sprayed on band-aid, a clear indication that something was seriously wrong.

When did that happened? Gino wondered. *Why was I not informed?*

"That little rash has inflamed my whole palm and it's creeping up my arm. See?" Light and dark gray splotches were visible on his wrist and forearm.

Gino's stomach tensed. Rona had mentioned that the colonists were ill. Here was his worse nightmare—literally. He almost asked the question *Is this the same disease the colonist have?* But thought better of it. This would be one more thing to upset the young ones. Olivia would become uncontrollable.

"I feel fine, but my palm looks like someone took a meat tenderizer to it," Zhoa said.

Not a pleasant thought, Gino cringed.

"Eew."

"Yuck."

"That's disgusting."

"You're not cooking with that hand, are you?" Olivia asked in repulsion. "You shouldn't even be allowed in the kitchen or near food for that matter."

"Not to worry, I'm supervising," Zhoa said. He smiled as he patted his younger brother on the back with his good hand.

Like a knight addressing royalty, Vong bowed deeply.

Zhoa and Vong were always in good humor. Not even Olivia's insensitivity seemed to bother them.

"I'm the cook," Vong said. "And I say we have breakfast. I promise to prepare a feast to make you forget your problems."

That should give us a chance to take a breath and cool down, Gino thought, then said, "A good meal will clear our heads. Even if we can't go outside for now, we all have plenty of material to work on in-house."

The crowd parted as Vong passed through.

"I'll help with breakfast."

"Me too."

"Help is always welcomed," Vong said cheerfully.

"I'm so hungry I don't know if I can wait."

Vong let out a little laugh. "I have appetizers to hold you over."

"Appetizers would be nice," Avil said. "But I'm hungry for eggs."

"How about I make little balls of meat? I'll use food coloring to make them yellow," Vong said. "They'll be like little egg yokes."

"Gee, thanks." Avil didn't sound enthused.

A few said they'd rather finish dressing first and would be back in time for breakfast.

Jorge took Olivia by the hand and tried to lead her away.

She started to join them, but when she saw Mathieu and Lesley move through the crowd toward Rona, she let his hand go and stopped to listen.

"Olivia," Jorge admonished.

"Go," she said, "I want to listen."

Gino also stopped. It might be a good idea if he stayed too. Knowing Olivia would not leave, he wave Jorge onward.

"Nothing we've done for Zhoa's hand has worked," Mathieu said.

"That doesn't sound good." Rona said.

Gino got close enough to hear Rona whisper, "You don't think what the colonists have might be contagious, do you?"

"Mathieu and I are a little worried," Mathieu said.

"Worried about what?" she asked as she stepped closer.

"Olivia, let the doctors have their discussion in private." Gino took her arm and tried to steer her away.

Olivia yanked her arm free. "I will not! If Zhao is ill, it concerns all of us."

Gino couldn't blame her. Still, there was nothing she could do, but make things worse. "Olivia, let the doctors figure things out before you announce this to the others."

"Are you accusing me of making things worse?"

"Yes, now go help Vong make breakfast and don't say anything," Gino commanded. "Let the doctors handle this."

"Fine, but if they don't say something soon, I will," she said.

"At least, give us a couple of days," Lesley said.

"I'll give you three," she said and left.

"Maybe this is something we should all know about," Mathieu said. "The colonists are clearly sick. If we'd known before we came, WSC would not have sent us."

"Now Zhoa has something that Mathieu and I can't seem to cure," Lesley said. "And there's a strong possibility that it could be related to what these people have." He paused and directed his next question to Rona and Lu. "Have you two been able to learn anything about the colonists' illness?"

"What we know so far is confusing," Rona said, "No one will allow us to examine them."

"We tried to secretly use the HMS, but we don't have anything conclusive." Lu shrugged her shoulders. "Sorry."

"Well, you can examine me," Zhoa said holding up his bandaged hand.

"In that case we'll run tests." Rona motioned for him to follow her.

Zhoa obediently followed. A big grin spread over his face. "The docs said you would."

Rona stopped and turned her attention to the doctors, placed her hands on her hips and glared at them. "I don't understand why you didn't order tests earlier."

"This is earlier," Lesley said in their defense. "We were in the process of bandaging his hand when Lu called us out here."

"The itching woke me," Zhoa said. He tried to scratch his hand though the gauze.

Mathieu's shoulders twitched with quiet laughter. "We knew it wouldn't take long before the two of you noticed the bandages and demand tests."

"Come on," Gino said. "There's nothing here for us. We were headed for breakfast."

With broad smiles, Lesley and Mathieu waved goodbye.

Rona waved back as if all was well, but Gino sensed she was secretly apprehensive.

Chapter 34

Larry Gino
Zhoa's Hand

LARRY GINO placed a hand on Rona's arm but waited until they were alone before he quietly said, "If Zhoa has an alien disease, he wouldn't be allowed on the next transport. He'd never be allowed to return to Earth. For that matter, if there is an alien disease, even it if was only a rash, this entire planet could be quarantined and none of us will ever be allowed to leave."

"I've been thinking the same thing. No one will risk the possibility of us bringing a pandemic back to Earth," Rona spoke softly. She didn't want her voice to across the room. "All of us will be stuck here for the rest of our lives."

"Evidently, a locked door isn't our most pressing issue," Gino said.

Lu scanned Zhoa with her HMS then she studied the results. "You do have a retrovirus."

"Should I be worried?"

"Let's finish with the tests first, before we hypothesize." Rona's voice and facial expression were natural.

Lu was not as calm. She fumbled with the HMS, almost dropped it but managed to catch it just in time. "It's the same retrovirus as what the dogs have."

Gino knew about the retrovirus but had not pursued the seriousness of the matter. *I've become too excited over my rocks,* he mentally reprimanded himself. *I should be more involved in everyone's projects.*

Perhaps it was time for a group meeting, where they all shared what they've learned. It would give all of them a better understanding of the planet and its people.

"I haven't been near them," Zhoa said. "I mean, I like dogs and I've always gotten along with them, but these seem to hate me. They stay clear of me." He held up his hand. "How could I have gotten this from them?"

"It's too early to tell, son." Gino looked at the women for confirmation.

They nodded. "Too early," Lu agreed.

Good, no use worrying the boy sooner than we have too. Gino scanned the room.

The colonists had taken all the dogs with them. Why? Did they know the dogs were contagious?

"Give me your arm." Rona took hold of Zhoa's arm with his bandaged hand, pricked it with a sterilized needle, then gently squeezed it.

One at a time, Lu gave her six small vials just large enough to hold a few drops of blood. Rona handed each back filled with Zhoa's blood. Lu corked and labeled them.

"I've never heard of anyone actually taking blood samples before," Gino said.

"Normally we don't have to," Rona said.

"The Handheld Medical Scanner does the work for us," Lu said. "All we have to do is swipe a person's palm and it tells us virtually everything physically about them."

"So why take blood now?" Zhoa asked.

"Because," Rona began, "you have something alien that the HMS is unfamiliar with."

"A sample of your blood will help us better understand it, identify it, and classify it," Lu said with a hint of excitement.

Zhoa cocked a worried eyebrow.

Even Gino tilted his head. A moment before they'd been disturbed at Zhoa's plight, now they seemed a little too enthusiastic about it.

Both women flushed with embarrassment.

"We don't mean to be delighted at your discomfort," Lu said. "We know this is serious. It's just that . . ." Her voice trailed off.

"Sorry," Rona grimaced. "It's just that the colonists won't let us examine them. What you have is new to us and the HMS. The scan is as good as the information programmed into it."

"Your blood will provide the information it needs to improve our analysis of the retrovirus, " Lu said. "It may help us diagnose the colonists' illness."

"In other words, Zhoa's discomfort could help you with your research and possibly save lives," Gino said.

"Yes," Lu and Rona chimed.

"I guess I can live with that," Zhoa said.

"Good," Rona said. "Go supervise breakfast. We'll put these in the Analyzer, then we'll join you. We'll discuss the results after we eat."

"Why so much blood?" Zhoa asked.

"So much blood?" Rona said with genuine surprise. "There was a time when a doctor would fill a vial of blood the length and size of a person's index finger. I don't think we have that much blood." Then she spoke in a mock hushed tone. "But Lu likes to drink what we don't use."

Zhoa gave her a fake expression of dismay.

"I do not," Lu said with pure innocence. "But I do like to run tests, lots of tests. And if it's needed, I'll ask for more." An evil grin crossed her face. "Then I'll drink what's left."

"Mmmm." Zhoa considered the women and said to Gino, "Those two are a little too bloodthirsty for me."

"I completely understand," Gino said. "I'll keep an eye on both of them just to be safe."

"I think I'll keep the rest of my blood, if you don't mind." Zhoa protectively held his bandaged hand against his chest.

They all laughed.

Lu placed the vials in the Analyzer and set it.

"Like all of us, you were given a thorough examination before you were approved for training, before you boarded the transport, and before you were allowed to land on Akiane," Rona said.

"And according to this." Lu had already opened her holo-screen and was comparing her scan of Zhoa with his medical records. "Everything seems to be exactly the same, except for the retrovirus." She tapped the screen a few times, pulling up more information. "It's not affecting your bodily functions, as of yet."

"As of yet?" This surprised Gino.

"We know Zhoa has an infection," Lu said. "It's only logical we keep an eye out for any other problems. Right now I don't see anything, so don't worry."

Lu smiled. Zhoa smiled. Neither seemed genuine.

"We'll also check DNA," Lu said.

"Why DNA?" Zhoa frowned.

"A retrovirus is programmed to infiltrate a cell and rewrite its DNA," Lu said. "We'll compare it to your original DNA."

"What?" Zhoa said. "Should I be worried?"

Gino placed a fatherly hand on Zhoa's arm.

"No," Lu said, shaking her head.

"This retrovirus started out with a few red bumps and it may still be no more harmful than a rash. But it is new to us Earthlings. We want to study it," Rona said. "Just to make sure."

Lu hit another button on the Analyzer and set it to map Zhoa's DNA.

"Fine," Zhoa said. "I'm going to supervise breakfast. Let me know what you find."

"Don't touch anything," Lu said. "Or Olivia will bite your good hand off."

"I won't." Zhoa promised.

Chapter 35

Jessica Hewitt
Twenty-Fifth Day on Expedition
The Storm

THE DOGS' whining mixed with the faint rumblings coming from deep within the ground pulled me from a deep sleep. But it was Nu Venia's coughing that alerted me to the chaos of the morning, and fully dragging me awake. I sat up reaching for the reason for all the commotion.

A light coating of dust filled the air and my eyes, making them blink several times. The ground shuddered. Rocks on the floor swayed, tilted, and rolled.

The blizzard had kept us in the cave for two days.

Our big project for this day was to dig the cave entrance clear of the snow and assess the situation. We'd kept an open place for fresh air and to use as an exit for the dogs when needed. Now the dogs were tearing the opening apart in a frantic effort to get outside.

Essal was gone. Where was he? Was he better?

"Ah." Nu Venia leaped out of her blankets. "There is something under me. I felt it move."

Cameron hurried out of his blankets and pulled the fur carpeting back. I held my breath at what he might find. Mud oozed up out of the ground where Nu Venia had been sleeping. A sigh of relief.

"We must move." Cameron pulled his pants and boots on and went outside.

Nu Venia did the same.

What now?

Reluctantly, I crawled out of my warm bedding and pull on my pants, boots, and jacket before I ventured outside.

The snow was more than knee deep.

Kahair hadn't risen as of yet.

Looming in the western sky was the gigantic gas planet. It was covered with angry orange-red clouds. Most of the planet covered the western half of the sky. The rest of the planet had yet to rise above the horizon. It appeared to be eating up the night sky along with its stars.

"Loki." Nu Venia's voice sounded strained with fear. "The planet is called Loki."

All of Akiane reflected Loki as if he was taking possession of her. Angry, wind driven clouds erased the horizon that separated the two planets and seemed to sweep across the ice ocean and over our snow-covered land. It gave the illusion that the two planets had become one and we were standing in knee-deep multi-colored snow.

"We must move." Cameron disappeared into the cave.

"Do we have time?" Nu Venia hastened after him.

"We will have to hurry," his voice echoed off the cave.

They were afraid.

I didn't ask why but did as I was told. I understood how serious the situation was, or at least I thought I did. Loki was too close. His and Kahair's gravity would pull on Akiane, each trying to pull her out of orbit. She would stand in the middle using all her strength to resist them.

Cameron attacked the snow at the cave entrance and cleared a path for us.

The cave might have been short on height, but it was long on room. Because we were able to make camp in the cave, the tents as well as most of our equipment were still packed on the sleds.

It was my job to pack what had been taken off the sleds. I threw everything on with no order in mind: our bedding furs and floor furs, cooking stove and food, and haphazardly strapped everything down.

Cameron was so particular about packing. He had to have everything in its exact, proper place before we continued our journey. Because he said nothing about my disorganized packing skills, I *knew* something was terribly wrong.

It was Nu Venia's job to convince the dogs to return to the cave so she could harness them in place. They obeyed with their tails tucked between their legs, and slunk into their respective places. As soon as one team was harnessed, it shot out of the cave and sped uphill. The other team did the same. We followed immediately after we'd strapped on our snowshoes.

The ground shook with little tremors. Dust flew. Bits of rock ceiling had begun crumbling. It was a relief to be in open air where I thought we'd be safe.

Note: "*thought* we'd be safe."

The entire island shuddered. We heard the crashing of rocks off in the distance. We stumbled, barely able to keep our balance. Once the ground settled, I half expected Cameron to stop and take stock. He didn't. The dogs kept moving uphill away from the ocean. We followed.

The ocean ice popped, quaked, and moaned. That's when Cameron and Nu Venia stopped. The dogs also froze. I followed their gaze seaward. Nothing. The ocean ice seemed fine to me. It always made those noises. It had never bothered my companions before. Why were they nervous now?

I didn't ask. I didn't want to know. I had a sick feeling that I'd find out soon enough.

The dogs moved on.

The depth of snow wasn't a bother to them. Without waiting for us to pack it down, they bounded over it and forged ahead. We hurried to keep up.

For the next hour, we continued uphill, crested it, and would have continued on to the next hill, but for a rockslide the blocked our way.

"Can we make camp here?" I asked.

"NO!" Cameron and Nu Venia yelled at the same time.

"Why?" I asked.

"We must get as high as possible from the ocean and volcano," Nu Venia said.

We looked back at out cave. It had crumpled. Smoke rose up from between the rocks.

"I do not believe the volcano is a threat. This one does not have the same smell," Cameron said.

"What volcano? What smell?" I asked.

"The mud in the cave was just the beginning of what will soon be lava," Cameron said.

I automatically turned to see where we'd just been sleeping. Somewhere underneath that pile of rocks, a volcano was forming.

Spago would have loved it, the beginning of a volcanic eruption. Too bad I didn't get some of that mud for him. Once things settled and the lava had cooled, I'd collect some rocks for him.

Cameron searched for a way around the rockslide.

"The volcano at Endurance emits large plumes of gas," Nu Venia said. "It smells like death and makes all who are outside extremely ill enough to wish for death. We close the entrance tunnels so the gas is unable to get into Endurance. There is much waiting until the air becomes breathable and we again open the entrances."

I hoped my friends were safe. Spago would know what to do.

Cameron kept speaking, "Most of the snow around Endurance will melt. There will be much water and ash from the volcano. Much mud. Good for the soil." He shook his head. "Messy for those who go outside."

It took some time, but eventually Cameron found a path wide enough for the sleds. While we cleared rocks, the ground continued to shake and settle. Then all was quiet for almost an hour. A wave of relief swept through me at the realization that it was over.

"What about breakfast? I'm hungry," I asked.

"No. One must hurry before the tremors worsen," Cameron said.

"Worsen?" I asked. "What we'd just experienced hadn't been bad enough?

"We must reach the other side of the rockslide before the quakes return," he said.

The sense of relief vanished. Now I was hungry *and* scared.

Nu Venia and I went first along the path. We encouraged the first team to follow us. With Imos now ran at Huth's side and were a better match than Huth and Addle.

Cameron pulled his team along. As the second team started through, we heard distant sounds of thunder. Black clouds with orange and red highlights were fast approaching.

"Loki disrupts weather," Nu Venia informed me.

Translation: we were in for some bad weather along with bad quakes.

The ice no longer popped. It shrieked in pain. Thunder became louder as the rolling clouds rushed closer. The ground rumbled from an inner-core disorder. Whatever was happening was just getting started.

Both dog teams froze in fear, dropped to the ground, and burrowed their noses under their paws and wrapped their tails around themselves. Neither team wanted to continue. Large rocks lined the path threatening to roll over the dogs. This was not a good place to stop.

"Huk! Huk!" Cameron yelled frantically.

Nu Venia grabbed Huth and I pulled Imos to their paws and dragged them along. If we could get them moving the others should follow.

"Huk! Huk!" Nu Venia echoed Cameron.

The rest of the team didn't move. We weren't sure what to do. We needed to get them moving.

Nu Venia stayed with the lead dogs while I moved along the line and pulled and prodded the rest of the team to their feet.

"Huk! Huk!" Nu Venia encouraged them forward.

During a moment of quiet, all at once, the dogs stood. They hunched their backs and pulled with all their might to get away from the rocks. Nu Venia jumped out of the way.

"Hurry up, move it along. Huk. Huk! HUK!" I yelled.

As soon as the first team was clear, they tried to run uphill, but the snow was deeper and hindered them. Nu Venia hurried to stop the team and hold them until Cameron and his team were freed.

I headed back to help Cameron, but he waved me off, so I caught up with Nu Venia and waited with her.

Cameron's team hurried after him in a frantic effort to clear the rocks. But Cameron was in their way and his snow shows slowed his progress.

A hefty boulder swayed, rolled, and pinned the sled against another rock. No longer able to hold on, a rock loosened itself and came crashing down, squashed Tipper, a wheel dog, killing her instantly and crushed Tiahissa's back legs, the turn dog that ran directly in front of her. She yelled in pain as she tried to crawl forward. The remaining dogs wailed in confusion and fear as they tried to escape their harnesses.

Mergite, the other wheel dog, leaped and pulled against her harness, which securely held her in place. Every few seconds, her head appeared over the boulder. Her eyes were wild with panic. Her fur stood on end.

Cameron quickly undid his snowshoes and ran to help the frenzied dogs. With a swipe of his knife, he cut the team loose. They ran tumbling over one another and tangling the harness. Then turned to free Mergite.

The team kept moving until they were well out of the way and uphill. They stopped and howled for us to join them.

Our team wanted to follow with the same gusto. I help Nu Venia hold them at bay.

Tiahissa was beyond saving. Cameron slit her throat and put her out of her misery.

The ground swayed. I checked my balance.

More rocks fell, narrowly missing Cameron. He prepared to leap over a rock, but another rock rolled and caught his right foot. He hit the rock he'd intended to jump over, and landed hard on his belly.

Nu Venia un-strapped her snowshoes and ran to help him. I stayed with our howling team.

As she ran, she grew in size. I mean literally. When she was standing next to me, we were the same height. Now she was as large as Cameron

This was not in the reports I'd read about Akiane. If anyone had told me, I would not have believed it. No one the habitat was going to believe me either.

How was it possible for her to change size like that? Could all the colonists do it? Cameron hadn't changed.

Another strong shake.

At the edge of the cliff, a large overhead bolder swayed toward Cameron's head, then tilted away.

"Cameron, get out of there," I yelled. He couldn't hear me. Even if he had, I knew his reaction. Chovis come first, even before his life.

The fact that he was caught didn't stop him. With knife in hand, he stretched as far as he could. I imagined the tip of his sharp knife just reaching the harness at the wheel dog's back. With the flick of his wrist, he freed Mergite. She jumped onto the rock beside Cameron. He tried to push himself up, but he was at an odd angle to his trapped foot. His hand slipped on the bouncing rock.

The overhead large rock swayed. The rocks holding the it in place tumbled over the edge of the cliff toward Cameron.

Nu Venia was not going to reach him in time. I couldn't bear to watch Cameron be pounded by rocks. And yet I was unable to look away.

Mergite sank her teeth into Cameron's jacket collar and pulled him clear as the rocks fell where his head had just been. He landed backward and flopped onto the rock that held his foot.

Nu Venia leapt over rocks and tore at the boulder trapping Cameron. She grabbed the back of his jacket and heaved him up, then flipped him over her shoulder.

He made himself smaller so she could better carry him.

How was that possible?

On the way out, Nu Venia stooped to pick up his snowshoes. She could not have moved like that if she was still as small as a twelve-year-old.

She carried Cameron as if he were no heaver than a sack of rice.

The larger overhead boulder fell and crashed where Cameron had just been, smashing the rock into many smaller pieces. The boulder cracked into several large pieces. A few of them dropped onto the sled.

Mergite soared like a small plane. One final leap and she was off the path, running full speed toward her teammates who were at the top of the hill yelping for her to hurry. The team I held wanted desperately to follow, but I stood between the lead dogs and firmly held them in place. Their howling objections pierced my eardrums.

The ground heaved, Nu Venia slipped on the snow and went down. Cameron fell on top of her. Immediately, he rolled off and stood on his one good leg and helped her stand. She helped him hobble to the sled.

The other sled buried in the rubble, carried our food.

"We will come back to salvage what we can," Cameron said.

We placed him on the sled with his snowshoes and continued uphill. I stopped on occasion to catch my breath. The climb was steep and difficult. Nu Venia and I walked first and packed down the snow.

Walking in snowshoes didn't make it any easier but it did help the dogs. They strained against the steep hill, but didn't complain.

After one more grueling climb, we reached the summit and stood on a flat piece of ground about half the size of the habitat. We looked around and realized we were on an island. The other side of it was no larger than the front half. We were as high as we could go.

"This will have to be enough. We can only hope and pray that we are safe," Cameron said.

I couldn't help wondering how much safer we would be if we were back at the habitat.

We had an amazing view of the multi-colored ice ocean, which that seemingly stretched all the way to Loki.

I noted that there was no other land in sight.

"How did you manage to find this lonely island in a blinding blizzard?" I asked.

"Chovis found land," Nu Venia said.

"Huth and Imos found you," I said.

"Just so," Cameron said.

"Chovis find chovis," I said.

"Just so."

"Amazing. Truly these animals are far superior to Earth dogs. Perhaps it is time I call them by their proper name."

Cameron proudly grinned at me but refrained from saying, "I told you so."

Chapter 36

Rona Montgomery
Akiane Quake

A LOW, barely audible rumble rose from the floor as if the ground was waking from a deep sleep. The sound rose until it filled the room.

"An Akiane quake," Spago shouted. "It should be over soon."

Within a few seconds, all was quiet.

"There," Spago said, "It's already finished. There might be a few aftershocks, but I doubt there will be anything more to worry about."

For the next few minutes, it seemed that Spago was right. Then the entire room shook as if trying to fling flies off its ceiling.

"Is there a possibility the habitat will come crashing down on top of us?" Rona yelled over the tumult.

Spago yelled back, "No, we're safe. The colonists have built this place to withstand quakes. Remember how the hexagons are fitted together?"

All eyes turned to the ceiling and walls. Rona vaguely remembered a discussion about the habitat's construction when she first entered the tunnel. Spago had said, or rather guessed, that the colonists reconfigured the basic elements of their building material down to the atoms so that the walls, ceiling, and floor were self-healing.

Rona closely examined the floor. She saw a tiny cracks no more than 5 centimeters long. Runners bolted like lightning.

In a blink of an eye, it was gone. She might have thought she'd imagined it if Spago had not spoken of it earlier.

The floor had just healed itself.

"They built the habitat to withstand quakes," Spago said.

Gino dropped his gruffness and assured them as a father would his children, "Don't worry, we're safe."

Rona hoped they were correct.

She'd never been in an earthquake before. Although the ground rumblings were unnerving, the planetary geological experts' composed attitude was helpful.

The tables lurched. One fell over scattering its occupants. Lunch plates clattered to the floor, sending bits of meat, vegetables, fruit, and rolls flying. Eating utensils clanged as they hit the floor. Stainless steel cups bounced. Coffee, juice, and water sprayed over surprised scientists.

This quake lasted almost half a minute.

Loud banging, clanking, and pinging sounds coming from the kitchen.

"My pans." Vong ran to the kitchen.

"There will be a mess to clean up after this." Zhoa rushed after his brother.

Attentions returned back to Spago. "I . . . ah . . . may have been wrong."

"You think?" Olivia shivered in fear.

"I suggest we put the rest of the dishes and such in the autobus." Gino called an autobus to him. An acrylic rectangle container floated over. He placed his eating utensils in it. Those near him hastily did the same.

Other autobuses were called and similarly filled.

"This does seem to be a little rougher than I thought, but it shouldn't last long." Spago didn't speak with the same confidence. "But it's a good idea to secure our equipment."

Rumblings started up again.

"Oh my," Beth yelled as one of her experiments skipped off a worktable and landed on the floor with a sickening thud.

"That can't be good," Rona said. She rose from her chair and headed for her workspace.

Everyone ran to secure his or her equipment. Rona knew that more than one experiment would be disrupted during the quakes and would have to be started over again. Still, moving the equipment was better than it being damaged.

Gino's rocks scattered as his table collapsed. He barely got there in time to catch his notebooks before they hit the floor and scattered. Who knew he could move that fast?

They'd used the packing crates to build cabinets for storage. The wall had been built and taken down three times before it was declared perfect. Now it took only a few minutes to take it apart and safely place crates around the room.

They turned tables upside down, folded chairs, and laid them on the floor. Then sat on the floor, some in silent prayer or meditation. Many eyes searched walls, the floor, and ceiling, waiting for what came next.

Time slowly stretched into five, six, 10 minutes. Nothing happened.

"See, I told you it wouldn't be so bad." Spago with a timid grin.

A collective sigh of relief drifted through the room just before another quake shook.

This one lasted longer than any quake on Earth. Nerves were coming undone.

"This was not normal according to Earth's standards," Spago declared. "I have no idea what's normal for Akiane."

One of Olivia's three aquaria swayed, water violently swished back and forth, unbalancing it. A leg buckled. It toppled into the aquarium next to it. They crashed to the floor, toppling into the third aquarium. Water gushed, sending fish skidding across the floor.

Mixed with fear and disappointment, Olivia's tough exterior crumbled. She stood as she hopelessly watched her research fall into ruins.

"They were my last aquaria," she said without feeling. Her hands covered her face as she cried.

"When is it going to stop?" Lu said between sobs.

Rona also felt like crying.

"It should have stopped already," Gino yelled over the quake noise. "This is odd." As a scientist, Gino emotions were a mix of miffed fascination.

Rona knew what he was thinking:

This was not scientifically possible.

It was worthy of study—if he survived it.

Quakes abruptly stopped, Gino and Spago exchanged worried glances as silent thoughts passed between them.

"What?" Rona asked.

Gino turned a light shade of green.

Spago was as white as a bed-sheet.

"That quake should not have lasted that long. That's not good," Gino said.

"Not good," Spago confirmed.

Rona shivered. *I hope I didn't come all this way to die in some cataclysmic volcanic explosion.*

The quiet continued for over an hour. Was that it? Or was the *big one* yet to come?

People stood and stretched.

Heads turned toward the bay door.

"If it's over, why is the door still closed?" Lesley asked.

"Maybe it takes a while to walk over here and open it," Beth said.

"Maybe they forgot," Olivia said.

Spago stood. He turned in a full circle so all could hear. "If that last quake was the big one, then there will be a few much smaller aftershocks." He paused and lowered his head. It was obvious that he didn't believe that was the last *big one*. He raised his head again. "If that was leading up to the big one, there could be several more . . . larger . . . louder. Each one will be more intense until . . ."

"This isn't a normal volcanic explosion, is it?" Olivia asked.

"No, it's not," Spago said.

"Tell us," Olivia demanded.

Spago closed his eyes. He wiped beads of sweat from his forehead with his shirt sleeve. He sighed heavily, opened his eyes, and said, "There's a gas planet that passes Akiane once every eleven years."

"We know this." Olivia was on the verge of panicking.

"There's no data," Spago said apologetically. "We didn't know how close it comes or what kind of gravitational pull it might have."

"You should have told us." Olivia yelled.

"Olivia," Gino reprimanded. "This is not anyone's fault. This is a natural phenomenon. This has been happening every eleven years for who knows how long."

"This explains why the aurora lights came down this far south," Bonga said. "The gravitational pull from the gas planet would have a huge effect on Akiane's star and the solar flares."

"Who cares about the stupid star," Olivia yelled.

Lu collapsed onto the floor, crying hysterically. Rona sat next to her and wrapped her arms around her, but Lu refused to be comforted. The fears of the quake and the possibility of death were too great.

"It's okay, it's okay," Rona said soothingly.

"We're going to die," Lu wailed.

"No, Lu, we're not." Rona tried to sound confident.

No sooner had the words exited Rona's mouth than the rumblings started up again followed by more shaking.

There wasn't anything Rona could say to calm Lu's hysteria. The best she could do was hold Lu close. At least they'd die together.

A loud explosion like a sonic boom shook the room.

Several asked, "What was that?"

There were a series of explosions with the same intensity as a jet breaking the sound barrier.

During a moment of quiet, Gino said, "Spago, tell us what's happening. Information is better than ignorance, even during a time like this."

Just as Spago yelled over the rumblings

Rona had to concentrate to hear him. It wasn't just because of the noise; her fear of death was more deafening than Akiane's quakes.

"The explosions are coming from the volcano. Gas is coming up through the magma flow creating large . . . " He paused. "Large doesn't fully explain—the magma flow is creating monstrous bubbles. The bubbles are exploding. At the same time they're throwing rocks the size of small hovercrafts out of the mountain." He paused. "I now know why the colonists closed the door."

"Why?" Jorge asked.

"The volcano is emitting plumes of ash, which could rise kilometers into the sky. When the ash comes down, it will cover everything. Anyone outside would have suffocated and died." Now he had everyone's full attention. "They closed the door to protect us and to make sure we stayed inside."

From under the bay door, ground waves moved across the floor much the way ripples moved over a quiet lake.

"This is going to be a long night." Spago sat.

The ground waves weren't large, but were unnerving. As they passed underfoot, Olivia screamed in fear as one thrown from a cliff. Lu whimpered. Cracks appeared throughout the room then disappeared just as quickly as the room healed itself.

More waves.

After the waves, came silence. If the end was coming, it wasn't immediate.

Everyone huddled in comforting groups.

Olivia remained standing, softly crying, and staring blankly at her fish flopping on the wet floor.

Jorge grabbed her arm and pulled her toward Rona and Lu and sat her down next to them. Rona reached around Lu and pulled Olivia closer. Olivia's terrified eyes focused on Rona. She grabbed at Rona digging her fingers into Rona's upper arms.

Lu sat between them, less hysterical, but still sobbing.

Jorge wrapped his arms around the three women and buried his face in their hair.

So this is what it takes to have his arms around me, a volcanic eruption? Rona thought. *It's not worth it.*

Underground rumblings, groans, and moans became louder. The habitat's trembling became more violent.

Lu's right. We're going to die, Rona thought. *We've come all this way and we're going to die. I'll never see Earth again. I'll never see my family.*

Mathieu joined their small group.

I should have thought this through more thoroughly, Rona reflected. But the possibility of dying had never occurred to her. Even though she knew the trip was dangerous and anything could happen, she never believed for one second that she would die. How naive. WSC told her to write a goodbye letter, just in case. She never thought that letter would be mailed. Now she wasn't so sure.

"Why did they lock us in here?" Olivia spoke too calmly, too vague. She was drifting away. Rona never thought Olivia could lose herself in any situation, but this wasn't just any situation.

Rona was on the verge of losing it herself. "Remember, Olivia, they told us when they locked the door. It's safer in here."

"And if it is, that means it's worse outside." Jorge's voice cracked as he spoke.

Rona and Jorge locked eyes. She knew exactly what he was thinking. Where was Jess? Akiane was mostly ocean. How could ice hold up to this? Had she found land? The fear in his heart plainly showed on his face. What if they never saw her again?

"It's lasting for hours," Olivia said.

"Quakes never last this long back on Earth," Jorge said, checking at his watch.

"It's getting worse." Olivia buried her face in Lu's back.

Rona leaned closer to the strong arms still holding her and rested her head on his shoulder. But it wasn't Jorge she had leaned into for comfort. It was Mathieu.

Chapter 37

Jessica Hewitt
The Storm

IT WASN'T one continuous quake. They came one at a time, some for only a few seconds, some for several minutes, some came so quickly, one after the other, they seemed like one continuous quake that lasted far too long.

There would be long moments of quiet and I'd think it was over, but as long as Loki remained in the sky it wasn't.

Caught between the gas giant's gravity and that of the star Kahair, Akiane was being pulled and stretched to her limits. It wouldn't be over until Loki had set in the eastern sky and moved on.

Akiane's sky filled with ominous storm clouds forming and swishing by the muscle of the wind, blocking Loki from view, but didn't ease the effects on the planet.

We tried to construct the tents, but gave up.

Rain came in large hard drops that beat at us. Wind flung raindrops downward at a 45-degree angle.

Great flashes of lightning repeatedly lit up the inside of storm clouds. Stretches of lightning streak across the sky or leaped downward to strike at Akiane.

Chovis cowered and loudly complained with whiny growls. They stepped on each other while searching for a place to settle and find emotional comfort. Their barking quieted to a soft pathetic whimpering.

"Where's Essal?" I asked. "Why isn't he here?" I couldn't see him in all that fur. Why wasn't he in my lap where he belonged? Where was he?

"Essal will return in time," Cameron said.

"We didn't leave him back in the cave did we?" I suddenly had a nightmarish picture of him crushed under a pile of rocks, then vaporized by molten lava.

"Essal will soon return." Cameron almost smiled, but it quickly vanished with the next rumblings.

Why was he being so mysterious about that dog?

The raindrops suddenly turned to ice and pounded us with pea-size hail, which quickly grew to golf ball size. There was nowhere go, no shelter to protect us. All we could do was sit and take it.

Chovis started barking—all at once.

The island's underground rumblings and the moaning of the ice made for a bad headache. Pounding my head against a rock would have been less painful.

"Arechit," Cameron yelled for the dogs to stop. They refused to obey, or maybe they couldn't hear him.

The winds sent the clouds tumbling and rolling. For a few minutes the clouds cleared, the rain and hail stopped. The sky filled with Aurora lights that angrily pulsed across the sky with lightning speed. Heaven itself was on fire.

We could now see the two moons. The smaller one was passing in front of the larger one. Loki was behind them. We saw Akiane and the moons' shadows on the giant gas planet's yellow-orange clouds.

Akiane's clouds returned this time filled with snow.

And all the while the quakes continued. Some were gentle but more seemed to shake entire planet at once.

Ocean ice rippled as if the waves under it were trying to get out.

It was a terrifying night, with no escape, and no warmth.

The fur suits kept us dry, but couldn't keep the cold out. Cameron gave us dried fish to keep hyperthermia at bay.

"What is all this?" I called.

"It is call *The Storm*. Loki tries to pull Akiane out of orbit, but Kahair wishes to keep her in place," Cameron said. "Loki brings blizzards, causes the ocean to mightily rise and fall. Even Kahair is affected."

"The star? How so?" I asked.

"Great star flares arise from Kahair," he said, "and bring dancing lights to the sky."

"This happens every eleven years," I said.

"Just so," Cameron said.

"Our window of opportunity to come here from Earth is once every eleven years," I said. "That window seems to coincide with when Akiane and Loki are the closest."

"I do not understand," Nu Venia said.

"The original crew must have arrived here just before or right at the time of Loki's arriving."

"Indeed, they did," Cameron said.

"WSC would have sent the robotic ships near the same time," I said.

"Is that why we received only one ship?" Nu Venia said. "The other two were lost in The Storm."

"Yes," I said. "And Loki is also the reason we never heard from you. Back on Earth, star flares used to disrupt communication. There have been entire cities very far north or very far south that have lost their electrical systems turning all lights and communications off."

Nu Venia's eyes narrowed.

"What?" I asked.

"If the flares stop communications, how is it you and Cameron were able to speak to Admiral Grossman?" she asked.

"We have developed technology that overcomes the disruption," I said. "That's why *Britannia* was able to communicate with WSC Moon Base."

Our summit gave a violent shake like a horse bucking. Thankfully, we were not thrown off the bucking island.

"Will Akiane hold together?" I feared it would split into millions of pieces and send us orbiting out into empty space.

"Akiane will hold."

At first, I doubted Cameron's confidence but he'd been through this before. All his life this storm had come and gone, and Akiane had remained intact.

Once in my lifetime would be more than enough for me. I couldn't imagine going through this over and over again. It made me even more determined to go home, as if I needed any more encouragement.

"Is it not the same on Earth?" Nu Venia asked.

"No, trust me, I've never seen anything like this before. We only have one moon and it orbits every twenty-eight days. It causes our oceans to rise and fall in tides. We never have anything like this. There's no gigantic gas planet to disrupt our gravity. How do you stand it?"

"It is part of living on Akiane," Cameron said. "But no one is ever outside when it happens."

We had to lean toward each other and yell at the top of our voices, which made out conversation difficult. My throat felt the effects of yelling. It would have been better to just be quiet. But we couldn't. We spoke for comfort. It was better than pulling our heads in our fur hoods like turtles.

That was what the dogs were doing. They whimpered to let the others know they were not alone. Cameron had stopped trying to quiet them. They'd become background noise.

"When The Storm is finished, the mountains near Endurance will appear differently," Cameron said. "There is much lava."

I would have thought that was another fable if I was not presently experiencing The Storm for myself.

"Will lava flow into the habitat?" I wanted assurance that my friends would be all right. If Spago was on the mountains, he could be dead by now. No, he was too smart for that. He'd know to return to the habitat.

"Endurance was built far enough away. There will be no lava damage," Cameron assured me.

I hoped he was right.

"Will this island hold up?" I asked. If a whole mountain range could rearrange itself, what would happen to this small island?

Cameron didn't answer. How could he know? He'd never been on it before.

"Are you always inside during this storm?" I asked.

"Always," he said. "It is the only safe place."

See, if we'd stayed just like I wanted, we'd be safe and would not have to endure all of this. I fumed.

Chovis lay so close to each other, they became a living carpet. They were finally silent, too scared to make a sound or maybe they knew something worse was coming.

No sign of Essal. What happened to him? When did he wander off? Why didn't he return? Why was he out there by himself? Maybe he couldn't find us. Maybe he was dead. What would I do then? I wanted Essal with me. In my lap so we could comfort each other.

I thought I saw the ocean ice rise, but it was just my imagination playing tricks on me. Then the ice settled with a tremendous, deafening swish. That wasn't my imagination.

The island shook sideways, up and down, and back and forth. Was it getting ready to sink into the ocean?

We heard a thunderous gurgling sound coming from behind us. We were curious about what it was but we'd have to walk to the other side of our summit to see what was going on.

No one moved.

The ocean ice swelled. Sank. Heaved. Slowly, settled back down. For one second it was still.

Then like a succession of grenades, ice cracked, and snapped. Hundreds of thousands of ocean geysers sprayed from between cracks. The entire ice covering, every bit of it, shattered. Chunks of ice went flying as waves exploded free and reached for the moons. Akiane's gravity pulled the water back with a cannonball splash. The ocean raged. Not just one section of it but the entire ocean seemed to boil as water rose and fell.

Tsunami size waves moved at unbelievable speeds across the ocean. But there was no order to them. They crashed into each other, ran over each other, joined together, doubling in size.

Phyllis Moore

Waves from every direction slammed into our island flooding the hills, the rockslide we'd passed through, and came within meters of our summit.

Chapter 38

Rona Montgomery
Morning After
Zhoa

LU JERKED, waking Rona with a start. She quickly sat up and took stock of the situation. To her amazement, their living quarters was intact. Not one piece of the ceiling, wall, or floor had come loose, not even a crack remained. The self-healing habitat was a success. There was not so much as a blemish to be seen.

As gradually as it started, the rumblings had slowed.

"Is it over?" Lu's eyes were still swollen. She'd been crying in her sleep.

"I think so, Lu." Rona was exhausted from her fitful night. She was stiff from stress. Her rump was sore from sitting in the same position.

Even though all had been near exhaustion, no one had thought to go to bed. They'd fallen asleep huddled in small groups.

Despite her fatigue, Roan felt a wave of relief that she'd survived the worst traumatic event of her life. It was almost like being reborn. She'd been so scared and convinced she was going to die. Yet, she woke to a new day with her whole life ahead of her.

Her next thought was to wonder if she'd do better this time around.

Olivia had been leaning against Lu; she moved away. Lu sat up. Jorge was asleep on the floor next to the women. At the sound of their voices, he bolted upright.

"We survive?" he asked.

"Is anyone hurt?" Mathieu laid a comforting hand on Rona's arm.

"I'm okay," Lu said.

"Me too," Olivia said.

"I'm fine." Rona patted his hand and softly said, "Thank you for staying."

His smile warmed her more that Jorge's ever had. She'd been chasing after an illusion when she should have been seeking something real—someone real.

Rona tried to unfold herself and extended her legs. Her whole body ached from the tension.

"I wonder how Jessica is doing," Olivia said.

Despair stabbed at Rona. She at least had the comfort of friends. Was Jess even alive? Suddenly the relief of surviving seemed small compared to what Jess must have endured. Even more sickening—Rona had no means to learn if she was alive or not.

"I should never have let her go," Jorge moaned. "I can't imagine she lived through that."

Rona feared he was right. Jess couldn't have survived if she were out on the ocean.

"She might," Olivia said. "I mean these people knew the Akiane quake was coming, they acted accordingly, when they built this place. They even locked us inside for our protection." She nodded toward the closed bay door. "It stands to reason that Cameron also knew about it and would have known what to do. I'm sure Jessica is safe."

Who would have thought Olivia would be the one to encourage them about Jess.

"Olivia has a point," Mathieu said.

Rona hoped they were right.

People stood stunned, ragged, and relieved. They spoke in hushed tones fearful the rumbling might start up again.

A wail shattered the muted atmosphere.

Vong sat on the floor and held his brother in his arms clamped against his chest. "Zhoa. Zhoa. Dead. My God, Zhoa's dead. My brother," he wailed.

No one moved.

They were too shocked to fully understand.

Zhoa can't be dead, Rona thought. *Vong must be wrong. Perhaps the infection progressed, placing Zhoa in a coma-like state. He can't be dead.*

Rona tried to stand. She'd been sitting curled in a ball for too long. Her legs were not ready to hold her. She tried again. This time she managed to get to her feet and awkwardly walk. But her legs gave way unceremoniously as she plopped next to the brothers.

Mathieu and Lesley joined her. Gently, the men tried to pull the brothers apart, but Vong refused.

"NO!" He held Zhoa tighter.

"Vong, let the doctors examine him," Rona spoke smoothly in the hopes of calming him. "Maybe they can help him." His tears stopped. Had she reached him?

Vong yelled at her. "Zhoa is dead! They can't help."

Unintimidated, Rona wrapped an arm around his shoulders.

"Please, let the doctors examine him."

"No," he whimpered as tears streamed down his cheeks. Zhoa was the only close relative he had left. His parents and sister were dead. Neither brother had married.

Too exhausted herself, Rona cried with him. "Let Mathieu and Lesley examine him."

Finally, reluctantly, Vong slowly dropped his arms.

Eyes wide, staring at nothing, Zhoa rolled away. The gray blotches on his wrist ran up his arm, disappeared under his sleeve and reappeared at his collar, ran along his neck and face.

Rona recognized those blotches. She'd seen them on sick colonists.

Confirmation: Zhoa had the same disease as the colonists.

Mathieu and Lesley pulled his to one side and checked his pulse, his eyes and face, his breathing, and his heart.

They shook their heads.

Vong buried his face in Rona's shoulder. She rested the side of her face on the top of his head, and rocked him. Rona couldn't begin to imagine how he felt.

Lu knelt next to Lesley. "Is that the same thing the colonists have?" she whispered.

"Think one of the hunters gave it to him?" Lesley asked.

"Hunters?" Lu asked.

"You know, when they bring meat," Lesley said.

"Without more information, it's difficult to say." Lu shrugged her shoulders.

Hunters brought meat and hung it on hooks just inside the door of their living area. Both brothers had little physical contact with the hunters. But they did have plenty of contact with raw meat.

Zhoa had the same disease as the colonists. Was the meat contaminated? Rona gave the thought serious consideration.

"Would an autopsy help?" Mathieu asked.

"Yes," Lu said. "It would also give us an insight as to what the colonists have. I hate that he's dead. I'd much rather he still be alive, but an autopsy would helpful."

Vong didn't respond to their conversation. Rona hoped he hadn't heard.

The doctors stood and proposed to move Zhoa to the kitchen where they would perform the autopsy.

"What?" Olivia objected. "You're going to perform an autopsy where our meals are prepared?"

Nerves were still too frayed to start an argument over where to lay Zhoa.

Vong angrily pulled away from Rona.

"Don't mind her." Rona tried to console him. "She's still stressed from the gravitational storm. She doesn't know what she's saying."

"I do too," Olivia snapped.

Vong snarled.

Of course Olivia was right. The food-preparing table shouldn't be used as an autopsy table. But Mathieu and Lesley would know what to do. Still, Olivia could have waited until Vong was out of the way and then quietly spoken to the doctors. Instead, she was upsetting him and everyone else. Why couldn't she just be quiet?

Vong stood feet shoulder width apart. He clenched and unclenched his fists. His muscles ready to do battle, which could be with Olivia if she didn't shut up.

"Would you prefer we do it here on the floor, or in the dorm room?" Lesley stood also ready for a fight. "How about if we do it on your bed."

Fire blazed in Olivia's eyes. How could she be so compassionate and encouraging one moment, then in the next become so unreasonable?

"Olivia, please," Rona said. "You're upsetting Vong."

"Vong? What about me?" she exploded.

"What about you?" Always calm and understanding Mathieu had also had it with Olivia. "He just lost his brother."

"Well I don't want to die of the same thing as Zhoa because my dinner was prepared on an autopsy table," Olivia yelled.

Vong rubbed the side of his head with the heel of his hand. He was fast. If he wanted, he could reach Olivia before anyone could stop him. If he hit her, he could seriously injure her. With his strength, it would take several men to pull him off of her.

"Olivia, there's more than one table in the kitchen. I doubt Vong will want to prepare food on the same table we used for his brother." Lesley said. "This is a fruitless conversation."

"Olivia," Rona said. "Mathieu and Lesley know what they're doing. Leave them alone."

But Olivia wouldn't stop. "Mark the table so Vong knows which one you used."

"Olivia," Gino said. "I doubt Vong is in any condition to cook for us right now."

"Mark the table so no matter who's cooking, they will not use an autopsy table to prepare our meals," she demanded.

"We'll turn the table upside down," Mathieu yelled. "Will that satisfy you?"

"Yes," she said. "And you don't have to yell."

Mathieu's jaw tightened. His eyes narrowed. Rona feared Vong might not be the only one to throttle Olivia.

"I won't leave my brother here," Vong said.

Rona had thought Vong was angry with Olivia, but he hadn't been following the conversation.

"What do you mean?" she asked.

"When the transport gets here, we're leaving. I'm burying my brother on Earth and I'm never coming back here again." He held his head high. His jaw set. His eyes brimmed with tears.

Lesley raised his hand. "We'll embalm him. We'll wrap Zhoa in bed sheets and place him in the freezer until the transport comes."

"With the meat?"

"Shut up, Olivia," Mathieu said.

Jorge gently tried to pull Olivia away. "Come. Let them sort everything out."

"No!" She tried to pull her arm out of his grip, but he didn't let go.

"Keep this up, Olivia and you're liable to get slugged," Jorge said.

"Am I the only reasonable one here?" She continued to struggle with him.

"In case you haven't noticed," Mathieu yelled, "we're all scientists. You're not the only one who graduated at the top of your class. All of us were chosen because we're the best in our field."

"What's that supposed to mean?" she yelled back.

"It means, we know what we're doing, Olivia," Mathieu said. "We don't need your know-it-all attitude."

Olivia finally yanked her arm out of Jorge's hand. "Know-it-all attitude? Is that what you think?" She spoke to all in the room. "You all think that?" No one answered.

Mathieu stepped directly in front of her, daring her to say another word.

"Fine." Olivia stomped to the women's dorm walking through the clumps of people in her path, who quickly parted for her.

"Maybe now we can get to work," Mathieu said.

Vong stood and swayed. Rona was fearful he might topple over.

Gino moved to his side. "I'll take him to his bunk." He led Vong away.

"Maybe we should get food and drink out of the kitchen before they start the autopsy," Jorge said.

"Good idea," Mathieu said.

Food? All Rona wanted to do was lie down and sleep for a week. Maybe the gravitational storm was over, but the storm inside her head was still raging. She was too stressed from the night before and too shocked over Zhoa's death to care about food.

No one noticed when the bay door had opened.

Chapter 39

Jessica Hewitt
Twenty-Sixth Day on Expedition

I WOKE to the sound of waves crashing against our island. Apparently, I'd survived. But how was it possible that I'd fallen asleep draped over a rock? Evidently, after such an emotional event, I was too exhausted to care.

The moons had set. Loki had disappeared.

Kahair's morning light had welcomed a new day.

Tsunami waves had given way to huge Hawai'i waves.

I half expected to hear birds happily chirping and feel a gentle breeze on my face, the calm after the storm.

But, this was an alien world.

There were no more thunderclouds or lightning. No birds and no breeze, just the relief that I'd lived through the night. Loki didn't stay long, but he certainly made his presence known.

I took a deep breath, inhaling the new day. At that peaceful moment, it was difficult to worry about the future. There was something awe inspiring about surviving a tempest night that put me in a surprisingly good mood.

Well, why not? I was still alive. We all were.

Nu Venia was making tea.

Cameron was trying to stretch out the kinks from his injury of the day before. Yesterday, he could barely walk. Today, he's ready to lift boulders. Incredible recovery.

Hearing a familiar sound, I turned to see Essal lying close by. He jumped to his feet the second my eyes were on him.

"There you are." I reached out to scratch his head.

Essal barked loudly and took two four-legged bounces away from me. He crouched low to the ground. Barked. Leaped up and stood expectantly.

"Essal wishes you to follow," Cameron said.

"Why?" I asked. "What's got him in a tizzy?"

He would have to wait. I needed to work the stiffness of sleeping on a rock out of my back and shoulders. I stood, stretched backwards and forwards, then twisted from side to side. It felt good.

Impatient, Essal barked more intensely. Whatever his problem was, it was important, at least to him.

"All right, all right," I said. "I'm coming." I really wasn't in the mood for a walk. I wanted a nice bed with uninterrupted sleep. A hot bath would have been nice, too.

Several more barks to hurry me up.

"You're becoming a bit bossy for one who completely deserted me during my night of terror. What's so important?"

Cameron let out a little chuckle.

"This is funny?" I asked.

"The night has passed. New matters are needing attention," he said.

"What matters?" I asked.

They both laughed.

"You will see," Nu Venia said.

"We all go," Cameron said. "You will need help."

Help with what? I wondered. Somehow I knew not to ask. Clearly they and Essal wanted to surprise me.

One would have thought last night had never happened. I thought there'd be some discussion of what we felt. Didn't people usually revisit traumas in great detail? Not these people. The night was over. The was a new day with new adventures.

Essal took the lead, and was soon several meters ahead, barking furiously for us to hurry.

We followed to him to a small cave with a cluster of rocks and in the cluster were six puppies, all about the size of my palm.

"What's that?" I asked.

"New born pups," my companions proudly announced.

"New born pups?" I asked, full of disbelief. They looked weeks old. Their eyes were opened, they had fur, and made squeaky noises.

Essal seemed to be broadly smiling. His tongue hung out of the corner of his mouth. His ears pointed straight up and his tail vigorously wagged his rear.

"Pups are in need of care. We will bring them back to our camp," Nu Venia said.

We carried the six puppies back with Essal trailing at my heels.

Cameron pulled a fur like nest from under the sled's tarp. All six pups neatly fit inside with room to grow.

He also pulled out a plastic rectangle that was longer than it was wide. He poured creamy white liquid in it and set it before the puppies. They bounced out of the fur nest to lap up their first meal.

"Pups must be fed like this," Cameron said.

Essal watched intensely as he sniffed each pup.

"One must feed them daily," Cameron said directly to me, which meant I to feed them.

"Why me?"

"Bringing forth of pups is to please you," Nu Venia said.

"Why me?" I asked again.

"No doubt seeking your approval," he said.

My approval.

Giving birth to pups was a biological event, not an act of praise.

"I thought humans and chovis were born in cocoons," I said.

"Most of the time, yes," Nu Venia said.

"Most of the time?" I asked. "What does that mean?"

"There are times when pups are born with or without a cocoon," Cameron said, "but it is unknown as to why."

"OK, who's the mom?" I asked as I scratched Essal's head.

It was only right they both received congratulations for a job well done.

Nu Venia and Cameron gave me a look that asked, *What are you talking about?*

One of us should have brought an interpreter.

"Who gave birth?" I asked. "Where was the mother? Why isn't she here?"

"Essal brought forth," Nu Venia said.

"Yes, I know he's the father, but who's the mother?"

"Essal brought forth," she repeated.

"He had to have help." These people were frustrating. They made every conversation difficult.

"Essal had no help," Cameron said.

"Sure he did. He didn't do it by himself."

"She needs no help," Nu Venia insisted. "If there is another to mate, chovis will mate, but when there is not, they bring forth alone."

These people were serious. They actually believed their dogs were hermaphrodites. How was that possible?

"What?" I asked.

"Chovis bring forth puppies alone," Nu Venia said.

"What?" It just wasn't sinking in. It wasn't possible!

"When it is time, chovis bring forth puppies," she said very deliberately.

Could that be true? Did anyone back at the habitat know? Was anyone even interested enough to study the dogs? By the time I got back, I'd have a story to tell them.

"So let me get this straight. Your dogs, I mean, female chovis do not need partners to have puppies."

"Indeed," Nu Venia said.

"They never use partners?" I wanted to be perfectly clear that I understood them correctly.

"They will join if there is one to join with, but those are few, and there are no males with us on this journey," Cameron said. "When there is not a male, a chovis will bring forth alone."

Alone or with another? Jorge had said something about worms that could reproduce alone, but preferred a partner. Chovis might interest him more than worms.

"So why are there no males with us now?" I asked.

"Males are not loyal or as reliable as females," Nu Venia said. "As soon as males become full grown, they mate and leave us for the ocean."

Chovis are certainly not Earth dogs. I had assumed chovis were descended from the dogs the first crew had brought with them. Could they have evolved into hermaphrodites? No. That was ridiculous. Besides, only Captain Assetti brought a dog, although the other ships brought livestock DNA with them. After they landed they'd planned to raise farm animals. There could have been pets included in the DNA stock.

That still didn't explain how dogs became chovis.

There was the only logical explanation.

"Are chovis native to Akiane?" I asked.

"What is native?" Nu Venia asked.

"Were chovis here when the first crew landed?"

Nu Venia blinked. "Chovis came with Captain Assetti."

"You mean the one dog the captain brought with her?" I asked. "A little white Spitz is the mother of all these dogs? How?"

"Fish," they said.

Fish? The same fish I'd eaten? They'd said fish changes people.

Before that thought completely solidified in my brain, I remembered Olivia saying something about her fish being all female. Lu said the same thing about the dogs. She couldn't find an adult male. If all dogs were female, that meant Essal had given birth to these puppies because he was really a she.

I was flabbergasted. How could a dog clone herself like that? I was . . . I was . . . There were no words.

"On this day, Endurance celebrates New Beginnings. We too celebrate," he said.

Celebrate? These people had just dropped the most amazing bit of information on me. But to them, it was everyday news. Puppies were born and they moved on. Were we to now have balloons, Champagne, music, and dancing?

"Is everyone in Endurance celebrating?" I asked.

"Indeed," Cameron said. "But we were outside during The Storm and we live. We have more than usual to celebrate."

"Well, I'm ready for a good party," I said clapping my hands in anticipation.

I had a flashback to *Britannia* where I'd avoided most social gatherings. Before my father's death, I'd been reasonably social, but afterward, I became moody and kept to myself. I continued to do so while on the transport.

When the captain reassigned me to the civilian quarters Rona introduced me to the rest of her friends and Jorge. They had tried to encourage me to attend many of the scientists' social gatherings. I didn't want to be with all those strangers, but I did want to be with Jorge, so I went.

Cameron said with glee, "We wash our underclothes."

Oh, be still my heart. "What?"

"Are you not in need of clean underclothes?" Nu Venia asked with big smile.

"Right. Clean underwear. Just my idea of celebrating." So much for Champaign and dancing.

Despite the disappointment, I had to admit clean underclothes would be nice. Mine were feeling a bit grimy. For that matter, so was I. A hot bath would have been heavenly and would definitely have been something worth celebrating.

"Underclothes first, then . . ." Cameron smiled as if I understood.

I didn't.

Chapter 40

Qorow Low
The Day of Celebration

THE DAY after Loki's visit was supposed to be a celebration of survival. But surviving this Storm had taken on a whole new meaning.

Instead of a day of celebration, Community prepared for the funeral march.

The eight who had died were wrapped in the yellow cloth of death and placed upon a moss mat to be carried out to the waters and laid to rest in the ocean. Six would stay behind to care for the twelve near death. No one died alone.

Qorow Low realized she had given birth too early. She should have waited until after The Storm. But to her relief, her little, one and only love, had survived the night.

Qorow Low lovingly held her daughter, Sharhr. "Fear no longer, my beloved. All is well. I am here. The Storm has passed."

What did Sharhr think when she was shaken with such force? Qorow Low had no words to comfort a child who could not possibly understand.

Her baby girl often whimpered in her sleep. She was awake for only a few moments at a time. When she was close enough for her eyes to focus on Qorow Low, Sharhr smiled ever so sweetly.

Qorow Low would remember that smile for all time.

"Who are you, little one? What do you think about? Do you dream when you sleep?"

An hour after a healthy child comes forth, she is walking and talking. Sharhr was four days old. She had not yet talked, laughed, walked, nor ran. All her energy was focused on holding death at bay.

But she could smile.

"Sharhr, I am your life-giver." Qorow Low often reminded her, just in case she forgot.

Then just as Sharhr was about to close her cloudy eyes to once again sleep, Qorow Low hurriedly said, "I love you," just in case those were the last words she heard.

Chapter 41

Jessica Hewitt
Twenty-Seventh Day on Expedition

EVERYTHING ON Akiane takes time. I certainly didn't have other plans. There wasn't a concert or a movie to go to or friends to visit. I wasn't planning on taking a trip somewhere.

The first thing we did before we began our day of celebration was to rescue the other sled. It had our provisions.

After all, what's a celebration without food?

The sled was still wedged between two boulders. The tarp was still securely tied to the sled, but it had been torn to shreds and most of our food had been swept away by the waves, as was the bag of dried fish.

We retuned to the summit with our sled, half a bag dried tupilak, half a bag blubber for cooking, and some dried fruit and frozen vegetables.

On the other side of our island, the gravitational forces of The Storm had produced hot springs. The trek going down was much easier than our path going up.

So we set up camp near the hot springs. The heat from the springs warmed the air almost enough to make us forget just how cold Akiane actually was.

But before we did anything else, we went fishing. Chovis always came first.

"If we don't feed them," Cameron said, "they will leave us."

Once chovis were well fed and happily napping, Cameron decided we should dig a series of pools so the hot water could pour from one pool to another. Thanks to thermal heat, the ground wasn't frozen. The water in each succeeding pool was a little cooler than in the one before it. We washed our clothes in the last pool, then draped them over rocks to dry.

By the time we were done, I was ready for a nap and was willing to sleep through whatever celebration Cameron had planned.

However, Cameron proudly held up what looked like a *wine bottle*. As he gently swayed it back and forth, the glass coloring drifted into different shades of carroty-orange to almost crimson. I was surprised the colonists had the means to make fermented drink.

"What is that?" I asked.

"We drink and we bathe," he said.

"While we bathe? Why not drink it after we're finished bathing?" Drinking alone, while I took a bath, wasn't my idea of a celebration. To me, a celebration was a group of people drinking together even if it was with the two of the most boring people on this planet.

They gave me that look. The one that said we needed a translator—again.

Then the worlds 'we bathe' hit the back of my brain and a cold feeling ran down my spine. "When you say 'we bathe' what do you mean?" I was a bit worried about the answer.

"One does not bathe alone," Cameron said, a little too cheerfully.

"Where I come from, one does!" I said none too pleased at the thought of bathing with strangers. "At least I do!"

"You bathe alone?" To Nu Venia this was as foreign to her as a communal bath was to me.

"I take it you don't," I said.

"Why would one?" she asked.

"Well, we . . . I mean . . ." This was *Akiane*, where *everything* was different. Even so, this was one area in which I had no intention of conforming.

"What?" Cameron asked.

248

I glanced over my shoulder at the hot springs pools of water. "You're planning on the three of us getting in the same pool?"

"Indeed."

"Together?"

"Just so."

"At the same time?"

"Is there a problem?" he asked. His arm and bottle now disappointedly hung at his side.

I know, I shouldn't have been so prudish, but I wasn't going to bathe with aliens.

Cameron gave me his best smile. It was supposed to reassure me. It didn't. "You keep your back to us as we get in. Nu Venia and I will turn our backs as you get in."

I stared up at him, considering. An image of him naked started to form in my mind's eye. I shook it out of my head before it had time to fully form.

"I usually bathe alone," I insisted.

"We have traveled and lived together for some time," Nu Venia said. "I should think we are comfortable enough to bathe together."

I'd lived with Rona for over a year. We'd become reasonably good friends. We ate almost all our meals together. Loved the same man. It never occurred to us to bathe together.

Why would I want to bathe with these people? I cringed at the thought. Up until now I'd been out of the tent when they changed their underclothes. I had been changing under my blankets. There had been no nakedness. I wanted none now.

"You are welcome to remain grimy," he said.

Not a pleasant thought.

"Or you can wait until we are finished and then bathe by yourself," Nu Venia said. "But I cannot guarantee that there will be Laszar left for you."

Cameron held the bottle up and gave it one good shake. Liquid inside swished.

"Laszar?" I asked.

"Drink for warmth of heart," Cameron said. I'd not seen this smile before. It was mysterious and one of expectant pleasure.

That wasn't a bottle filled with just any liquid. It was liquor. He was talking about getting drunk. A hot bath and a strong buzz. That would certainly put a smile on my face and improve my good nature. Tempting. But I'd have to *bathe* with them.

"You may have one taste to see what it is like. But if you do not join us . . ." He shrugged. "I cannot guarantee there will be any left when it is your turn to bathe."

I had a vision of them drinking and laughing in a hot tub and me sitting alone at camp with Essal and her pups.

"Why wait to bring it out now?" I asked.

"What better way to celebrate the day after The Storm than a hot bath with friends and a bottle of Laszar?" Cameron opened the bottle and handed it to me.

I took a tentative sip. Delicious. The inside of my mouth felt warm and tingly. A hot bath and a bottle of liquor would be a true celebration. Akiane's cold and the tediousness of this expedition would be expelled and forgotten, at least for a while.

One of the pools we'd dug was deep and wide enough for all three of us to comfortably fit in. This was the pool Cameron had us work on the hardest.

At the time, I was annoyed and almost quit on him. Now I knew why. The water was hot and welcoming. I gave in.

Chapter 42

Jessica Hewitt
Laszar

I SAT on one of the three rocks Cameron had secured for seating in the pool, and leaned back and let the warm water swirl around me, caressing my body, legs, arms, toes and fingers.

Heavenly.

It was even better after I'd soaped and washed my hair and was clean again. Who would have thought a bath could become such luxury?

"Jessica, would you like a drink?" Cameron held the bottle of Laszar out for me.

"Indeed," I said and gratefully took it.

I was not so timid this time. I drank deeply.

Before it was all the way down my throat, it started back up. I coughed and wheezed as it spilled out my mouth and nose.

"Are you in need of assistance?" Nu Venia asked.

Unashamed of her nakedness, she half-rose with the intention of helping me in my time of need.

Quickly, I waved her away. "I'm fine," I said hoarsely.

She hesitated just a second before settling back down.

Cameron smiled when I took another swallow. Now that I knew what to expect, I drank more carefully. The liquid awakened the inside of my mouth with indescribable flavor sweet and pungent at the same time.

"Takes a little getting used to," I croaked, and handed the bottle back to him. I felt the aftertaste all they way down my throat. One more cough. Then it hit bottom and awakened every fiber of my body

What a pleasant feeling. It was better than when the fish stew warmed me.

"It really wakes up the insides. With a bottle like this, I could spend the rest of my life right here in the hot springs warm and safe," I said.

"It pleases the mind and opens the tongue." Cameron held the bottle high and took a deep drink.

"Loosens the tongue," I corrected, remembering the American idiom.

"What?" he asked.

I thought better of it. "Nothing."

He passed the bottle to Nu Venia.

I closed my eyes. All terror of The Storm drifted away. The torture of this expedition evaporated. For the first time since I'd set foot on this planet, maybe even for the first time in years, I was at peace.

Nu Venia nudged my arm with the bottle. I took it and drank.

"This doesn't bother you, either of you, taking a bath like this, together?" I asked.

Cameron began to un-braid his hair. It was going to take a long time to undo all those braids.

In a very serious tone, Nu Venia said, "Children grow up bathing together. There is no shame, but few life-givers would allow me to bathe or play with their children. Only Cameron's life-giver accepted me." She readjusted her sitting position and helped unbraid Cameron's hair.

"My life-giver believed every child was a gift," Cameron said.

"When my life-giver died," Nu Venia said, "Cameron's life-giver took me in."

Cameron nodded. "Nu Venia and I have been together since I came forth."

"You came forth?" I sat up in surprise. "Who is older?" All this time, I thought he was the older and she was *his* charge.

"I am," Nu Venia said, "by 2 years."

"How old are the two of you?" I casually asked. I figured a little exchange of personal information couldn't hurt.

"He's twelve," Nu Venia said.

My head popped up, my eyes widened.

"Is something wrong?" Cameron asked.

"I'll say. I thought you were 30."

"How old is Adumie?" I asked.

"Adumie is 37 years of age," Cameron said.

"I'd have guessed he was much older," I said.

That couldn't be possible. How could they be so young, but appear so much older? Akiane's years must be different from Earth's.

"Do you consider one rotation around Kahair as a year?"

"No," he said, "we break up the rotation into 11 years."

"So this is your second time experiencing The Storm," I said.

"That is so," Nu Venia said. "The first time, I was very scared, but Cameron . . ." She giggled. "Could not stop crying. He thought his time of living was over. He was too little to understand."

"Nu Venia has raised me since my life-giver died," Cameron said.

"And you're still together," I said.

Nu Venia lowered her head. "No one else will stand with me."

"Why?" I asked. "What makes you different?"

She spoke softly and blushed with shame. "There are two who brought me forth, but I do not know who the other is."

I wanted to reassure her. I certainly wasn't going to judge by an archaic attitude. I was surprised her people still acted like she was an outcast just because her mother had an affair and didn't want to disclose the father's name.

But things were different here and I didn't want to pry and make her feel more uneasy.

"Yeah, that happens. My parents split up because of me," I said. "Sometimes, things just don't work out."

"Your parents?" They exchanged glances.

I kept talking. I figured they'd catch up. "Dad was a good man, kind and gentle. He never yelled or spanked. And believe me, there were times when I rightly deserved it. The only time I ever saw him get angry was when Mom suggested I go to a boarding school. Dad wouldn't send me."

"What is 'boarding school'?" Cameron asked.

Because of the Laszar, I forgot they didn't understand everything I said.

"It's where parents send their children away to get an education. The child only comes home when school is on vacation," I said.

I still remembered the feeling of relief when Dad told me I wasn't going. I had no idea of the coming repercussions of that decision.

"Mom was the one who was usually angry, but for that conversation, she was calm and reasonable. She claimed the boarding school had a better education than public school. I'd make influential friends. It would be good for my future. Now I know she just wanted to be rid of me," I finished. Talking about it wasn't as bad as I thought. There were no tears. No emotion, just words. "Sometimes late at night, I can still hear angry voices,"

For some reason, it felt good to talk. My words were like the steam coming out of a pressure cooker. They eased the tension of the emotions that rambled inside my head.

"Dad turned red-faced with fury. I'd never seen him so angry. Most other arguments, he'd give in to her with an indifferent shrug. That would infuriate her. She said he couldn't stand up and fight like a man. But she'd be just as angry when he did stand up to her. She was always angry about something."

She was always angry with me about everything. I just couldn't get anything right.

"When I asked Dad about it, he'd say if you love someone, you overlook their faults. He really loved Mom. But, Mom didn't return his affection with the same intensity. They fought a lot. Not just because of me. They fought about most everything. If Dad said the sky was blue, she insisted it was gray."

"Is not the sky of your world blue?" Nu Venia asked.

I half smiled. "It's an expression that means they fought for the sake of fighting."

She nodded her understanding.

"One day, Mom had enough and left. Dad quit his teaching job in St. Paul. We moved to Woodlands Village where he could be a stay-at-home dad, and write young adults novels."

"Sounds like Dad loved you very much," Cameron said.

He used Dad as if it was my father's proper name. I didn't bother to explain that Dad was a nickname for father and father was a designation.

Dad's name was Loy Hewitt, which meant nothing to them.

"Yes, but he loved Mom more. He missed her terribly. Sometimes I heard him talking to her picture." And just in case they didn't know what a picture was, I said, "He kept a likeness of her on a small table next to his bed."

I didn't know why I was telling them this. I'd never told anyone else, not my fiancé, not Rona, not even Jorge, but for some reason, I couldn't stop talking.

"He changed after Mom left. It was a long time before his old-self returned and he laughed again. Even then, he was never truly the same." I still felt bad about that. "It was my fault they split up. If not for me, they'd have stayed together."

"How was it your fault?" Nu Venia asked.

"I was born. I was an accident. Mom never wanted children. I don't think they argued before I came along. Dad kept me out of obligation, which I'm sure he often regretted. I was a pretty horrid teenager."

"I don't believe that is true," Cameron said.

"What, that I was a horrid teenager?"

"No, that Dad preferred Mom over you."

"Oh. That. Why not?" What did he know? Telling them was a mistake. I should have kept my mouth shut. I took another drink and passed the bottle on.

"Dad loved you more than Mom, or Dad would have sent you to boarding school and stayed with Mom," Cameron said. He took a drink. "But he kept you and declined to send you away."

He passed the bottle to Nu Venia.

"I'd never thought of it like that," I said a bit surprise. I'd always thought Dad didn't have a choice, but I guess he did. He could have sent me away. He chose to keep me instead.

That was a profound revelation.

But just as I was accepting the fact that Dad might have really loved me, Mom's angry face loomed. Rejection settled in like an old unwelcome friend. It hit me harder than the Laszar.

More words came out. "I wrote Mom a letter asking her why she left, but I didn't know where to send it. I placed the letter in a book for safekeeping. Dad found it. I thought he'd scold me. Instead, he held me in his arms. We sat in a rocking chair and cried together."

I paused, remembering that moment, the warmth of his body, his strong arms, his smell. He used to hold me when he'd read one of my books to me, but that night was the last time we sat like that. I didn't remember if that was by his choice or mine.

Probably mine.

"Dad said crying wouldn't bring Mom back."

Then I remembered. It *was* my choice.

"It hurt to see him crying. It hurt him to see me crying. I didn't want to hurt him ever again, so I stopped asking about Mom. I stopped crying and haven't cried since."

And I never sat in his lap again. He must have thought I was rejecting him, when in reality, I was trying to give him space.

"You cannot make a person hate you any more than you can make a person love you. Neither you nor Mom were at fault," Cameron said. "Mom's heart was too small and incapable of loving. There was nothing you could do about it."

"It's not my fault." That revelation flipped over and over inside my brain.

Dad had tried to tell me. I'd tried to convince myself, but somehow it just wouldn't sink in, not until that moment, on an alien planet, bathing with aliens, drinking alien liquor. Was it that easy? Tears threatened. Nu Venia handed me the bottle. I took another long swig. Tears vanished. I passed the bottle on.

The emotional turmoil in my heart was truly a Storm moment for me. I felt old crusty guilt and rejection crumbling from my heart. For one second, I thought I was free. Ah, but then shame came tumbling in, laughing at me. *"You may have beat Rejection, but you will never be free of me. It is your fault he's dead. You killed him."*

"Jessica?" Nu Venia softly asked.

"I was so mean to him, so uncooperative," I said. "Every day, I let Dad know I hated Woodlands Village. I couldn't wait to get out of there and leave it and him behind." My heart constricted at the shame. Dad let the love of his life leave so he could keep me, and I walked out on him as soon as I was old enough. I truly was a horrid daughter.

"He gave up everything for me, and I gave him up for adventure. Then I betrayed him for love," I said.

Shame pulled me back to the worst day of my life, the moment of my betrayal and Dad's death.

It must have shown on my face. Cameron and Nu Venia stared at me, worried for my well-being. How could I tell them? How could I not?

Maybe if I had more courage.

I reached for the bottle, Nu Venia handed it to me. I took a long drink. Then another. The liquid forced its way down my throat, hit bottom, and the words came out of my mouth, before I had time to stop them. "Dad's dead because of me. I killed him."

There it was.

Everyone had said it was a tragic accident. I'd kept the truth hidden. My friends, family, and even the media. Now twenty-seven light-years away, the shame of the truth was out.

Shame was the real reason I'd kept everyone at arm's length. I couldn't bear them knowing. Seeing the truth on their faces, and the rejected of those I loved.

Even though we had lived in the same room for over a year, I'd never truly been Rona's friend. I had been afraid to let her in. Therefore, I rejected her. I criticized and belittled her as I did everyone. Maybe I didn't say it out loud but I certainly thought it.

Deep in my heart, I knew Jorge liked me best but I refused to give in to that belief or even pursue the possibility.

If I didn't like myself, how could I dare to hope that he'd love me? I feared if he truly knew me, he wouldn't be able to stand me.

My rock-hard heart cracked. Would shame seep out? It couldn't. I'd lived with it for so long. It owned me. It was the reason I'd run from Earth, family, and friends, joined the space program, and volunteered for the Akiane Project. How could I ever be free? How could I ever forgive myself?

"How did Dad die?" Nu Venia softly asked.

I knew I was drinking more than my share, but I couldn't help myself. Then it hit my brain and just like Cameron had said, my tongue loosened.

"I hate all dis, cold, snow, all dis." I waved my hand about, there seemed to be more than one hand on my wrist, but they moved too fast to count.

"When old, I moved sout. Far sout, to Bajaaa. The desert am ocean." I pointed over my shoulder. "Waves, year round. When torm comes waves gib." I swished all my hands up to show them. "Yours gibber." I sounded strange. Something was different about my speech, but I couldn't tell what.

Cameron's eyes narrowed. He reached for the bottle. I don't think he believed me about the waves. No matter.

He took the bottle from me.

"Dad lived far nort, lots of snnnow and coooldd. When thaw snows, gets muddy, mis ... mis ..." That wasn't right. "Mo..." that was it. "Mo-squi-toesss come. Suck blood dry.

Drives animmils crazy. Rive me crazy." I reached for the bottle.

Cameron shook his head. "Finish first."

"Ho Kayee. I visit-ted Dad between mooo-squitoo-esss and, and snnow. Never come to me." I shook my head as Nu Venia and Cameron swam around me. "Finally, I con . . ." What was that word? Ah. ". . . consenced him. He camed. Like desert. The rains, bloom every, everrry . . . where. Waves mall." I showed them by patting the air down.

In my memory, I saw Dad standing ankle deep in the Pacific Ocean. The little waves sweeping over the sand swirled around his feet. *That was the last time I saw him,* I remembered. The vision kicked the Laszar out of me.

"He stood in the water watching the waves come in. I should have been with him." I paused as emotion rose like one of Baja's winter waves. I hadn't cried since Mom's letter.

I thought I might cry right then, but tears stopped just short of reaching the outer rims of my eyes, and seemed to fall inward.

"I was in love. To be married. We were on the beach laughing about something. I don't remember what. I wasn't watching Dad. When I looked back—he was gone." I fell silent.

There. My sin was out. Dad had given up love for me and I'd let him die because of love.

"I don't understand," Nu Venia asked.

"He had never been in the ocean before. He didn't know how strong the current could be. He was old and frail. He must have fallen. It would have been easy for the current to drag him out to sea before anyone realized he was in trouble."

"Dad was an adult, not a child to be watched over," Cameron said. "You could not have known."

They were trying to use logic to convince me that Dad's death was not my fault, but they were wrong. It was my fault.

All my fault.

"I should have been with him," I said. "If I had been with him."

"Then what?" Cameron asked.

"Then he would be alive! And I would be on Earth. I wouldn't be here with . . ." I paused and sheepishly said, "with you."

"If Dad was old, he would have died at some point," Cameron said.

"Many of our people have died," Nu Venia said sadly. I thought she was sympathizing with me. "They die slow and painfully," she finished.

"So I'm supposed to be happy because he died quickly?" I asked, offended at her statement. "I didn't even get to say good-bye. You at least get to say good-bye. I didn't get to. One second he was there and the next he was gone." I snapped my fingers. "Just like that."

Cameron asked, "On the day, was Dad sad?"

"No." I shook my head. "It was the happiest week he'd had in a long time. We hadn't seen each other for a while. We hugged and laughed. He kept patting me on the arm, my leg, my cheek, like he couldn't believe we were finally together again. I was going to ask him to stay and not go back. I think he would have said yes. Dad loved the ocean. He was like a little kid, we couldn't get him out of the water."

"You couldn't get him out of the water?" Nu Venia asked. "I do not understand."

I stared at her. I didn't understand either. That day was like a fog. Perhaps because I never thought of it. I'd refused to. But now, for the very first time, I thought about the day my father died, then all those years faded and I remembered as if it were yesterday.

"I had been in the water with him. We'd walked up the beach to get ice cream. Chad stayed with our things." The scene unfolded before my eyes. "We walked back in the water because the sand was hot for his feet. I'd gone to get his shoes so he could walk to the blanket and sit. I gave Chad his drink. He said something funny. We laughed. I gave him a quick kiss, picked up Dad's shoes, and turned around. He was gone. Chad had been watching me, so he didn't see what had happened."

"It wasn't your fault," Cameron said. "You were taking care of him by retrieving his shoes."

"It wasn't your fault," Nu Venia confirmed.

I was confused. Their words . . . I heard their words. They made sense. Family members had said the same thing, but I just couldn't accept it. Shame wouldn't let the truth in.

Maybe it was the Laszar, because I said, "It's not my fault."

And for the first time, I believed.

"Dad died happy," Cameron said.

"Dad died happy." I'd never considered the possibility.

"A person cannot ask for a better end to one's life than to die happy. My life-giver died slowly, in agony," Cameron said.

"As did mine," Nu Venia said.

"All this time, I've been afraid that Dad was angry with me for neglecting him."

I blamed myself for Dad's death because I was sure he blamed me. But it was me who blamed me, not Dad. An enormous weight lifted from my shoulders. I felt so light! I was surprised I didn't float out of the pool.

Chapter 43

Jessica Hewitt
In the Tent

WE WERE dressed, sitting outside our tents, enjoying what little warmth Kahair had to offer.

Nu Venia was behind Cameron re-braiding the hair at back of his head while he braided the hair down his sides. They were meticulous. Each braid was the exact same size.

A pleasant smile lingered on his lips softening his face. I barely remembered what the hard-faced warrior looked like. Cameron had softened into a mellow teddy bear. Who would have thought?

Nu Venia finished a braid and separated the next set of strands. At almost the same moment, he too finished, but instead of starting another braid, he rested his hands in his lap.

"I am sorry for forcing the two of you on Woden," he said. "The importance of this Woden is not fully realized by those of Endurance. If there had been understanding, no one would have objected."

"What?" I asked, jumping out of my complacent mode. "Who objected?"

A guilty "oops" spread across his face. He tilted his head to one side and grinned sheepishly.

"Better tell me. I have the bottle." I held the long neck between my thumb and forefinger and swung it gently back and forth. We'd decided not to finish it in the bath but wait until we were sitting on the rocks, fully dressed, relaxing in Kahair's light.

"There is only a little left." I smiled as if we were long-time friends. It was a strange feeling, regarding them as friends. When we started this trip, I could barely stand to look at them, let alone have a civil conversation with them.

Nu Venia giggled. "One must enlighten Jessica before all is consumed."

Cameron hesitated. "There may be nothing left after certain words are spoken." His smile was warm and friendly.

I'd shivered the first time I saw him smile. Now, I smiled back. Had we become friends? They'd saved my life twice. We'd survived The Storm and taken a bath together. Perhaps it was time to be friends. How times had changed.

I brought the neck of the bottle up to my eye. "Mmmm, I think there's enough for several small drinks for each of us or just one long swig for me."

"Chances will have to be taken." Nu Venia spoke with the seriousness of one assisting in a delicate operation.

Gripping the neck and shaking the bottle at him, I threatened, "Tell me or I drink."

Cameron sighed as if being forced to do some terrible deed. "It was believed that you would want to follow in Striken's footsteps."

Striken was the priest and second in command to Captain Assetti. Assetti was the only captain to survive the first landing on Akiane. Those two had gone on the first Woden together. They were gone for so long the settlers feared they were dead. But they returned very much alive and victorious.

The colonists thought I wanted to be just like him? Why?

"And just how did such a belief come into existence?" Surprisingly, I wasn't angry. It must have been the liquor, or perhaps it was our new friendship. Stranger things had happened.

Cameron gave me another sheepish grin. He didn't need to say. I knew he was the one. I shook my head.

"An Earth priest was requested," he said. "It was thought such a one would bring healing and life to those of Endurance as Striken once had."

My arm dropped to my knee. "What Earth priest?"

Nu Venia froze in mid braid. Cameron leaned slightly forward. They got that all too familiar, *we need a translator,* look.

"Are you not the Earth priest?" Cameron asked as if his bubble of hope had burst. "An Earth priest was requested."

"Well, you got me instead." I shrugged. "As far as I know, the ship's priest, now called counselor, and he or she might be of any religion, is still onboard ship." I shook my head. "Sorry."

"It was thought that you spoke for the Holy One. That you would want to make such a journey," he said.

"See, that doesn't make sense. Adumie is so against me and my friends, why would he ask the captain for a priest from Earth?"

"Adumie did not request your presence, the request was Jecidia's," Nu Venia said.

That old man sure got around. When I first met him, he, Adumie, and Cameron escorted us through the habitat to our living area. A couple of days later, Jecidia walked me into one of the main buildings, down a hall to the commons area, where all the colonists, Cameron and Nu Venia, were waiting for me. From that conversation I got conned into Woden.

Now I learn that old man ordered me up and served me like an old fashioned cheeseburger to his people.

"Why Jecidia?" I asked.

"Jecidia was leader," Cameron said with pride. "Now Adumie is leader." The same pride did not linger on Adumie's name.

"Because Jecidia became too old to lead," I guessed.

"Jecidia is younger than Adumie," Nu Venia said.

"Younger? How is that possible?" Did age mean nothing to these people?

"Jecidia is sick," Cameron said, "and became too fragile to lead."

"Rona saw some children who were sick," I said. "You also mentioned this illness before. What is it?"

Nu Venia retuned to braiding Cameron's hair.

"We do not know the source," Cameron said. "It kills slowly. Some die more slowly than others. No one knows why. Jecidia has been sick for a very long time. There is much pain, much difficulty in walking, breathing, eating, and living. Death comes very slowly for Jecidia."

That didn't sound good. I couldn't begin to imagine living like that, in constant pain where the only relief is death.

"But I was told he asked for me by name. How did he know I was onboard ship?" I asked.

"He didn't," Cameron said.

"I don't understand." I truly didn't.

"Jecidia wanted one like Father Striken who hears Holy One's voice and spoke for him. Jecidia asked for a Jezhuit."

I stared at him for a long time before I finally understood what he meant by Jezhuit.

"Do you mean Jesuit?" I asked. "A Jesuit is a Catholic priest. I'm not Catholic, I'm not a Jesuit, and I'm certainly no priest. So how come *I'm* here?"

Now it was their time to stare at me in disbelief.

Finally, Cameron said, "A Jezhuit was requested."

When he said Jesuit, he stressed the S into a Z and dropped in the hint of a W behind a silent H. Jezhuit sounded lot like Jess Hewitt.

So I asked, "Did Jecidia send text?"

"Text? I am unsure. I was not there. I always believed Jecidia spoke with your captain."

"He did not speak directly to my captain. He spoke to a communication tech, who relayed the message to Captain Norris. Somehow the tech misunderstood and told the captain that he asked for me by name."

We stared at each other stunned by this new revelation.

I broke the silence. "I'm here by mistake!"

Unbelievable.

So many things had gone wrong in my life because of the bad choices I'd made. Now I find my life had been turned upside down because someone was too dumb to know what a Jesuit priest is.

I placed the bottle on the ground, stood, and paced.

"I didn't belong on this trip," I said. "You're wrong about God wanting *me*. I'm not the one you were hoping for!"

"When we return victorious, you will speak to the Community," Cameron said.

"I'm here by mistake. What would God have me say?"

"That my people must accept help from Earth." He didn't wait for me to object. "We are a dying people. I have prayed. We have all prayed. Holy One has sent you to bring the cure to save us."

"You mean the scientists from Earth," I corrected him.

"No, you The Jezhuit."

I burst into laughter at the absurdity. "Me, a priest?" I said with full sarcasm. "I don't think God would have me." I would have continued to laugh, but for the seriousness of their hurt expressions.

The shock of my denial seemed to have frozen them in place. Nu Venia held a braid in her hands. Cameron sat so still, he appeared to have turned to stone.

"I'm sorry, but I'm not a priest. I don't understand why you would think I am."

"Jecidia asked for a Jezhuit," Cameron said. "You came."

"I know but that's not what happened," I said. "The radio person misunderstood Jecidia. When he mispronounced Jesuit, the technician thought he said Jess Hewitt. I'm out here because of some idiot's mistake."

"Mistakes are not made by Holy One," Cameron said.

"What?" I sat down. "You've got to be kidding me. It's as plain as Kahair's rising in the eastern sky: I'm the wrong person for the job."

"There was a person on that transport named Jess Hewitt," he said.

Now it was my turn to freeze at his words. He was right. For my entire life, I had been Jessica. The only time I'd been called Jess was on that ship. Someone got sick at the last minute, and I was assigned to the bridge.

There were two other Jessicas by the time I arrived. On duty we were referred to by our last name or rank, but there were those who called us by our first names when off duty.

Phyllis Moore

Since I was the last to arrive, I lost the right to be called Jessica or even Jessie. My name became Jess.

I was sitting right under the captain's nose as Jess Hewitt when Jecidia's request arrived.

"But I'm not a priest. Why would God want me?" I asked.

For all my life, I'd been unimportant. The thought of God wanting me for anything made me feel even more insignificant. I knew I wasn't capable of fulfilling His mission. I couldn't take care of my own life. How was I going to take care of something He wanted?

"Holy One knows what you are capable of," Cameron said as if he'd heard my thoughts.

Reassured, they returned to braiding his hair. It might have been that simple for them, but it wasn't for me.

I stared at them. "I don't understand. What can I do that no one else could?"

"You will save my people," Cameron said as if it was the most natural thing for me to do.

"How am I supposed to do that?" I insisted.

"When the time comes, you will know," he said.

"Saving people is Rona's job, *not mine!*" I firmly protested. "I'm no medic. I don't have the training or knowledge."

He simply smiled.

I was just beginning to like that smile but, right then, it was most annoying.

Blind faith. What a fruitless way to conduct one's life.

"Your people hate me!" I exclaimed.

"You are feared," Cameron said, "not hated."

"Explain." I took my last swig. Then handed the bottle to him.

He accepted, drank, and passed it to Nu Venia. She finished it.

"Earth is powerful enough to trek across space and heartless enough to abandon its own," he said.

"But we didn't..." I started to explain.

Cameron cut me off. "Yes, I know. You believed all were dead. Yet, we are not. With your arrival comes much fear of who you are and what you desire of us. Woden is a journey to overcome that fear."

"Explain," I repeated.

"Assetti and Striken made a dangerous and impossible walk across Akiane to learn of the land and bring back knowledge of this planet," Nu Venia said. "They returned from the dead. There was much rejoicing and honor."

"When they began Woden, we were not in Community," Cameron said. "Upon their return, there was understanding between those two that spread to the rest of our people."

"There must be more to the story," I said.

"They brought with them the food of life," Cameron said.

"What is that?" I asked.

"The first settlers also developed an illness and were dying," Cameron said. "That which Assetti and Striken found cured them."

When we first met back at the habitat, in the commons room, Nu Venia spoke with such passion of how Earth had abandoned Pegasus Colony as if it had happened yesterday. Now Cameron spoke with the same intensity about the future. His eyes were bright with excitement and faith that we would succeed, that I would succeed.

"You're expecting us to do the same thing?" I asked.

"Indeed," he said. "When we return, we will receive great honor, as did Assetti and Striken. Community will listen when we speak."

"Cameron expects too much." Nu Venia dropped her head in sadness and sat back.

He seemed to shrink under her disapproval.

"Sorry, Cameron, but I agree with her," I said. "We—I've barely survived this trip. I'm not sure I'll survive the rest of it."

That of course depended on just how much longer Cameron wanted to continue Woden. I wasn't sure how much more of it I could take.

He stared at me.

Maybe if Nu Venia and I worked together, we might convince him to turn back.

"I'm here under false pretences. You didn't even ask me if I wanted to come along," I continued. "You tricked me."

"It was not meant to be a trick. You were the one who suggested Woden," he said.

"I didn't know what I was saying or what was at stake. All I wanted to do was finish negotiations so I could be on *Britannia* when she returned to WSC Moon Base. I didn't know what a Woden was. I still don't."

"Woden is a journey to prove one's worth and to make Community," he said. "When we return, we prove we are worthy to be heard when we speak."

"And what are the stakes?" I asked.

"Stakes?" Cameron asked.

"What happens if we don't finish the journey?" I asked.

"My people's lives are at stake," he said. "All will die."

"Even so, you didn't ask for my help, *you tricked me.*"

Despite his reasoning, I wanted some acknowledgment of what he'd done.

"I am repentant," he said, and bowed his head.

His apology was a bit late considering all we'd been through. I should have still been upset with him. He needed to pay. But I forgave him.

"Nevertheless, I'm here by mistake. I don't hear from God and I don't speak for God. That throws your whole plan out in the snow. I don't know what good I can do to help your people," I said. "What good will I be if I freeze to death or drown out here?" If only he understood what I was trying to say.

I watched as he considered my words. Was I getting through to him? His face shifted as he processed his thoughts. At first he seemed confused, then resolved. Was this it? Had he decided in my favor?

He smiled reassuringly and his eyes were determined.

"There was prayer by Community. Jecidia requested a priest. You came."

Incredible.

He had not heard a word I'd said. For a second, I thought I'd convinced him. Instead, he was more convinced.

"How many times must I tell you, *I'm here by mistake,*" I desperately tried to get through to him. "I know nothing."

"Holy One does not make mistakes but has chosen you to save my people."

"And just how am I supposed to do that?"

"When we return, you will know," he said.

Not the answer I wanted.

We were two immovable forces, his blind faith versus my lack of it.

We were doomed.

Chapter 44

Rona Montgomery
Alien Retrovirus

TWENTY-SEVEN light-years from home and Rona was reliving a recurring nightmare, where she stood in front of the class without the answers and everyone was laughing at her.

She had parts of the problem to Zhoa's death, not the whole picture. She could conjure up theories, but was unable to come to a definite conclusion. Her mission for this meeting was to pick her words carefully and reassure her friends they were safe.

I wish I had more information to give them. She sighed.

People settled into chairs or sat on the floor. Normally, dogs didn't come into the eating area, but since no one was eating, they were everywhere, reminding her of an old saying, *Lie down with dogs and you'll get up with fleas.* It was in reference to making the wrong kinds of friends. She couldn't help but wonder if, in this case, the *fleas* might just be the retrovirus.

Olivia sat on a chair while her dog companion lay at her feet. One dog rested her head on Beth's thigh. Another lay across Tam's outstretched legs as he sat on the floor. Dogs walked around sniffing at chairs, legs, feet, and each other. Occasionally, one nudged another out of the way. That one would get up and sniff the area again before settling in a new place.

Lu pulled her hair behind her right ear. The tip of her tongue peeked from between her lips. Her fingers sped over the wireless keyboard. An image of the retrovirus that had killed Zhoa appeared on the wall behind Rona.

Spago sat with his arm draped over the back of Lu's chair and watched her.

Those two were becoming close. Rona was sure that hug of relief Lu gave Spago when he came in from the blizzard had not been the beginning of their relationship but it did bring it out into the open. And there was that kiss he'd given her. Since then, they'd spent more time together and were showing more signs of public affection.

Angrily, Vong slumped back on the chair next to Lesley, folded his arms over his chest, and hung his head. Showing he didn't care what Rona had to say. Zhoa's death had changed the normally good-natured Vong. Now, he was perpetually angry and often spoke coarsely. He hated Akiane and its people. He wanted to go home. Rona wasn't about to tell him that might not be possible.

Depending on the outcome of the final analysis, if the retrovirus was contagious, WSC would quarantine everyone to the planet for fear of transporting the retrovirus to Earth and causing a pandemic. There was a strong possibility that none of them would ever leave Akiane.

Another Earthling would never set foot on the planet again.

This was definitely not what Rona had signed up for.

What did I expect? She reprimanded herself, *that none of us would die? That Akiane would be a bed of roses? That all of us would return home safe and sound? Yes. That's exactly what I expected.* What she hadn't expected were the thorns. This was not supposed to be a dangerous mission. Unfortunately, things had become dangerous.

These were her friends—no, they were family. She'd cried when Jess left, but at least there was the possibility of her returning, no matter how remote. Zhoa was gone and would never return. He was wrapped in a makeshift body bag, in the cooler, waiting for his return to Earth. How could Rona stand it if anyone else died?

The crowd settled, patiently waiting for her to begin. She took a deep breath.

"Zhoa died of a retroviral infection that's native to Akiane. We've never seen anything like it before. It's not in our database, and we're not completely sure how it works, at least not yet. Lu and I are still doing research."

It stood to reason that the colonists' DNA would be slightly different. When a populace is isolated from the general population, as the colonists had been isolated from Earth for 318 years, the colonists' DNA would have mutated naturally, which is call a genetic divergence.

That's what Rona had come to Akiane to study, the colonists' genetic differences. Now she was about to speak on the genetic mutation of a retrovirus, which had caused Zhoa's death. She didn't understand the retrovirus well enough to come to a clear conclusion, nor formulate a hypothesis.

The image on the wall from Lu's computer showed a bright green-yellow disk with tiny spikes protruding from it. The middle sank in, thickening the outer edges.

Olivia rose from her seat. Her copper curls bounced as she hurried to her workspace.

What was she up to? Rona wondered. *Surely she wasn't so heartless as to just walk away.*

"Here," Rona pointed to the image on the wall while she kept an eye on Olivia. "This is the culprit. Interestingly, we found the same thing in the dogs."

Olivia returned with her com wristband.

"When we first examined the dogs, the HMS couldn't identify the retrovirus because it wasn't in its database. As we continued to examine dogs, we came to the conclusion that the retrovirus is natural to them."

"What is the bases for your conclusion?" Mathieu asked.

"There are no signs of illness. As an example, their white blood count is low," Lu said.

"And the HMS accepted the retrovirus as normal for the dogs," Rona said. "HMS identified the same retrovirus in Zhoa. We took samples of his blood and entered the data into the HMS. We have since sedated three dogs and taken a sample of their blood."

"So you thought three dogs were a good start," Olivia asked. She retook her seat next to Jorge. Her keypad appeared. She began tapping.

Puzzled, Jorge strained his neck to see what she was doing.

"No. What we wanted was a live sample of the retrovirus from the dogs," Rona said.

"But Zhoa didn't have any contact with the dogs." Vong spoke as if defending his brother's honor from a distasteful deed.

Then his voice softened as he fondly remembered his brother. "He liked dogs, but Akiane dogs seemed to hate him." Vong's head rose, then quickly hung back down. "They avoided him, me too, for that matter."

Rona thought she saw his eyes glisten. That was the real reason Vong was surly; he was fighting his emotions. Yet, a good healthy cry was just what he needed.

"We don't think he got it from the dogs," Rona said. "If they were contagious, most of us would have similar symptoms."

"We've checked all of us; no one is ill," Lu said.

Olivia projected a new image onto the wall next to the image of the retrovirus already there.

"This retrovirus comes from the fish," she said.

The images were identical.

"But Zhoa never touched a fish," Vong objected loudly. He sat on the edge of his chair and intently examined the slides.

"Tupilak must eat fish," Olivia said. "We should check the meat for retrovirus."

"We considered the tupilak," Rona said, "but all the meat has been cooked, dried, or smoked. There's nothing raw for us to examine. And since the colonists have stopped bringing us meat . . ." She shrugged. "So unless they drag another tupilak into the bay area, we can only speculate." She paused before she continued. "But Lu and I agree that the tupilak could be the cause for the colonists' illness and for Zhoa's . . ." she couldn't bring herself to say death.

"Zhoa was wearing his antimicrobial clothing. He always did." Vong objected to Zhoa getting the retrovirus from the meat.

"Yes," Mathieu said. "We all do. Antimicrobial clothing protects us from viruses, retrovirus, germs, and allergens that we know about on Earth. We know nothing about alien retroviruses, germs, and allergens. Even though the clothing was designed to protect us from the unknown, we are on an alien planet. Something could easily get through and infect us."

"But if it's in the meat, shouldn't all of us be sick?" Avil sounded alarmed.

Many were frightened by the possibility.

They know this, Rona thought, *but they're still scared, and want me to reassurance them.*

Something else she hadn't expected.

"Cooking makes meat safe," Rona said.

"How long does the meat have to be cooked?"

"Yes, and at what temperature?" another asked.

Twice, we've told them they are safe, Rona thought. *But they're not listening. They've got cotton in their ears.*

"As Lu and I have just said, we've checked everyone. All of us are healthy."

"Zhoa insisted we cook everything thoroughly," Vong said. "We never served anything raw or rare. Not even the vegetables. He said it was a precaution just in case there was something that didn't agree with us Earthlings." He leaned forward and rested his elbows on his knees, hiding his face in his hands.

Many shifted uneasily in their chairs. A few checked their hands and arms for the same tiny red bumps that Zhoa had when his rash first started.

"Mathieu and Lesley helped butcher the meat," Jorge said. "They aren't sick."

"We wore scrubs." Mathieu said. "We did it as a joke, but it may have saved our lives." He ran a trembling hand over his face.

"What do you mean?" Jorge asked.

"Zhoa cut his hand," Lesley said. "He cleaned up right away and sprayed a protective band aid on the cut but he kept working bare-handed."

"It happened sometime when we first started butchering the meat," Mathieu said.

Vong examined his hands. He stared at his left hand for a long time.

"We think that's how the retrovirus got into his system, through the cut," Rona said. "And since he continued to work barehanded, he continued to re-infect himself. But unless we get the chance to test raw meat, we can only speculate."

That bit of information seemed to settle the group, just a little. None of them had handled raw meat.

"A virus breaks down DNA and inserts new information into the it, thereby changing the course of the host's DNA and its function. It's usually no more serious than a bad flu." Rona pointed to the images behind her. "This is a retrovirus."

"What's a retrovirus?" Olivia asked in the same tone a teacher would test her student.

She knew but she asked so Rona would define the retrovirus in more detail. It was annoying but Olivia was right, not everyone would know what a retrovirus was.

"A retrovirus infects the host's genome and tricks the host's DNA into replicating the retrovirus. This retrovirus is more aggressive than anything we've ever seen on Earth," Rona said. "It took over Zhoa's body faster than any one of us could have predicted."

"We think the stress of the gravitational storm may have accelerated the infection," Lu said.

"A retrovirus synthesis an enzyme called reverse-transcriptase before it can begin the process of duplicating itself," Lesley said. "The retrovirus infected Zhoa's DNA but the DNA message to duplicate it got confused."

Vong's left hand dropped. He head popped up. "What does that mean?"

"The enzyme isn't working," Rona said. "The retrovirus started to recode Zhoa's DNA but it never finished the process, His DNA just fell apart."

"Zhoa's insides were . . ." Lesley paused unsure if he should continue.

Mathieu shrugged. "Might as well tell them, it's vital information to help solve the problem," he said. "Sorry, Vong. If it wasn't important, we wouldn't say anything."

"I understand."

Lesley continued, "It was the worst we've ever seen. His heart was mush. His pancreas and spleen were like jelly. His liver had completely dissolved."

"We agree that it may have been fear spiking his adrenalin, because of the ground-quakes, that accelerated the spread of the infection," Mathieu said. "But still . . ." He shook his head. "There's got to be more to the story."

"How could the retrovirus infect his whole body if it wasn't duplicating it self?" Gino asked.

"That's the problem," Rona said. "We don't know. We need more time to fully understand it."

"How come the colonists aren't all dead?" Vong spoke accusingly.

"They're already dying," Rona said gently.

"Many of them have the same gray blotchy skin as Zhoa did," Lu said. "The mystery is how have they managed to survive for three centuries without dying out."

"Are the parents passing the retrovirus to their children?" Jorge asked.

"Retrovirus are not inherited by the next generations," Rona said. "But this retrovirus is new to us. We're not sure what it does. There's more to this story that we don't understand. It would help if we could examine the colonists but I don't think they're going to let Lu or me do that anytime soon. The only thing we know for sure is that they're dying. And if they won't let us help, there's nothing we can do to save them."

Chapter 45

Rona Montgomery
Tupilak

RONA AND Lu were sitting on the floor excitedly leaning in toward their holo-screen. The first two chovis to disappear off their tracking radar had reappeared. Their bleeps came from the ocean heading directly to the habitat.

"They're not returning from the same place they entered the ocean," Lu said.

"Well, the snow and ice are gone so I guess they had to come back on shore from some place else," Rona said. "It's good to know they're not dead after all."

"If only we could ask them where they'd been," Lu said.

She did a happy wiggle with her arms and shoulders, her upper body swayed in rhythm while her bottom remained firmly settled on the floor.

"Now if they let us scan them, we'll see if there's anything new about their physiology since we first examined them as puppies," Rona said.

The bleeps moved around the habitat to the southeast side. The dogs were headed for the tunnel entrance closest to the scientists' living quarters.

Rona straightened her back. "Don't you think it's odd how unswervingly they're traveling," she said. "Dogs usually roam and backtrack."

"Yes, and they aren't stopping to examine or sniff anything along the way." Lu tapped the screen. "They don't seem to have a heartbeat, or blood pressure, either. If I didn't know any better, I'd say they're dead."

"See, Lu, now that's odd. Don't you think?" Rona said with a grin.

Without changing pace, the bleeps entered the southeast entrance and moved through the garden toward the bay door.

"They seem to be headed directly toward us. Maybe they know we want to examine them," Rona said teasingly.

Lu giggled. "Maybe, they're zombies come to eat us."

Rona didn't laugh. "Guess we'll find out, they're almost here."

The women turned to faced the bay door.

Eight colonists—eight *angry* colonists—entered the scientists' living quarters dragging two un-gutted, un-skinned tupilak behind them.

A dozen adult dogs and puppies trotted alongside.

"Great," Rona whispered. "Two of those dogs are ours, but we can't check to see which ones. Their owners won't let us."

Leading the group was Adumie. Like a massive angry bull, he was a man out to roll heads.

He stopped, held something for all to see and demanded, "What is this?" It was too small to see between his thick green-gloved fingers.

But Rona knew it was the radio tags that she and Lu had been following. He must have found them and taken the tags off the dogs. Since they were no longer properly attached, it would explain why they'd stopped recording vital signs.

Rona started to stand.

To her surprise, usually timid Lu stood first and said, "That's ours."

"Why?" Adumie yelled and growled at the same time.

Rona cringed. Why is he so angry?

Lu took a step backward as if his voice had pushed her.

Their friends stopped what they were doing. Mathieu moved to stand next to Rona and helped her to her feet. Gino and Jorge flanked her and Lu. More friends gathered around for moral support.

"W-we are tr-r-acking the d-dogs to see where they tr-r-raveled." Lu stuttered.

"What is ours is none of your concern." Adumie took several threatening steps directly toward her.

Lu was like a delicate rose in a charging bull's path.

Ever-gallant Jorge moved to stand in front of Lu. She peeked around him. Spago and a teammate joined him. Were they planning to fight this man? The colonist was a full head taller than Jorge with a hundred pounds more muscle and he was not alone.

In a confident swagger, Vong joined the men. After Zhoa's death, he'd been passionately practicing his martial arts with such intensity that none dared spar with him. If the rumors about his abilities were true, he might easily bring Adumie down. A warrior smile creased Vong's face. He was ready for battle. The fact that Adumie was at least twice his size didn't hamper his confidence.

"What's the problem?" Gino casually asked. He patted Vong on the back as he passed him. Gino motioned for rest to fall back. Reluctantly, they obeyed.

Disappointed at the loss of a good fight, Vong was the last to retreat.

"You have no right to claim what is ours as yours," Adumie yelled. "We have freely given you tupilak and a place to live. You have no need to steal from us."

Rona wished he'd explain exactly what he meant. Then maybe they could rectify the situation and mend a few fences.

"I don't believe the women were trying to claim anything as theirs." Gino motioned to the women to confirm.

"No," Rona and Lu said together. Rona gave him a quick, grateful smile. Gino could be playfully gruff, but when he wanted to, he easily took control of a situation and made everything better.

"Why?" Adumie asked with the same intense anger.

Gino motioned for Rona to stand next to Lu. Mathieu followed. Jorge stepped aside.

"I ... we ...," Lu began.

Rona said, "Lu and I were tracking your male dogs."

"Male dogs?" Adumie asked.

Rona pointed to a dog.

"Chovis," Adumie roughly corrected her.

Chovis. Rona remembered the colonists telling them that chovis ate fish. No wonder the dogs never begged for meat. It was logical since tupilak were marine animals that they ate fish. Now she learned chovis also eat fish. Olivia said the fish had the retrovirus. Since both tupilak and chovis have the retrovirus, it was also a logical to assume that fish must be the source. She and Lu would have to examine some of Olivia's fish more closely.

"Lu noticed that all your chovis are female." Rona finally found her voice. "We were curious to learn what happened to the males."

Adumie shook his head as if her words made no sense. She would explain it to him if she knew what it was he didn't understand.

"Chovis and tupilak belong to us. They are none of your concern," Adumie said. He threw a tracker at her.

Rona tried to catch it, but it bounced off her shoulder and continued to fly past her.

"How many more of these are there?" he fumed.

"There are eight more that are here in the habitat," Rona said. "Six others left the area and are in the ocean."

She and Lu had managed to find 16 pups, but in each case as a pup became an adult, he mated, left the area, and their tags went offline.

"You will gather all of them," Adumie said.

"We can't get the tags from the chovis that have gone into the ocean," Rona quickly said.

Unyielding, he continued to speak, "You will leave what is ours alone. You will no longer steal fish from our waters, rocks from our mountains, or algae from our ashag."

He was so angry it was evident that he had not heard Rona.

"You will receive no more meat from us. When your transport returns, *all* of you will leave on it and *none* of you will ever return again." he turned to leave, then stopped.

He jabbed a finger in the direction of the tupilak and said, "Everything you touch is defiled. It is now your duty to dispose of these."

The colonists vacated the area, leaving the two un-butchered tupilak behind.

A disgruntled murmur ran through the crowd of scientists.

"How could he do that?"

Rona ran after Adumie. "We know why your people are dying." She stopped at the bay entrance and waited to see if he would turn back. Perhaps if he knew she and Lu wanted to help, he might not be quite so angry.

His next step faltered.

"We can find a cure," Rona said. "If you let us."

He steps slowed. Was he considering her words? No. His steps hurried on.

Another walking at his side did stop and turned around.

Even though it was difficult to tell who were men and who were women, for some reason, Rona was sure this person was a woman. She was as tall as Adumie's shoulder. Her arms were short and fat like her stout body. Her black eyes locked with Rona's.

For a second, Rona thought she might say something.

"Qorow Low," Adumie roughly said.

The woman quickly followed after him.

"Wait." Jorge had joined Rona. "What about Jessie? What if she's not back by the time the ship arrives."

Without slowing his angry, long-legged stride, Adumie said, "Those outside during The Storm no longer live."

"What?" Jorge exclaimed.

Adumie and his assembly turned right and disappeared between unkempt trees.

"How does he know Jessie's dead?" Jorge asked.

No. Dead? No! Rona didn't, wouldn't believe it.

Soon all of everyone was gathered at the door.

"He doesn't care about Jessica any more than he cares about his own people," Lu said in disbelief.

"I can understand Jess, but his people? Why would he not want a cure?" Mathieu asked.

"He doesn't want to believe," Gino softly said.

"Then we'll have to prove to him," Rona said. She was not going to be thrown out without a fight. It would be two years before the next transport arrived, plenty of time—if she worked hard.

And Jess? Jess would return. She would. She wasn't dead. She couldn't be dead.

"Before you start on that cure, explain what just happened." Gino scolded them. He wouldn't be pleased if forced to return to WSC Moon Base empty handed.

Maybe Rona and Lu deserved it; the others didn't.

She and Lu had moved too quickly and had not asked permission from the colonists to study their dogs. But the colonists would have said no. They didn't ask because they didn't want another rejection. She and Lu wanted to do the research.

"This is all my fault," Lu burst into tears. "The Canini Project was my idea."

Spago hesitated unsure as to how to comfort her. Then he placed a consoling hand on Lu's back. Lu dropped her head on his shoulder. He wrapped his arms around her and held her close.

"I'm to blame. We worked on the project together, but I'm team leader," Rona said. "We'll do what it takes to make amends."

"But what were you trying to accomplish?" Gino asked.

"We've checked every day, and so far all the adult dogs, chovis, are female," Rona said. She took a deep breath of frustration. "We wanted to know what happened to the male chovis."

"And?"

"Nothing conclusive." Everyone turned an accusingly eye on Rona and Lu. "I'm sorry. We didn't know this would happen." She nodded toward the tupilak. "I have no idea why they left them here."

"This is not your fault," Gino said. Resolve replaced the anger on his face. "Neither of you are to blame. The colonists have been against our being here from the beginning. If you hadn't placed tags on their dogs, they would have found another reason to exile us."

Everyone agreed.

"Sounds like they don't like us examining rock, fish, or algae," Avil said.

"As far as they're concerned, we can't do anything right," Olivia said.

To Rona's relief, Gino wasn't angry with them after all, and neither was anyone else. They were angry at the situation.

"What about Jessie?" Jorge sounded fearful that she'd been forgotten.

"She'll be back before the transport arrives. If not, we'll ask the captain for a shuttle to search for her," Gino said.

"That's two years from now!" Jorge declared. "She'll be dead by then."

Placing a fatherly hand on Jorge's arm, Gino looked up at him, and said, "There's nothing we can do, son. We don't have the means to search for Jessica or the others."

Jorge dropped his head. "I don't care about the others."

Silence swelled until it filled the room. Everyone was thinking about Jess, but there was nothing any of them could do to help her. And if Adumie was right, it might too late.

"So what did you learn from your tags," Mathieu asked, breaking the uncomfortable stillness.

Ever so slightly, Lu pushed herself away from Spago. She sniffled. "What difference does it make?"

"You must have gotten some data," Mathieu said.

"Might as well tell us what got the colonists all riled up," Olivia said.

It was comforting to know the others cared about their research. Rona hoped Lu felt the same.

"The chovis are descendants from the captain's Spitz. Their overall mitochondria structure does match," Lu said. "But there is a strange mutation in the mitochondria we've not yet been able to explain."

"But Spitz are lap dogs," Spago exclaimed. "These dogs are huge in comparison. Some of them are the size of a Newfoundland."

"We think their DNA was altered," Rona said. "But we're not sure how or why. Along with the mutations, there are new alleles in their chromosomes unlike anything we've seen before."

"Alleles?" Vong asked.

"A genetic definition," Lu said. "It's in every pair of genes that's located in a specific chromosome. They pass specific traits to the next generation."

"And these genetic definitions are different how?" Jorge asked.

"That's what we don't know," Rona said. "There are some things we'd like to study, but to do so . . ." Her voice trailed off.

"You need better means of getting the information from the dogs," Jorge finished for her.

"Chovis," Rona corrected. Lu nodded.

Avil had been examining the tupilak. "Hey, what's this?"

He held up a tupilak ear, detached something, and handed it to Rona.

"It's a radio tag," she said, in surprise. "Did you find a tag on the other tupilak?"

"No." Avil shook his head. "I checked. I bet the other tag is what Adumie threw at you."

Several people in the area searched the floor where the tag might have landed.

"Here's the other." Beth held it up.

"I don't understand. How did the radio tags get on the tupilak," Olivia said.

"I have no idea." Rona said. "We only tagged puppies."

"We need a show and tell of what you've found," Gino said.

"Shouldn't we retrieve radio tags first?" Lu asked.

"Yes," Gino said. "Who gave you the tags?"

"I did," Olivia said.

"Then we'll work with Olivia to find them," Gino said.

"Shouldn't we do that?" Lu asked.

"You and Rona will test the tupilak," Gino said.

"Why?" Rona asked.

"To solve the mystery of how the tags that were placed on puppies ended up on full-grown tupilak," Gino said.

"There are more chovis that have disappeared off our radar," Rona said. "We've no idea where they are."

"We'll worry about that later," Gino said.

"What do we do with the tupilak once we're finished with them?" Lu asked.

"I'm not butchering them," Vong loudly declared.

"Bury them," Mathieu said.

"And where do you plan to do that?" Jorge asked.

"Outside," Mathieu said.

"Permafrost," Jorge reminded him. "Frozen ground."

"Oh," Mathieu gave him a big dim-witted grin. He tilted his head to the side as a new thought hit him. "If the ground is frozen for years at a time, where do these people bury their dead?"

No one answered. Several brows furrowed.

"In the complex?" a voice suggested.

"They've buried their dead in the complex for over 300 years?" Mathieu asked. "There were originally more than 2,000 settlers. Who knows how many have been born and have died since then. That's a lot of graves." He consulted Jorge, Spago, and Gino. "When you or your teams were outside, did you see anything that remotely resembles a cemetery?"

They exchanged glances.

"No." They agreed.

"So, I ask again, what do they do with their dead?"

"Who cares what they do with their dead or what to do with the tupilak? Drag them outside and leave them to rot," Vong angrily said.

"We might have to do that," Jorge said.

"The colonists will be insulted," Rona objected.

"They're already insulted," Vong said. "What difference does it make?"

"But if we just dump the tupilak like that, it will make things worse," Rona said.

"We just got kicked off this planet, Rona, how much worse can it get?" Vong asked. "You've got more important things to worry about anyway."

"Like what?" Rona asked.

Suddenly, the anger evaporated from Vong's continence. "What about a cure for the retroviral?" he quietly asked.

"We'll get to it. Nothing will distract us from that," Rona said. *Why does he suddenly care about a cure?*

"It might not make any difference if we do find a cure. Not if the colonists won't let us help them," Lu said. "We won't even know if the cure works since we don't have a test subject."

"Well, Lu," Vong said.

Something twisted in Rona's stomach.

"I'll be your lab rat." He raised his hand, palm facing them. It was filled with tiny red bumps.

Chapter 46

Qorow Low
Watching, Waiting, Learning

QOROW LOW WANTED understanding of off-worlders. She also wanted understanding as to why Adumie mistrusted them. Perhaps she wanted to see and have agreement with Adumie. Yet her greatest fear was that he might have the true discernment about them. Perhaps she came to find proof that he was wrong.

What if Cameron was the one with understanding?

Adumie wanted to banish those of Earth.

Cameron wanted to forgive, put the past behind, and welcome those of Earth as part of Community.

How was Qorow Low to know which was correct?

She had a need to know for herself, therefore she watched, listened and learned.

Off-worlders easily laughed and talked. They were not overshadowed by death. Some never touched, but there were those who did. They didn't just hold hands they pressed bodies without shame or embarrassment. One might have thought their actions were natural.

Such watching caused wondering.

At first, Qorow Low diverted her eyes but she became more comfortable with watching. She noticed not all off-worlders touched. But for those who did, it seemed loving. They took pleasure in the touching and very often smiled at each other.

Such watching reminded Qorow Low of past times when there was much smiling and laughing among her people. But that was before the slow-dying death.

Life-givers only touched their children in the caring of them, but as the child became older, the child was taught not to touch.

Because of these people, Qorow Low began to wonder why it was permissible for them to touch, but not permissible for those of Akiane.

Adumie said off-worlders were blasphemous.

How could such loving actions be wrong?

The watching woke desires. Qorow Low wished she could walk with Adumie while holding his hand. Ah, but such thoughts were irreverent. She cringed in shame.

Of all those she watched, it was the dark-skinned one, and the small one that walked at her side, who most interested her.

The dark one said she could cure the slow killing illness. Did she speak truth? Was there a cure? Could this be the answer to some many prayers for a cure?

If Adumie was right, she should not approach the dark one, but if he were wrong, her child would die. She prayed with all her heart that he was wrong.

No one in Community knew where the sickness came from or how to stop it. She desperately wanted off-worlders to have the knowledge.

Adumie was so angry. Not just about the deaths, but with Holy One as well. He no longer spoke Holy One's name in reverence, but spoke the name God with distrust, as one would insult.

He never spoke harshly or criticized Qorow Low, at least not out loud. In truth, she had no idea what he thought of her. Nevertheless, she had a deep affection for him, and wanted him to be happy, yet that seemed impossible.

She bowed her head. Adumie would be disapproving of her thoughts. She greatly wanted to please him. By that desire alone, Qorow Low should not speak to the dark one.

But...

She wanted to have children—many children. If this child died, she knew she would never try again.

Qorow Low had been watching the dark-skinned one and the small one in the hopes of learning if they could be trusted. By logic, she should not approach those two.

And yet, her heart compelled her, pushed her, willed her forward.

She wanted her child to live that was why she named her Sharhr, which means to *live forever*.

The baby girl whimpered and twitched.

Qorow Low opened her fur jacket to check on her. She slept in the scarf that secured her to her chest.

If off-worlders could help, was it not her responsibility to give her child a chance at life?

Adumie would be angry. He was always angry.

I will go in secret. If it does not work, he need never know, Qorow Low reasoned. *If they do have a cure, how can he be angry then?*

The decision was clear; she would secretly contact the dark one.

Chapter 47

Rona Montgomery
The Colonist

NO MATTER how many times Rona walked the paths though the habitat she never tired of the beauty of alien plant life. The garden eased Rona's homesickness for the lush forests of semi-tropical Georgia. She missed her family and she missed Jess. The quiet walks helped her think. But this time instead of ruminating over what she'd given up, missed, or perhaps gained with Mathieu, Rona sorted the facts about the retrovirus that had killed Zhoa and had infected Vong.

Thanks to what they'd learned from Zhoa's autopsy, Rona and Lu had stopped the retrovirus in Vong's system. The HMS revealed that the retrovirus was in both his hands. The hand with the rash was more infected, but the retrovirus had not yet moved beyond his palms.

Fearful of how quickly it could spread, Rona and Lu decided to use the fastest method to eliminate it.

Nano-computers.

The nano-computers were programmed to attach themselves to the retrovirus. Hundreds of thousands of them were placed in a saline solution.

If the retrovirus had spread throughout his body, they would have injected the solution directly into a main artery. But because the retrovirus was localized, they only injected his infected palms.

Each nano-computer attached itself to an infected cell, and injected it with an anti-drug killing the retrovirus.

Within a few hours, Vong's palm looked normal.

One more check with the HMS confirmed that Vong was free of the retrovirus.

If only they could examine a colonist and run tests. Rona was sure modern medical technology could easily defeat any alien illness.

Rona froze. Among the tiny leaves and orange jewel-like flowers growing along the ground were two fur maroon boots, one had a white spot near the toe of the left boot. With one thin green gloved, stubby-fingered hand, a woman held the top edge of the enormous leaf down so her shoulders and head were visible. Like so many of her people, had similar features as that of an Eskimo, a flat face, and wide nose, but unlike Eskimos, she and her people were maroon.

"Hello," Rona greeted. She was both surprised and overjoyed that a colonist would be so bold. Was this the breakthrough she was hoping for?

"Good light," the colonist timidly said. She did not step out into the open. With the fear of a timid rabbit, her eyes darted around examining the immediate vicinity.

Following her gaze, Rona also quickly inspected the surrounding area.

"We're alone," Rona softly assured her.

The woman took a halting breath. "You said you have a cure."

This was it. The scientist in Rona wanted to shout for joy. She forced herself to remain calm and not allow her face to break into a grin let alone a broad smile.

"Yes, I do." Rona didn't rush the conversation, but when the woman didn't speak, she asked, "What's your name?"

The woman hesitated then asked, "What does my name have to do with a cure?"

"Nothing. But it's nice to know. My name is Rona." She extended her hand as a gesture of greeting expecting the woman to reach around the leaf with her free hand.

Instead, the woman jumped back in revulsion. Rona had done something wrong. The leaf gently swayed back in place as the woman disappeared behind it.

"I'm sorry." Rona withdrew her hand.

Rona saw the top of the woman's head turn side to side. "Oh," she exclaimed. "I should not have come."

Rona feared she might bolt. "Wait," she said.

The top of the woman's head turned. She was leaving. Rona might not have another chance to talk to her or to any other colonist. She had to stop her before she left. The survival of the colony might depend on it.

Instinctively, Rona pushed the large leaf out of the way and grabbed the woman's arm.

The woman let out a squeak of terror. "No, no." She roughly yanked her arm free.

Rona released her. Taking a step back, she almost tripped over the stones at her feet.

Lu came running. "Rona, are you all right?" She stood on the path breathless. "What are you doing in there?"

"Lu, I've done something terrible but I don't know what I did wrong."

"We do not touch," the woman said, backing away. "It is forbidden."

"I meant no harm." Rona clasped her hands at her back. "Please don't leave."

"Rona, who are you talking to?" Lu asked.

They could hear many footsteps running along the path towards them.

"Oh." The woman slipped farther into the dense garden.

"Rona, come out of there," Lu insisted.

"I have to go after her. Cover me, Lu."

As Rona moved more deeply in to the thick undergrowth, she heard, "Lu, are you all right?" It was Jorge.

"Yes," Lu said with a nervous laugh.

"Why were you screaming," Olivia asked. She sounded more annoyed than worried. She had little empathy for others.

"A chovis ran across the path and surprised me." Lu laughed nervously.

She's a pretty good little actress, Rona mused.

"You?" Olivia questioned. "Little miss tom-boy?"

Rona feared Olivia would once again cause trouble.

Lu wasn't afraid of the dogs. She'd almost become a veterinarian, instead of human genetics.

"Well, I was deep in thought," Lu said. "And we are on an alien plant. One's imagination tends to run away in strange directions."

Rustling tree leaves muted the rest of the conversation.

"Wait, wait," Rona called, hopefully loud enough for the woman to hear but not so loud that her friends might hear.

Evidently, this woman didn't want anyone to know she'd come. Rona had to do something before she was gone for good. "Are you sick? I can help. You don't have to die. Let me help."

The woman abruptly stopped. Rona almost ran into her. She jumped back just in time to what she hoped she was a respectable distance.

They stared at each other, each breathing heavily.

"My name is Qorow Low," she finally said.

"Pretty. Unusual, but pretty."

"Here, Rona is uncommon."

"Yes, of course. I keep offending you. I don't mean to. Honest."

"My name means cutie."

Rona observed her stout body, short arms and legs, deep pink skin, straight black, chin length hair, flat face, and large nose.

"Yes," she said. "I can see it."

"What does your name mean?" Qorow Low asked.

"I, uh, don't know," Rona said. "I never checked."

"How can you not know what your name means?"

"Does the meaning of my name have anything to do with my curing you?" Rona smiled.

Qorow Low smiled weakly. "No." She studied Rona. "Can you heal us?" There was such hope in her face of what might be and fear that there might be no hope.

"One of our people died. Another became ill, but my friend Lu . . ." Rona pointed back towards Lu. " . . . and I healed him. Now he's healthy."

Qorow Low's black eyebrows creased her deep pink forehead as she debated what to do next. Then slowly, she opened the front of her fur jacket to reveal a small sleeping child strapped to her chest.

The mother wouldn't take the child out of her jacket or allow Rona to touch it. She had to examine the baby while it rested against her mother's chest.

Baby's eyes: watery; arms: limp; no hair; skin lacked color; hearing: inconclusive, it didn't respond to sound, but it didn't respond to movement in front of its eyes either; breathing: shallow.

"May I draw blood?" Rona asked. If she couldn't do a proper physical examination, blood testing would have to do. She could tell a lot about blood, by color, texture, and smell, even before it was processed.

She wished she had her Hand Held Medical Scanner. It would have helped her know something defined that she could have told the mother.

"What is 'drawblood'?" Qorow Low said it as one word.

"Blood," Rona said, "in your veins."

"Yes."

"I want to take some."

Qorow Low eyes widened, she quickly closed her jacket, and took a step away. "Why would you do such a thing?"

"No, don't be afraid," Rona said. "I just want a little bit. It will allow me to obtain information that will tell me what's wrong with your child."

"How will you do this?"

"I have equipment in my lab back in my living quarters."

Her face crinkled in dismay. "I cannot go to your living area." She spoke softly anxious that someone might hear. "No one must know I have come to you."

"Yes, yes, I know. If you stay here, I'll go get what I need and come back."

Qorow Low hesitated.

"It will help me help your child," Rona said.

Leaves rustled. *Now what*, Rona wondered.

Lu stepped beside her.

At first sight of Lu, Qorow Low stiffened. If she ran, Rona was sure she never get another chance to speak to her.

"Please," Rona said. She raised her hands in a gesture of calm, but this time, she kept her hands to herself. "This is Lu. She's my teammate and will help me find a cure for your child."

Already half turned, Qorow Low hesitated when her child made a little squeaky noise. One hand came to her mouth. The other rested on her jacket over the baby's back.

Rona sympathized.

She was a mother in turmoil, torn between honoring her people and saving her child. It was not right to force a mother to make that kind of decision.

"We will do our best to help," Rona assured her.

Lu asked, "What's that on your ear?"

Rona cringed. Why had she come? Lu should have waited until Rona returned with the blood samples. Now she would mess everything up. If only she'd be quiet and let Rona do the talking.

Quickly, Qorow Low's hand rose to her ear and pulled her black hair over her face.

In that split second, Rona saw something on Qorow Low's ear, she hadn't noticed earlier.

"Please, let us examine your ear," Rona said.

"I wish you to help my child."

Before Lu could say another word, Rona placed a hand on her arm. She didn't take the hint.

"Yes, but if you're sick, who will care for your child?" Lu asked.

The mother stared at Lu then at Rona. "There are many who would care for her if I were to die."

"But you're her mother. You should care for her."

Lu's words seem to soften Qorow Low. Her shoulders dropped slightly.

"We only want to help," Rona guaranteed.

After another moment of consideration, Qorow Low pushed her hair behind her ear to reveal the skin along her hairline.

Rona and Lu moved closer.

Lu's hand reached up to touch.

Qorow Low cringed.

Rona grabbed Lu's hand and shook her head, "No."

Lu's hand retreated.

The ear was dull gray, and was spreading into little blotches over her skin to the edge of her temple. The illness was just beginning to reveal itself.

There were so many questions Rona wanted to ask: When did the disease first appear? What about the rest of her family? Did her husband have it? Were her parents still alive? But if they bombarded her with questions, Rona was certain she'd run.

Lu must have had the same thoughts and questions, but to Rona's surprise, she also restrained herself.

"Would it be all right if we also drew some of your blood as well as your baby's?" Rona asked.

Slowly, Qorow Low nodded. Tears ran down her cheeks. Rona watched as the mother's face scrunched up. Then it relaxed just a bit as she came to a decision. "I will stay here and wait for you."

Like snow melting under a warm star, relief spread over Rona. Her first colonist was agreeing to an examined. It had taken almost a month, but her human genome project was finally starting.

Chapter 48

Jessica Hewitt
Thirtieth Day on Expedition

"NOT ALL of the ocean is ready to be free of ice. It will not completely thaw for many more months," Cameron said. "Ice will return to the waters surrounding this island. We will start back as soon as the ice is strong enough to hold us."

Cameron's words shocked me.

"I don't understand," I said. "I thought we were headed north."

"Only if you wish to continue Woden." Then to my complete shock, he said, "We head back to Endurance."

"What? We are?" I wanted to hug him, to kiss him. I could barely believe my ears. I could barely contain my joy. I do believe that moment was the happiest I'd ever experienced in my entire life.

"We have accomplished our goals," he said mater-of-factly.

"What goals?" I asked. *Who cared, we were going back.*

An expression of wonderment crossed his face. "Trust," he said.

"Excuse me? What trust?" I had no idea what he was talking about.

"There was drinking of Laszar," he said. "There was sharing of hearts."

Oh that. That was it? One swift drink and we could go home? I truly did not understand.

"If all it took was a drink, why didn't we do that back at Endurance?" I asked more than a little annoyed. "Why did we have to endure all of this?"

"Laszar does not bring forth trust. Laszar helps release developing of trust," he said.

"You mean, no matter how drunk I got before Woden, I would never have confided in you about my parents, but once we'd developed a relationship of sorts, the drink helped to bring my innermost thoughts to the surface," I translated.

Yeah, that's right, I was finally beginning to understand Cameron and his reasoning.

Scary.

"Indeed." He gave me a slight bow. "We have shared with you about the slow-dying illness. We have come to an understanding as to why you are the chosen one."

We hadn't done that. Well, I hadn't, but I wasn't gong to tell him.

"Now we will return to Endurance. You will speak to the Community. They will listen," he finished.

And my joy evaporated.

He still expected some sort of miracle from me.

I was convinced I didn't have one.

But as I thought about it, I realized, if the colonists, or rather—if Cameron's community was willing to listen to me, I might be able to persuade them to let our medical team examine them. They might be able to discover a cure.

I could do that.

If I facilitated the medical team and the colony getting together, I might also be able smooth the progress of two worlds reuniting.

And with that, I too felt I'd accomplished something of my own Woden to be proud of.

I would be returning to Endurance with a mission and fulfilling my orders to negotiate WSC's takeover of the colony.

I'd have a long discussion with my admiral about these people and explain their reasons for rejecting us. If he was reasonable—if he was reasonable . . . yeah.

It would be a long discussion, but it was important for me to convince him not to forcibly takeover Akiane as a WSC colony, but accept Akiane as a sister world of humans populating the Milky Way.

If we could do it here, we could do it elsewhere.

I'd travel twenty-seven light-years seeking for a way to escape my life.

Instead, I'd found myself and my life's mission.

And it was one hell of a mission.

The End

Phyllis Moore

All my books are in paperback, ebook, and Prime Reads on Amazon.

Reviews are important.

If you enjoyed *Storm's Coming*, please consider writing a review. If you think you don't know what to write, you do. What you would say to a friend is perfect for a review.

Thank you for being a fan.

Phyllis Moore MythRider

Send an email if you would like to be on my email lest: PhyllisMooreMythRider@gmail.com

Follow Phyllis Moore at:
Blog: MythRider.WordPress.com
FB: Phyllis Moore MythRider
Goodreads: https://www.goodreads.com/phyllis_moore

Why MythRider? Because there is more than one author named Phyllis Moore. But I'm the only MythRider.

www.ingramcontent.com/pod-product-compliance
Lightning Source LLC
Chambersburg PA
CBHW070224260626

47160CB00002B/687